# BY DELILAH S. DAWSON

*Minecraft: Mob Squad*

*Minecraft: Mob Squad: Never Say Nether*

*Mine*

*Camp Scare*

*Servants of the Storm*

*Hit*

*Strike*

*The Violence*

Star Wars

*Phasma*

*Galaxy's Edge: Black Spire*

*The Skywalker Saga*

Blud

*Wicked as They Come*

*Wicked as She Wants*

*Wicked After Midnight*

*Wicked Ever After*

The Tales of Pell (with Kevin Hearne)

*Kill the Farm Boy*

*No Country for Old Gnomes*

*The Princess Beard*

The Shadow (as Lila Bowen)

*Wake of Vultures*

*Conspiracy of Ravens*

*Malice of Crows*

*Treason of Hawks*

# MINECRAFT™
# MOB SQUAD
## NEVER SAY NETHER

# MINECRAFT™
## MOB SQUAD
### NEVER SAY NETHER

## DELILAH S. DAWSON

NEW YORK

Copyright © 2022 Mojang AB. All Rights Reserved.
Minecraft, the Minecraft logo, and the Mojang Studios logo
are trademarks of the Microsoft group of companies.

Published in the United States by Del Rey,
an imprint of Random House, a division of
Penguin Random House LLC, New York.

DEL REY is a registered trademark and the CIRCLE colophon
is a trademark of Penguin Random House LLC.

Hardback ISBN 978-0-593-35579-4
International edition ISBN 978-0-593-49913-9
Ebook ISBN 978-0-593-35580-0

Endpaper art: M. S. Corley

Printed in the United States of America on acid-free paper

randomhousebooks.com

2 4 6 8 9 7 5 3 1

First Edition

Book design by Elizabeth A. D. Eno

For the kids who know what it's like to be
bullied. I was bullied, too.

# MINECRAFT™
## MOB SQUAD
### NEVER SAY NETHER

# 1

# CHUG

So here's what you need to know: My name is Chug, I'm the greatest fighter around, and I have the four best friends in all the Overworld, one of whom is a pig. We live in a town called Cornucopia, which used to be entirely contained within tall, impenetrable walls. Our ancestors, the eight Founders, built it all by hand long ago to keep us safe, and our Elders have always been strict about the rules the Founders left behind.

Maybe too strict.

For generations, no one knew what was outside the wall—except Nan, the oldest person in town, and she never told anyone anything because she's a feisty old bird. But then a vex started poisoning our crops, and the town Elders were going to send all the families away forever, so my friends and I had to go on an adventure to a woodland mansion to save our town from a bunch of illagers and this beet farmer dressed as a witch, and these brigands stole our llamas and threatened to throw us into a river, and—

Yeah, that's the past, and the past is boring. All you need to know is that now our town has opened up the wall, and life is different—better. My brother Tok and I live outside the wall in New Cornucopia, where he uses his big ol' brain to craft items, and I use my big ol' personality to sell them in our shop. It's called the Stack Shack. I wanted to call it ChugTokMart, but Tok said it sounded like I was choking on an apple, and he was probably right.

It's morning, and my brother's bed is empty. Tok is always awake before me. He says the early morning quiet helps him concentrate as he dreams up new recipes for tools and tries to master the art of brewing potions. I think he wants privacy so if he sets something on fire again, I won't freak out. He makes lots of great things, but he also makes lots of huge messes—and loud, echoing booms. As I lie in my bed, curling and uncurling my toes against the blankets and thinking about breakfast, I strain my senses to figure out what Tok is working on. Bad smells usually indicate potions, while hammering suggests tools or armor and—

*Boom!*

I leap out of bed and run for Tok's workshop. When I throw open the door, I'm relieved to see he's been working outside in the yard and has therefore not damaged the roof. Again.

"Gunpowder?" I ask.

"Gunpowder," he confirms, looking a little dazed.

"One of your eyebrows is sizzling, bro."

He swipes at it and shakes his head. Gray powder surrounds his shoulder-length black hair like a cloud.

"I'm getting closer," he says. "I just need to tweak the recipe."

The problem is, he doesn't *have* any recipes. Elder Gabe is the only person in town who can make potions, and he won't tell Tok anything. I step closer and look at his brewing stand, but whatever ingredients he was working with are now various blackened stains. "Or you could make some nice, safe, unexploding pickaxes today. Or armor. People love your armor."

Tok's cats, Candor and Clarity, meow plaintively from around the corner, where they've wisely been hiding. He kneels and holds out his arms, and they run up to rub worriedly against him. "We have enough armor. The shop is fully stocked. But these potions—I'm so close! Elder Gabe won't share his recipes or give me any ingredients, and I've pored through all Nan's books, but there's just so much I don't know. I've studied all the potions I can find, and I keep trying random concoctions, but it's like I'm missing some vital ingredients, and just . . . ugh!"

"You're obsessed, bro," I say softly, patting him on the shoulder.

He's always been like this. Before he learned about crafting tables from Nan, he was constantly trying to construct machines to save time on chores—to weed our parents' pumpkin patches or pluck the eggs from underneath our fussier hens—but something always went wrong. I guess now that he's mastered crafting, his brain still needs something tough to chew on.

He stands up and gazes toward the mountains in the distance. "I wish we could go back to the woodland mansion library, see what's on the shelves. I bet there are loads of books on potions."

"The Elders ordered us not to go back to the woodland mansion," I remind him. "They agreed to open the walls, they understand that people need freedom to come and go, but—"

"We're still kids," he finishes for me. "And it's not safe."

I nod. It's kind of funny—I used to be the one who got us in trouble, whether I was mouthing off when I shouldn't or getting in fights with this bully named Jarro and his toadies downtown. But now I've settled down, and Tok is the wild card, because once he's at his crafting table or brewing stand, it's like he goes into a trance and doesn't think about safety—or flammability. As I like to remind our parents, who still live on the much more boring pumpkin farm in town, I'm now the good son who hasn't blown up a single thing.

"Maybe we could get permission to go on an expedition," Tok says, getting that mad gleam in his eye that makes me want to put on a helmet and duck. "Now that Lenna is compiling a library, surely everyone would benefit from new books."

"Did I hear my name?"

We both look up, and I grin when I see Lenna jogging toward us, along with her pet wolf, Poppy, and our other friend, Mal. Lenna has oak-brown skin and styles her hair in two puffs. She used to wear stone gray hand-me-down clothes from her nine other siblings, but now that she's moved away from her strict family and their beloved mine and is working as Nan's apprentice, she chooses bright colors that usually clash.

"Tok wants to go back to the woodland mansion to find a book on potions," I explain.

Our other friend, Mal, has red hair in a braid and matching freckles, and she's pretty much our leader. She's also Nan's great-great-granddaughter. She looks Tok up and down, hands on her hips, noting the charcoal smudges on his face and the combination of bed head and gunpowder in his blue-black hair. "We came running when we heard the latest explosion. I guess your neighbors don't even bother getting out of bed anymore, do they?"

"Let's just say the folks next door don't pay to have their hoes fixed," Tok says sheepishly. "Could you really hear it all the way from the cow farm?"

Mal nods. "I was milking at the time." She swipes at a wet smear in her red hair. "The cow and I were both surprised. That seemed like a bigger boom than usual."

"I'm so close!" Tok paces around his workshop yard, and Candor jumps down from his shoulder to lick rogue gunpowder out of her orange-striped fur. "I mean, sure, Elder Gabe can make Potions of Healing and Regeneration, but I'm trying to create something totally new. It's going to make you completely resistant to fire."

Mal and I exchange a look; she's my best friend, and we can pretty much read each other's thoughts.

"But is fire really that big of a problem around here?" she asks gently.

Tok ducks his head. "I accidentally set the workshop on fire once, and Candor's tail caught—"

I pat him on the shoulder. "Bro, that was an accident. She's forgiven you. And her tail tip grew back as good as new." The poor cat looked like a candle there for a minute, but I don't mention that. Tok loves his cats more than anything.

"I could use an expedition, though." Mal's hand goes to her pocket and pulls out her diamond pickaxe, which was crafted by her great-great-great-grandmother, one of our town's founders—and Nan's mom, because that's how old Nan is. "The new mine is going well, but I miss—"

"The discoveries," Lenna breathes. "New places, new animals, new plants, the smell of fresh wind."

"The loot," Tok agrees. "Opening chests. Trading in the village. Picking up all the ingredients witches drop. Books galore!"

"Fighting hostile mobs." I gaze off into the distance. "I haven't seen a zombie in weeks. My sword arm sure could use some exercise."

Mal hooks an arm around my neck. "Oh, selling shovels isn't good enough for you?"

"Shovels!" Tok rolls his eyes. "Old Stu can make shovels. I want to make new things. I want to create new potions no one has ever seen before." He sighs and gazes out at the mountains beyond. "It's funny. We used to live within the walls, and we were happy, but we wanted more. Then we left home and had an adventure, and now we live beyond the walls. And I still want more."

Lenna sits on the floor, rubbing Poppy's soft gray wolf belly. "It's like Nan says: Everyone in Cornucopia is descended from adventurers. Maybe some people are content to stay here, but we're different." Poppy wiggles happily, like she wants an adventure, too. "I say we go ask her to send us on an important expedition to the woodland mansion. It's safe enough. We've been there before. And Nan is in a good mood today. Oh! I forgot." She reaches into her enchanted, nearly bottomless pocket—a neat magic trick Nan taught us so we could carry loads of stuff—and pulls out four cookies. "She told me to give you plenty of cookies and said . . ." She looks up, thinking, and then draws her eyebrows down and says in a Nan-ish voice, "Tell that crafting boy to stop blowing things up before noon. Us old folks need our beauty sleep."

After we eat our cookies and help Tok clean up the brewing mess, we follow the path through New Cornucopia and wave at the guard as we pass through the break in the giant wall to enter the older part of town. Tok's cats pace beside him, Poppy runs up ahead to scout, and my pet pig, Thingy, runs along behind us, oinking to be included. I scratch his head the way he likes and wish I'd saved him some cookie. We amble past farms and fields and navigate the busy downtown crossroads everyone calls the Hub.

"Ow!" Lenna cries.

I spin around, and she's rubbing the back of her head with a grimace of pain. Going on full alert, I pull my sword out of my pocket—because of course I always have a sword in my enchanted pocket, both for self-defense in case of random zombies and for sales demonstrations in case of random customers. Tok and I do a ton of trading in the shop and whenever we're in the Hub, so I always have my pockets loaded with a variety of goods. Beside me, Mal has her pickaxe out and ready. Tok snatches something from the ground at Lenna's feet.

"A poisonous potato?" he asks, holding it up to show us.

Muffled snickering from a nearby alley draws my attention, and Mal and I nod at each other and run for it. All we find, of course, are the retreating backs of the town bully, Jarro, and his two minions, Remy and Edd, disappearing around the corner.

"I wish he would grow up," Mal mutters.

"He makes me want to throw up," I respond.

I put my sword away as we return to Tok and Lenna. "You know who," I confirm.

"We saved the town—*we literally saved his life*—and he's still bullying us." Lenna shakes her head. She used to be the weakest of us, and everyone in town thinks she's weird, but now she's a whiz with her bow and arrows, even if she focuses more on books these days. If Jarro knew the true depth of her skills, there's no way he'd single her out.

He'd go back to focusing on my brother.

"An ocelot can't change its spots," Tok reminds her.

Not that we've ever seen an ocelot, but Nan's books make them sound pretty cool.

With Jarro's Big Potato Gambit out of the way, we continue our trek to Nan's cottage. See, Jarro's mom always makes him stay downtown. These days, she'll tell anyone who'll listen about how it was wrong to open the wall and that now everything is less safe. For us, at least, her paranoia is really useful: She keeps Jarro with her almost all the time, which means it's been a while since I've gotten in trouble for punching him in the kidneys. But when we come downtown, he always tries something like this, something rude and sneaky and hard to prove, should we involve the adults. Not that the adults would do anything to help. They didn't before we saved the town, and they still don't. That's how scared they are of Jarro's mom—and the fact that she controls all the sweet berries in Cornucopia. Even Nan is a little scared of her.

I can relax a little once we're out of the Hub and entering the carefully planted forest that hides Nan's house. When Lenna moved in with her to become her apprentice, Nan had some of her nephews add a new room on to her small cottage. As soon as I see its tidy brick chimney poking up from the trees, I can smell more cookies baking. Thingy and I hurry ahead and knock on the door.

"Go away," Nan shouts. "We're full."

"It's me, Nan," Mal calls. "The great-great-granddaughter you don't mind."

The door opens. Nan's ancient, wrinkled face peers out. "You." She points at Tok. "No explosions in my cottage. And you." She points at me, and my heart nearly stops. "Four cookies is the limit, and that includes the pig. Got it?"

"Yes, Nan," we chorus as she steps back to let us inside.

I'm pretty sure she doesn't even know my name. She just calls me "the beefy one."

Nan offers her cheek to Mal for a kiss, and we settle into our usual places around her table. Lenna is at home here now, and she brings us glasses of milk as Nan serves yet more of her cookies, which are the best ones in town.

"I'm guessing this isn't a social call," Nan says. "Children don't visit old people for no reason."

Mal sits up. "We'd like to go on an expedition to the woodland mansion. If Tok had the right books and could learn more about potion recipes, his experiments wouldn't be so dangerous. And noisy."

"And Lenna could find more books for the town library you're building," Tok adds, and I can tell he's embarrassed by the suggestion that he's causing problems that need to be solved. "You could give us a list of things to look for."

Nan raises one tufty white eyebrow and pins each of us with a sharp look. "What do you really want?"

"Wildness," Lenna says with her usual dreaminess. "It's nice here, but too tame. The air doesn't move. Even the bees are bored."

If Lenna said that at home with her family, they would all laugh at her and call her Loony Lenna, and she would end up alone and crying under her bed. But here, with us and Nan, her words make perfect sense.

Some adults just automatically say no, but Nan isn't one of them. Her lips twitch this way and that as she chews a cookie and thinks about it. "Bad idea, just now," she finally says, and my heart sinks. "When they opened the wall, the Elders unanimously decided to restrict travel, especially for kids. You all know that. Your parents were worried sick, and a couple of you—I can't remember which ones—nearly died the last time you left town. But I'll send Stu a letter, see if some of the adults have time for a trip. We can tell them to look for books on potions and fire prevention."

"But we know the way to the woodland mansion," I argue. "We know more about the Overworld than anyone else in town! Have you seen these people fight with swords? They have little flower stem arms. Wibble wobble flobble. The mobs will destroy them!"

Nan snorts. "Yeah, I've seen. Downright embarrassing, especially when they're related to me. But here's the thing: Last time, when you kids left, the town was in danger. Your expedition was a last resort. Now that everything's peaceful, there's no way your parents would give you permission to go back out there."

I hate it, but I know she's right. We all do. Our parents love their safe, comfy life on the pumpkin farm, and they only agreed to let Tok and me open our shop outside the wall if we promised to come home for dinner every day. Mal is an important part of her family's cow farm, and Nan needs Lenna's help here. Apparently no one else can come up with a sufficient argument, so Tok just writes out a list of book topics to look for, and he and I trudge back to our shop while Mal heads out to the mine in her backyard and Lenna stays with Nan.

It's a pretty day, and business is brisk, but we're both droopy. Tok got excited about the possibility of getting his hands on that library, and I got excited about getting my hands on a sword that I could then swing at zombies and vindicators. At dinner with our parents, we're quieter than usual, but they kind of prefer us that way. It's like a little spark in Tok has gone out, and I hate that.

As we snuggle down in our identical, side-by-side beds and the cats curl up to sleep on Tok's feet, I say, "Hey, bro, I'm sorry the trip's not going to work out. But maybe the adults will bring back the books you need, and you can make a potion that'll turn Elder Stu into a llama."

I can tell Tok is still down because he doesn't even laugh. He just says, "Maybe."

Tok has a hard time quieting his mind, but I can fall right asleep. My last thought is that in the morning, I'm going to make his favorite breakfast to cheer him up.

But when I wake up, Tok's bed is empty. There are no booms. He's not in his workshop. The cats pace outside, crying.

My brother is gone.

# 2

# MAL

So here's what you need to know: My name is Mal, I live on my parents' cow farm but I prefer working in my mine, I love my friends more than anything, and I have an adventurer's heart. After yesterday's discussion about a possible mission to the woodland mansion, I can't stop daydreaming about what it would feel like to walk out the gate and into the big, wide Overworld on another grand quest. Sure, I spend less time with the cows these days and more time on my own, mining a small plot of land in our back pasture, where I have a knack for finding rare ores, but my parents still count on me. Thanks to a dangerous potion, I nearly died the last time I went on an adventure, so it's no wonder they want to keep me close and safe.

But still, I can't help staring at the mountains and thinking about llamas and wondering what else there might be out there, what else I might be missing. The Elders may have opened up our town, but there are still rules, and I still feel pressure to be a good daughter, a good kid, a good cowherd.

I'm milking Henrietta when Chug bursts into the barn looking terrified, which is not normal for him. Chug will mouth off against the biggest bully in town, he'll run right at a zombie while throwing insults, and on our last adventure, he even stood up to adult brigands with swords who stole our llamas and loot and tried to steal his pet pig, so the fact that he's frantic and fighting tears definitely has my attention.

"Chug, what's wrong?"

"It's Tok," he says, breathless. "He's gone."

My mind is immediately hunting for the answer. "Maybe he went into town for ingredients?"

"None of the shops are open yet. I don't even think Elder Gabe is awake. I banged on his door for ten minutes. So his neighbors are awake now, I guess."

"Maybe he went to visit Nan, check her library again for something he missed?"

Chug's brow rumples. "That's a good idea. Let's go check there."

I leave the bucket of milk by the barn door and follow Chug as he runs down the road that leads back to the Hub. It's a cloudy day, and the air is thick with the promise of rain. As we get closer, I notice that several adults are standing in the street, looking angry and confused, our town Elders among them. Elder Gabe stands in front of the open door of his potions shop, shaking the walking stick in his gnarled fist and shouting, "Thief! Thief!"

"Elder Gabe, what's going on?" I ask as we slow down, because I know that I'll get better results than Chug. When he's upset, he has even less of a filter than usual.

"I've been robbed!" Elder Gabe squeaks, shaking his stick at me. "Someone broke into my shop and stole everything! Every potion! All my ingredients! I'm finished! We're all finished! The town is helpless and doomed!" His beady little eyes narrow on Chug. "Speaking of which, where's your brother?"

Chug's jaw drops. "Are you accusing Tok of stealing?"

"I'm considering all possibilities. Where is he?"

Chug deflates. "I don't know. I woke up, and he was missing."

"Aha!" Gabe cries. "So he *is* the thief!"

Uh-oh. I step in front of Chug before he goes on autopilot and punches one of our town leaders in the nose.

"Tok wouldn't steal," I say, hands up. "Ask anyone. He's never stolen anything."

"It just adds up." Gabe shakes his head. "The only person in town who constantly begs me for potion ingredients and recipes disappears on the day my shop is burgled, and if you ask me, there's really only one answer."

"I can think of another answer," Chug says, hands in fists.

Before I have to restrain him, we're interrupted by one of my least favorite people in town: Jarro's mother, Dawna. She bursts out of her gate, flailing, wearing a pink bathrobe and curlers.

"Help! Help!" she screeches, waving her arms. "There's been a crime!"

She runs up to the eldest Elder, Elder Stu, and when Elder Gabe joins them, we follow along.

"What's the problem?" Elder Stu asks.

"I need to know what you're going to do about the crime in this town!"

It's barely dawn, and Elder Stu already looks exhausted. Then again, most people do after dealing with Dawna or her son, Jarro. "We didn't have any crime until today. What happened?"

Dawna takes a big breath. "I woke up, and all my sweet berry bushes were gone! All of them! And when I went to ask Jarro if he'd heard anything, he was gone, too!"

I definitely notice that she mentions the missing bushes before the missing kid.

Elder Stu and Elder Gabe exchange a glance. "So we've got two missing boys, missing sweet berries, and missing potions."

"Who else is missing?" Dawna squawks.

"My brother," Chug breaks in.

Dawna looks at him like he's a talking pig. "There you go! I knew it was one of you Bad Apples, always making trouble around town! That little pyromaniac kidnapped my son and stole my berries! I demand you put this one in jail right now."

Chug can't stand Dawna, and he hates being blamed for things he didn't do, and he really hates it when Dawna—or anyone—calls us Bad Apples. We might be different and we might accidentally cause a little trouble here or there, but none of us are bad.

"My brother didn't steal anything! He never has! He never would! And if he did, he definitely wouldn't steal your nasty kid, unless it was to feed him to wolves!"

"How dare you!" Dawna shrieks.

"Pretty easily! How dare you?" Chug barks back.

Elder Stu moves between them, which I have to admit is pretty brave.

"Now, now. This is all most unusual. First of all, we need to spread the word, have everyone in town looking for those missing boys. They're probably hiding somewhere—"

"That's what you said last time, when we were fighting zombies in a dark forest to save you!" Chug wails.

I clap a hand over his mouth, and Elder Stu nods at me gratefully and continues.

"Nevertheless, we need a hard target search of every farmhouse, henhouse, cowhouse—just all the houses, really. All the structures. There are only so many places to hide in Cornucopia."

He's wrong, though. The wall is open, and the town is no longer contained. But I don't say that. I don't say anything.

"You have to find my berries! And my boy!" Dawna screeches, as no one has really paid her any attention for a few minutes, and she hates that. "He's so innocent—"

"Ha!" Chug barks behind my hand.

"What's going on?" Lenna has appeared beside me, Poppy dancing around our feet. "Nan sent me to get some flour, and all the shops are closed."

"That's because everyone is here," I tell her, still holding Chug's mouth shut. "Tok and Jarro disappeared last night, and Elder Gabe and Dawna were robbed."

Chug licks my palm, and I whip my hand off his mouth. "We have to find Tok," he says before making a face. "Ew. Mal. Ever heard of washing your hands? You taste like cow butt."

A hand lands on my shoulder. It's Elder Stu. "You kids go home and tell your parents what happened. Look over every inch of your farms. That's how you can help—by staying put and doing what you're told." His face, somehow, manages to look even more stern than usual. "And tell your parents to lock up any healing potions they might have on hand. With Elder Gabe's potions and ingredients gone, we're all in grave danger. If anyone gets hurt . . ." He shakes his head. "You kids just be extra careful, okay? No climbing trees, no riding cows. No shenanigans!"

Chug is about to say something snarky, but I grab his arm and yank him away. "Yes, Elder Stu. Will do," I call over my shoulder. Lenna follows me as I lead my friends away from Dawna's hysterics and the Elders' annoyance—and worry. It feels off, not having Tok with us, like a table missing a leg.

"Tok wouldn't hide out with Jarro," Chug growls. "If anything, Jarro kidnapped him. He's probably torturing him! He's—"

"He's too stupid to even think about doing that," I remind him. "Jarro's never even been outside the city walls. There's no way he could find your house, much less steal Tok out of his bed."

"The cats would've let you know if Jarro was around," Lenna adds. "Candor hates him."

"And look at Remy and Edd." I point at the two kids fidgeting across the street. "Jarro's toadies don't look like they're in on a joke—they look worried."

And they do. Like Jarro, they're not very smart, and they're not good actors. They generally have two modes—bully and run—but now they're skulking around, uncertain what to do without their leader.

Elder Gabe gives us a harsh look for continuing to exist in his presence, and I say, "C'mon," and lead Chug and Lenna down the road. "Let's go look for clues in Tok's workshop." If I know Chug, and I know Chug better than anyone other than his own brother, he probably didn't look around very well before running to my house. He's got a ton of great qualities—he's loyal, he's funny, he's a great cook, he's a great fighter, he's a great friend— but he's not big on attention to detail.

When we get to New Cornucopia, everything looks normal. There are a few small family farms out here, mostly younger families who got sick of how crowded things were getting inside the walls. There are a couple of shops along the main drag, including a bakery and a farm stand, but no one is freaking out like the folks in the Hub. Chug puts Thingy back in his little paddock, and I pause at the fence to scratch the adorable pig behind his ears. "Okay, so we all agree that there's no way Tok would just get up and leave on his own, not without telling us, right?" Chug and Lenna nod emphatically. "Then we just need to figure out what happened. Thingy didn't squeal, and the cats didn't meow, right?" I ask Chug.

His head hangs. "I sleep pretty hard. You know that."

"It wasn't your fault," Lenna says. She reaches under the fence and pulls the feathery green end of a carrot out of the mud. It's not the only one. "Looks like someone kept Thingy busy last night."

Chug turns red. "ARE YOU TELLING ME SOMEONE MADE THINGY INTO AN ACCOMPLICE?" he howls.

Thingy oinks indignantly, and Chug scratches his back. "It's not your fault," he croons. "The carrots were just too good."

Lenna walks under the awning where Tok does most of his work and pokes at something in the dirt. "And here. Fish bones—to keep the cats quiet." She looks up, troubled. "Whoever took Tok knew what they were doing."

Chug drops to the ground on his rump, his head in his hands. "I can't believe I let this happen. I should've protected him. I was right there, just a few feet away! Why didn't I wake up? He's got to be so scared—"

I sit next to him and lean against him. "There's no way you could've known. Nothing like this has ever happened before."

When Chug looks up, his eyes shine fiercely. "It's still our fault, though. We're the reason the wall is open. We live outside it. Before, we knew everybody in town. There were only so many suspects. But now, anyone could've snuck in here. Anyone could've taken my brother."

Lenna sits on the other side of him—sometimes Chug needs to be grounded. "It's not our fault. It's the fault of whoever did the bad thing." Tok's cats appear and butt their heads against Chug's leg, and Poppy whines softly and creeps forward to lick his cheek.

Chug sighs and sags against me. "Maybe that makes sense to my mind, but my heart doesn't buy it."

He sniffles and snuffles, and Lenna and I lean into him as he cries. Chug's a tough guy, but he's got a big heart, and his brother means the world to him. He means a lot to me, too. We've all been best friends forever. Maybe I'm an only child, but Tok is family.

"So we have to find him," I say. "The adults are going to look in barns and under tables, and they're going to assume it's just kids being kids, like they did last time."

"Like they always do." Lenna sighs.

"And that means it's up to us. We've already found two clues. Maybe we'll find more." I stand and pull Chug and Lenna up, too. "Come on. No more sitting around feeling sorry for yourself, bud. We've got to take action."

Chug looks around the workshop and exhales. "Yeah, probably better to do something than nothing. Should we gear up?"

"For what?" Lenna asks.

"I don't know! I just know that I always feel better when my pockets are stuffed with weapons and food. Someone took my brother, and I want to be ready to take him back, even if that involves a fight."

Now a man on a mission, Chug heads into his house, and we follow. He opens a chest and pulls out his old diamond-and-gold armor from our last expedition, plus his sword.

"Chug, that gold armor is basically useless," I say.

"Yeah, but it looks *sick*. And we don't have enough diamond for everybody."

When he takes out a saddle, I give him an odd look.

"In case someone gets hurt and needs to ride Thingy again," he explains. "I've been training him, you know. He can back up now."

He offers me a pickaxe, but I grin and pull my diamond pick-axe out of my pocket. "I'm kind of attached to this one. It makes me feel like my great-great-great-grandmother is always with me, you know?"

Lenna reaches into her own pocket and pulls out two of Nan's cookies. "I have a little food, but we should probably bring some more. And I always have my books and my bow and arrows."

Soon we're all loaded up with food for us and some potatoes for Thingy, who Chug simply can't leave behind—not with Tok gone. We lock Candor and Clarity inside the shop; even if they keep creepers away, Chug would never forgive himself if some-thing happened to Tok's cats because of him. We're not wearing our armor yet or wielding our weapons, because if anyone in town sees us kitted out for adventure, they'll surely go tell the Elders, and then they'll probably close up the wall again just to keep us from disobeying them. But when it's time to head out, we all just kind of . . . stand there.

"Which way do we think they went?" Chug asks.

"Away from the wall," Lenna murmurs.

I fetch the carrot nubbin Lenna found in Thingy's paddock and hold it out to Poppy. "Do you think she could track whoever held this carrot? Can she smell that well?"

"I don't know. I've never tried something like that." Lenna takes the bit of carrot and rubs it over Poppy's nose. "Poppy, find whoever touched this," she says.

Poppy licks her hand and wiggles excitedly.

"Oh," Lenna says, disappointed. "I guess I'm the last one who touched it."

Beyond the boys' house and shop and the single road of New Cornucopia, the Overworld spreads out just as big and wide and wild as the first day we saw it through Nan's secret window. The mountains rise, far out, jagged gray peaks topped with snow. Somewhere in that direction lie a beacon and a village, and beyond that a river and a dark forest. Since that last treacherous journey, we haven't gone farther than the bounds of New Cornucopia. We've played it safe, followed the rules laid out by our Elders and reinforced by our parents.

We've been good. We've done our chores and our jobs.

The whole world is out there, and we've been content enough to gaze at it.

Until now.

Now we have to go back out, even if we're not supposed to.

The last time we left, we saved our town.

This time, we have to save our friend.

"I guess we're ready," Chug says. He opens the gate to Thingy's paddock, and the pig trots out and dances around, oinking excitedly. "You've been feeling a little cooped up, too, haven't you, buddy?" Almost as an aside, he tells Lenna and me, "He likes to get into Dav's potato fields, so I have to save him from himself."

As if on cue, Thingy squeals and darts ahead, out of Chug's reach. But he doesn't go for the potatoes invitingly growing in rows next door.

He finds something on the ground and munches it delightedly.

"Hey, what is that?" Chug calls. "Are you eating garbage again, you naughty boy?"

He hurries to the pig and tries to pry open its mouth, but Thingy shakes him off and darts ahead again, plucking something from the dirt and slurping it up.

"What's he eating?" I ask as we hurry along behind him.

"I don't know, but his mouth is all red and sticky." Chug gasps. "Is it blood? Is it Tok's blood? Thingy, are you some kind of bloodthirsty monster? I know some people actually—ugh—eat pigs, but I didn't know pigs could eat people—"

But Lenna holds up a red-daubed finger from where she kneels on the ground. "It's sweet berries," she says.

As Thingy rushes ahead yet again, Chug worriedly trailing in his wake, I grin.

"It's a trail of Dawna's stolen sweet berries," I say. "And I bet whoever took Tok is dropping them."

## 3

# LENNA

 So here's what you should know: My name is Lenna, I work as the apprentice to the oldest, kookiest person in town because my family is boring and doesn't understand me, and now I'm overjoyed to be on an adventure again, covered in pig slobber and sweet berry juice. Maybe Mal thought Poppy would use her nose to sniff out the trail of the kidnappers, but I guess we all underestimated the powers of a hungry pig and a trail of delicious berries. We can barely keep up as Thingy darts ahead to his next treat, and Chug is half jubilant and half worried.

"He's going to get an upset tummy!" he calls back to us.

"So put him on a lead!" Mal calls back.

"Oh, yeah," he mutters, digging through his impossibly deep pockets. "I keep forgetting about the existence of anything that isn't Tok or Thingy." The next time the pig stops for a berry, Chug manages to get the lead on him, and it's pretty funny, watching big, burly Chug get dragged around by his excited pet.

Even if I would've preferred to stop at Nan's house for provisions, I guess gearing up at the Stack Shack is the next best thing. At least all our pockets are full, and we're not going out into the Overworld with nothing. We all feel the same urgency—Tok is in trouble, and he has to be at the end of this sweet berry trail.

Now that we're beyond the town walls, I reach into my own pocket and pull out my bow and arrows—or, to be more accurate, Nan's bow and the arrows I've learned to make myself. It's hard to believe that just a while ago, I didn't even know that weapons like this existed, and now I'm the best shot in town. It feels good to hold the bow again, and not just for practice, but for a good reason. Before my friends and I went on our first adventure, I was considered a lazy, loopy daydreamer, the girl who flapped her hands and slept under her bed instead of on top of it. My family wasn't particularly kind and constantly let me know that I was weird, annoying, and useless by their standards. But traveling the Overworld taught me my own value.

I'm a good shot, a good friend, a tamer of wolves, a fighter of mobs.

And since I've become Nan's apprentice, I've become so much more. I've studied her books, sung her songs, listened to her stories, learned about cities and ports and secret underwater ruins. I've learned to make arrows that fly true. I've learned what it feels like to receive praise from someone you respect. And, probably most importantly to my friends, I've learned how to replicate Nan's famous cookie recipe.

But now, I take up my post at the end of our adventuring caravan. That's where I feel most myself—trailing behind my friends, defending them from the back, and keeping my senses on alert for whatever will come at us next. It's a dark gray day, the clouds sitting low and the air so thick that it presses against my skin like a wet blanket. Poppy trots by my side, bright-eyed and happy, tongue lolling. I'm always calmer when she's within reach. She's been happy enough to follow me around Nan's cottage and forest and the town, but it's immediately clear that my wolf has missed traveling, too. Every now and then, she bounds into the grass, scattering rabbits. She keeps missing her quarry—maybe she's grown a little too tame. But I have full confidence that she'll soon be catching her own dinner, a wild thing again, happy to be along on the adventure. I know she won't leave my side, though—we're a team.

Normally, Mal is the first in line when we're adventuring, but now she follows Chug, who's being dragged along by a pig on a lead. I wonder if she's noticing the same thing I am, that our current path is suspiciously similar to the same one we took the last time we went on a quest. We're headed for the mountains, and if the berry trail continues on in the same manner, we'll soon see the beacon our town's founders erected outside the nearest village. We know our adults have gone there several times, but no one has let a single kid come along, even though we know perfectly well how to trade with the odd denizens there, who don't speak our language but are clearly intelligent, even if they can only communicate using the word "Hm."

Thunder rumbles overhead, and the sky goes a shade darker. I look around, but we're in a grassy area, nowhere close to trees or any kind of building.

"Should we stop and dig a shelter?" I ask.

"No way!" Chug shouts. "Every minute we spend waiting, Tok gets farther away. And if something else comes along and finds the sweet berries before Thingy does, we might never find him."

Thingy tugs him ahead, and Mal follows. She looks around nervously and reaches into her pocket, pulling out her diamond pickaxe. It's nice, knowing I'm not the only one who has a funny feeling about this prairie. We haven't seen any mobs bigger than the rabbits Poppy has failed to catch, but then again, smart animals take cover when a storm is about to strike.

The rain starts hesitantly at first, as if asking a question, then answers itself with a heavy downpour. Thunder booms, and lightning forks down, striking the grasses up ahead.

"Are you sure about not making a shelter?" I shout as water soaks me completely.

"We can't lose the trail!" Chug shouts back.

Mal looks to me and shrugs, and I shrug back. We both know there's no way to change Chug's mind, not when he's worried about his brother. We're going to be uncomfortable for a while, and that's that. I hate the feeling of being wet and cold, but I care about Tok and won't feel complete until we find him again.

Boom!

This time, the lightning cracks down close enough that I feel the ground quake. Thingy squeals, and Chug stumbles backward, landing on his rump.

There, exactly where the lightning struck, stands something Nan told us about, something so rare that I thought we would never see it.

A skeleton horse.

"Run away!" I scream. "Don't get any closer, don't let it see you—"

But it's too late.

Lightning strikes again, so loud that my eardrums feel like they're going to burst, and a flash of light reveals not the bone horse I briefly saw, but four skeleton horsemen, armed with bows and arrows and wearing helmets that will make it all the harder to vanquish them.

"What are those things?" Chug shouts from the ground.

Mal darts forward and tugs him to standing. "They're the reason you're carrying a sword. Run away, fast, and see if you can get your armor on while Lenna and I hold them off."

"But Thingy—"

"They want to hurt you, not him!" I shout, because Nan made me memorize everything about this rare mob.

Chug lets go of the pig's lead and runs behind me with Mal. I nock an arrow and release it, glad that I've only improved my bow skills. The hit lands, knocking the skeleton off the horse, and I fire again and again, aiming for the skeletons, which are already shooting back. An arrow glances off my shoulder, and I feel a hot sting and an electrifying jolt of energy. It hurts, and I'm in danger, but . . . I feel so alive, so awake. The Overworld might seem safe, when you view it from New Cornucopia, but there's always something new out here that wants to kill you in a whole new way.

Behind me, I hear Chug's armor clanking as Mal steps beside me and draws a bow of her own. I grin at her, glad she brought it along. We've been practicing together in Nan's forest. Her skills can't compare to mine, but she's pretty good at almost everything she tries, which adds up. I take down another skeleton, and Mal promptly shoots the skeletal horse that was underneath it.

"Oops," she says. "Don't tell Nan."

We've both heard Nan's stories of Helga, a beloved skeleton horse she had as a child.

"Okay, ready." Chug runs up between us, clad in a mishmash of armor—diamond, gold, and iron. When I raise an eyebrow, he shrugs. "You watched me pack it! We sell a little of everything, so I always have something in my pocket. At least my helmet is diamond, right?"

Before I can answer, he charges directly toward a skeleton horseman, howling furiously, and dispatches it with several swings of his diamond sword. I used to worry about Chug's habit of running headlong into trouble, but it really helps when fighting mobs. If only we were in sync like we used to be—I can't shoot arrows at something when he's blocking it. Mal and I focus on the fourth horseman, and again, she shoots the horse while I shoot the rider.

"Ow!" Chug screeches. "It hit me!"

"What did you think it was going to do—offer you a cookie?" Mal shoots back.

"I wish. But I'll settle for a free helmet." With a few more jabs and stabs, Chug has destroyed the skeleton and its mount, but the enchanted iron helmet disappears. Chug turns around, holding up a dropped bone. "Well that doesn't seem fair."

We're on high alert now as the rain pounds down, and I have an arrow ready as I spin, looking in every direction. I think there's one skeleton horseman still up and active, but it's so dark now and the rain is so heavy that it's hard to see anything.

Something growls to my left, and I pivot with my arrow drawn, but it's too close for me to hit. A zombie! I let the arrow fly off into nowhere and stumble back, but it gets in a hit, and my arm hurts so bad I almost drop my bow.

"Chug!" I screech. "Help!"

"Lenna, where are you?" he calls. I hear his sword thudding against bone, but the zombie is still after me, and I trip on something and tumble to the ground. Poppy stands over me, growling, and I toss my bow away and dig through my pocket until I find the axe Nan gave me for chopping firewood. Poppy lunges at the zombie as I struggle up and hack at it, but it doesn't want to go down. Lightning flashes, and I see Mal and Chug fighting a zombie of their own. Poppy and I finally beat our gruesome attacker, but as I struggle to keep upright, my heel lands on something, and I hear a snap.

My bow.

"We've got to get to shelter!" I shout.

"Then come help me protect Mal as she digs!" Chug shouts back.

When the next lightning strike reveals his position, I run over to stand back-to-back with him as Mal hacks into the ground with her diamond pickaxe. It's sharp and she's fast, but time seems to slow to a crawl as she digs down and widens a space for us. Poppy growls at an incoming mob, and I hear the twang of an arrow before I feel the hot punch of it in my leg and fall over. Screaming like an angry llama, Chug rushes the skeleton and beats it down with his sword. All I can do is lie on the ground, Poppy protecting me, and hope nothing worse comes.

"It should fit us all," Mal says.

She waves me over, and I lower myself into a hole hacked into the wet grass. It's far from the cozy shelters she made on our last adventure, even further from my snug little room in Nan's cottage, with my comfortable bed and work desk. My feet hit the ground, and I collapse and crawl to the side. There's barely enough room to stand, but it's wonderful, escaping the overloud onslaught of the rain and the way it pummels my body like a thousand poking fingers. Water pours in the hole, and then Mal and Chug leap down and huddle on the other side.

"Anybody got a door?" Chug asks.

We all droop a little at that. Tok always made our doors—beautiful, watertight wooden doors that kept out even the most persistent of zombies. I feel a pang of regret that I put Nan off whenever she offered to teach me how to craft—I wanted to learn the lore, practice my shooting, learn how to bake. I thought, why did I need to craft when Nan and Tok and Elder Stu always did that?

"Maybe I can . . ." Mal sifts through the stone she's mined and picks up a block. She stares up at the hole in the ceiling—er, ground. "Do we at least have torches?"

Chug digs around in his pocket and pulls out an old torch, which he attaches to the wall. With the space lit up warmly, we can see how small and rough it is. Mal fits the block into the ceiling, and the air goes still and silent. It's a nice reprieve from the rain, but it's also . . . scary. We're trapped underground now, with no way out until Mal mines that block or digs back up elsewhere.

"I left Thingy out there!" Chug says as distressed realization breaks across his face.

"Poppy, too," I add, feeling guilty.

"It's okay," Mal says, doing that thing where she steps up as our leader. When she gets this way, it's almost like she's put on armor made of sunshine, like she has the ability to fix us and make us see the silver lining again. "They're animals—the mobs don't care about them. They'll be fine. And they won't go far. The storm will be over soon, and then we can go outside and find our trail. If we'd stayed out there, the mobs would've swarmed us."

"But what if Thingy just keeps following the sweet berries?" Chug leaps to his feet. "What if he finds the kidnappers, but he's so far away that we can't follow, and then they have Tok *and* Thingy? What if they eat him?"

"I don't think they would eat Tok," I assure him.

"No, Lenna, I know. I mean Thingy."

I grimace. "Good point." Even if no one in Cornucopia would ever dream of eating Chug's pig, Nan tells me pork is delicious, when you're not so attached to the pig in question.

Chug looks like he wants to break down the ceiling with his bare hands, but Mal puts a hand on his shoulder, and he slides back down the ragged wall to a sitting position. I'm already on the ground, and Mal joins us. I can feel Chug's sadness filling the little cave like rising water, cold and gray and ready to suck everyone down. There has to be something I can do, but I'm injured and I feel just as terrible as everyone else, especially since my bow is broken. I feel like my main contribution, my main skill, is now completely off the table. Like I'm useless.

I dig through my pockets, wishing I'd brought another bow, but I know full well it's on my desk back home at Nan's house. Ah! But I do have something I can offer.

"Here. Eat up." When I hold out the cookies, Chug and Mal both light up, grinning.

"Good ol' Nan," Chug says, happily munching, before hurriedly adding, "Uh, but don't tell her I called her ol'."

"Actually, I made these." I feel a little shy saying it, but it's true, and the truth is important.

"Whoa, really? Good job, Lenna! They taste just as good as Nan's!" He clears his throat. "But don't tell her I said that, either."

As we eat, I can feel my wounds throbbing just a little bit less. I wish we'd brought along some healing potions, but, well, all of the potions in town were stolen by whoever took Tok, weren't they? All the ones we carried on our last journey came from Nan or witches or snatching the loot out of chests. When things go wrong, or when we're in the middle of a fight, we depend on the ability to heal quick. Sure, food can heal us, but slowly. I prefer having the safety net of potions, just in case catastrophe strikes. If we had Tok—

Nope. I'm not going to start thinking things like that.

We need to look on the bright side.

"Maybe the rain has slowed down," I say, in part because if we stay down here much longer, Chug is going to ask for more cookies, and I'm more aware than ever that we're going to need them. With just the three of us, we're so much more vulnerable than when we had Tok. And we never encountered a storm so dark that mobs were able to spawn last time, either. I'd thought this adventure would be easy, but . . . well, what adventures worth having are?

Mal picks out the block in the ceiling with her pickaxe, opening up a square-shaped hole. A few drops of rain patter down, but the sky is noticeably brighter. Chug collects the torch, stows it in his pocket, and boosts Mal out of the hole so she can clamber out onto the grass. I go up next, and Mal and I pull Chug up behind us. I feel better after my cookie, even if my leg still stings a little. The heavy clouds have moved off, leaving everything glittering with raindrops. Far off, a zombie has caught fire and is moaning as it ambles around like a walking torch.

I hear a yip of joy and see Poppy racing toward me. Much to my surprise, Thingy is by her side. They cavort around us, barking and oinking respectively, and Chug is so happy that it makes me think we can do this—we can navigate this world and find Tok and get back home, even if we are a bit rusty.

"Where's the next berry, Thingy?" Chug says, looking deep into his pig's eyes.

"Oink," Thingy says with an equal level of seriousness.

"Maybe the rain makes it harder to smell things," Chug says, looking around. "Or maybe there was so much water that it floated the berries away. I can't even remember which direction we were going."

"Me neither," Mal says. "It got so confusing and dark there, and we were fighting, and now I have no idea which way is which."

But Poppy hasn't calmed down. She's pawing at me and yipping excitedly.

"What?" I ask her.

In reply, she bounds away, toward a little hill up ahead. I follow her, and Mal and Chug follow me. As I pass by my broken bow, I grab it and shove it in my pocket. Hopefully, somehow, we'll be able to fix it later.

As for my wolf, she's really focused on something, and my heart sings with hope as I think that maybe it's Tok, maybe he's escaped his captors and is out here all alone, confused, looking for us. If so, he can have every cookie in my pockets.

Poppy leads me through the grass, and I don't see any more sweet berries, and I begin to wonder if maybe she's leading us toward the village, where the scent of cooking meat and fish is always present. I can see the beacon way up ahead, a glowing crystal blue light towering up into the sky. The prairie gives way to a few scattered trees and boulders, and the cows and sheep there assure me that if nothing else, we'll be able to eat today. Poppy passes by everything that might be food, growing ever more excited.

I hurry around a boulder, and through the underbrush I see a shape that takes a moment to come into focus. It's a person walking a tree on a lead.

Or—maybe a person *attached* to a tree *by* a lead?

"Tok?" I shout, breaking into a run.

Behind me, Chug whoops and runs faster, zooming right past me with Mal by his side. I try to speed up, but that cookie didn't fully heal me from the damage I took in that fight. When I finally catch up, I can see who it is.

My heart sinks.

It's not Tok.

It's Jarro.

# 4

# JARRO

 So here's what you need to know: My name is Jarro, and when my mom hears about this, somebody's going to be in really, really big trouble. I've almost got my hands untied from this stupid rope, when—

"Jarro?" someone shouts.

"Mom?!" I cry, looking around the endless sea of grass.

And then I spot a shape running toward me.

To my absolute horror, it's the last person I want to see: that goody-goody Mal. And her stupid friends. And their stupid, scary wolf.

I want to shout at them, tell them to go away. But I'm tied to a tree in the middle of nowhere, surrounded by monsters, and if there's one thing I know about the group of kids my town calls the Bad Apples, it's that even if they hate me, they won't let me die out here.

"A little help?" I drawl with my usual brand of smugness, hiding the fact that I'm terrified.

"I say we leave him here," Chug says, his blocky hands in fists.

"We can't," Mal says, almost sadly. "The zombies will get him."

"Zombies?" I look around, my heart clattering around like crazy. "What's a zombie? Are they the things that moan or the things that rattle? Are they nearby? Do you idiots have swords?"

Chug looks at me like I'm an idiot. "Of course we have swords. What kind of dingus goes into the Overworld without a sword?"

I don't have a good answer to that, so I go for his weak spot. "What kind of a dingus goes into the Overworld without his brother? With Tok around, it's almost like you have half a brain. On your own, I'm surprised you can even figure out which boot goes on which foot."

Success! Chug looks like I just punched him in the face, which is as gratifying as if I'd really punched him. "You mean he wasn't with you? Or whoever did this to you?"

I look down at my ropes, then back up at Chug. "Untie me and maybe I'll tell you."

Chug looks to Mal because he's a wimp who can't think for himself. "I dunno, Mal. He's a lot easier to kick this way."

Mal shakes her head and unties my hands. I flex my fingers as the blood runs back into them, making them tingle. But I don't thank her, because then it's like she's won. "They took your brother. They had us both blindfolded and gagged, but I saw him before they caught me." I kick the wet lead, now lying on the ground. Once I've made sure my arms and legs work, I look back the way they came. "Home's that way, right?" And I start walking.

After a few beats of stunned silence, they follow me. Chug runs around to block me, and I try to go around him, but his dumb girlfriends box me in.

"Where is he?" Chug bellows.

I turn away, wincing at his breath. "Where is your toothpaste?" When I try to walk again, his hand lands on my chest, and my anger starts to build. "Bro, get your hand off me."

"You're not my bro, bro," he says menacingly.

Normally, I'd look to my sides and see Edd and Remy closing in, but out here, there's a whole lot of nothing. Just my least favorite people and me. And, yeah, they think they're so tough because they've been out here before, beyond the Cornucopia wall, but I'm not impressed.

"Get your hand off me, and let me leave, or I won't tell you which direction they went."

Chug's face screws up, and his fist starts to rear back, and Mal grabs his shoulder.

"You catch more bees with honey than beetroot," she says softly, making me snicker.

His fist cocks back just a little more.

"Listen to your girlfriend," I say with a sneer.

"Just a little punch?" he asks. "Somewhere soft?"

But I can tell he's given up. This always happens when Mal's around. Which I like, because not only do I get hit less, but I also get to make fun of their friendship in a way that makes Chug even angrier.

Mal steps between us as Loony Lenna stares off into nowhere. Her brother Lugh says she does this all the time, and everyone in their family thinks she's pretty useless.

"We want to find Tok," Mal says in that bossy voice of hers. "And you know where he went."

"Maybe," I allow.

"And you want to get back home alive and not in zombie-chewed chunks."

"I—" I swallow. "What's a zombie? Do they really . . . eat people?"

I don't like her answering smile, which suggests she's superior just because she knows something I don't.

"Zombies are monsters that want to hurt people. They only show up when it's dark."

I nod. "During the storm. The growling things and the rattling things."

"The zombies growl and the skeletons rattle," Lenna adds dreamily. "The zombies will bite you, but the skeletons have bows and arrows. So I guess they twang, too."

During the storm, everything got really dark, and I heard the scariest sounds. The people who kidnapped me fought them off, shouting and grunting, and I only now realize that when they tied me to this tree, they basically left me here to die, because anything could attack me and I couldn't defend myself. It's lighter outside now, the rain gone and the clouds lifting, but at any moment . . . those things, those monsters, could come back. And I don't have a single weapon. I was ready to walk back home, ready to do it alone, but now I'm frozen in place. Still, I can't let the Bad Apples see my fear.

"Take me home, and I'll tell you where they took your brother," I say.

Chug and Mal share a look. "Tell us where they took Tok, and we'll take you home," Mal shoots back.

And then we go silent. My mom is a savvy businesswoman, with her sweet berry empire, and she once told me that when you're negotiating, forcing the other person to talk first makes them lose power. I've got all day—whereas every moment they try to gain the upper hand, Tok gets farther and farther away.

"We can't take you back," Lenna finally says, breaking the standoff. We all stare at her, and she continues. "We don't have time. We'll lose their trail if we double back to town."

Chug gasps and stares over my shoulder, toward the tree I was recently tied to. I can see his dumb face trying to figure out what to say, and it's taking him forever just to formulate words.

Finally, he says, "So do we tie him back to the tree or what?"

It's my turn to gasp. "No! That would be murder! The skelbies and zombletons or whatever—they'll come back after dark. You can't just tie me to a tree and leave! And if you did, I'd never tell you which way they took Tok. Never." Normally, I put a lot of energy into not sounding scared, but I can tell that Chug would do it. He would tie me to the tree and walk away, and then he'd think he'd won.

"We're not going to tie him to a tree." Mal taps her chin. "But we're absolutely not taking him home. Lenna's right. If we double back to town, we lose hours and hours, plus the berry trail, and someone back home might try to stop us." She frowns at me. "Especially if Jarro runs back to his mommy and tells her what we're doing. They'd never let us leave again."

Now they're all staring at me, and I hate it. I've somehow lost the upper hand.

"So what do you propose?" I say.

"Dig a hole, throw him in, seal it up, come back for him later," Chug suggests.

"Stick him *in* the tree?" Lenna offers.

"No," Mal says before I can protest. "We have to take him with us."

"No!" Chug and I both howl at the same time.

"He'll ruin everything! He's useless out here! He'll slow us down!" Chug screeches, right as I bark, "This is a big waste of my time! Take me back home or I'll tell the Elders!"

It's an empty threat and we all know it, but it's just what pops out whenever I'm around these jerks.

Mal steps up to me and really looks at me. I don't think any of us ever really look at each other. We've known one another since we were babies, we're in the same class at school, nothing about any of us ever changes—or it didn't, until these kids left town and learned how to live in the Overworld outside the wall. I guess I haven't really looked at them, either. I just see them as the same Mal, Chug, Tok, and Lenna I've always known—or Bossy, Jerky, Wimpy, and Loony, as I like to think of them. But now we regard each other, and it's almost like Mal is sizing me up. I tower over her; I could crush her like a bug. I resist the urge to throw my shoulders back and stand taller. I don't owe her anything.

"Do you think you can learn to survive in the Overworld?" she asks me.

I snort. "If you guys can do it, it can't be that hard."

Chug snorts, too. "We've nearly died ten times, dude. Everything out here wants to kill you."

I shrug. "So give me a sword. I'm not scared."

"If you're smart, you should be scared." Lenna's smile is pitying, which I hate. "It's actually pretty scary. My first night out here, I was scared. And I was scared today, too. The fear doesn't go away—you just get more skills, experience, and loot."

I can't believe I'm listening to Loony Lenna, but . . . well, the Bad Apples just seem different, ever since they went on their stupid adventure. Tok and Chug own their own shop, like adults, and make their own profits. Even my mom has to admire that, and she hates them. Mal is allowed to do her own mining—and, again, keep the profits. And Lenna has this weird importance, I guess because she works for one of the most important people in town and is set to inherit Nan's job one day. If I'm honest, and I would never admit this to anyone, I'm kind of jealous. My mom doesn't even let me leave the Hub. She says the world is dangerous, and I need to stay where she can protect me. Even Edd and Remy get to roam farther than I can.

It hits me then, like a slap across the face—I'm *outside*.

Outside the Hub, outside the wall, outside the town.

Outside what has been, up until this moment, my entire world.

Outside of my mom's carefully designated limits.

I take a deep breath and just look. At the uneven ground, the wildflowers, the passing birds, the mountains in the distance. Things outside just smell different. Even the air feels different on my skin. I never, ever thought that in all my life I would be this far away from my mom, or my town.

I just wish it didn't have to happen with these particular people, under these particular circumstances.

"So let's say I go with you . . ." I put my hands behind my back and pace. My mom says it makes you look important when you're doing a deal. "And let's say I tell you which way they took Tok. What do I get out of it?"

"I don't punch out all your teeth, to start with!" Chug roars.

Mal holds up a hand to him, and his jaw obediently snaps shut. "If you help us find Tok, and you aren't too much of a jerk, we'll teach you what we know. These skills are valuable back home."

Chug shakes his head like a confused chicken. "Mal, you can't be serious. You want to give Jarro—our enemy, the jerk—a *weapon*?"

She ignores me to face him. "What else are we going to do? If we take him back, we lose the trail and half a day, and someone in town will stop us. If we leave him here, he dies. If we take him with us, we're more likely to achieve our goal, because he knows he can't go home until we have Tok. And when we encounter hostile mobs, we'll have one more fighter."

Chug deflates, and I've got to admit—it's gratifying. "If he doesn't stab me in the liver," he groans.

Mal pats his arm. "We'll start him off with a wooden sword."

"Great! Liver splinters!" Chug throws his hands up in the air and walks around, muttering angrily to himself.

Mal steps closer and stares me right in the eyes. "Can you behave?"

My head jerks back. "I always behave! It's you guys who—"

"Zip it." Her fingers snap nearly on my nose, and to my surprise, my mouth, too, clicks shut. "We're going to have to call a truce. You need us and we need you. As long as we're outside the walls, you're on our side." She picks up the lead that tethered me and swings it in front of my face. "Betray us, and we really will tie you to a tree. Got it?"

I'm kind of speechless. She's right about us needing one another, and I hate that. But I also . . . kind of . . . want to know what they know. And out here, away from Edd and Remy and my mom and all the other nosy neighbors, with no one watching me and judging me . . . maybe I could try.

When she drops the lead at my feet, I pick it up and stuff it in my pocket. It barely fits, and it makes me feel dumb, but I don't want her to threaten me with it again.

"But you have to give me a real weapon, and you have to teach me how to fight," I say, nose in the air.

"Deal."

Mal sticks out her hand, and I shake it.

# 5

# TOK

 Here's what you need to know:

No, wait.

Here's what I need to know:

WHAT IS EVEN HAPPENING?

Where am I? Who is dragging me around? Where's Chug? Are my cats okay?

I'm blindfolded and gagged. I can't see anything.

My feet are killing me, I'm still in my pajamas, and the only thing I'm really sure of is that every step takes me farther and farther away from home.

I'm just a kid.

What do they even want with me?

And even worse, what are they going to do with me after they get it?

# 6
## CHUG

This is the worst day of my life, and that includes the day Mom made beetroot soup for dinner. First my brother disappears, and now I'm stuck with my worst enemy. Mal made me promise not to hurt Jarro, and she made him promise not to hurt me, and now we're just glaring at each other in a meadow, wishing we could hurt each other.

"So which way did they take Tok?" Mal asks, right back to business.

Jarro points — in the same direction Thingy is straining toward, testing the strength of his lead. "That way."

"Obviously," I mutter under my breath.

I take Thingy off the lead, and he jogs to the next dropped sweet berry. He happily gulps it down and trots on to the next one. Mal gives me a pleading look and follows him. I'd like to be up there with my best friend and my best pig, but there's no way I can trust Jarro enough to leave him alone. He doesn't like any of us, and he certainly doesn't know how to defend us. He doesn't know anything about life outside of Cornucopia—he doesn't even know what zombies and skeletons are. He might be so busy bullying Lenna that a witch surprises us. Or he might steal Mal's pickaxe. I don't know his full capabilities. I just know he's trouble.

So it's Thingy, then Mal, then Jarro and me, then Lenna and Poppy. Every now and then, Mal looks back to check on us, brow drawn down as she stares at me and Jarro as we silently, angrily march side by side. Whenever he pulls ahead, I hurry to keep up. I don't want him to get too close to Mal.

"Back off!" Jarro grumbles as I pick up the pace.

"You back off!" I mutter. "Stop trying to get ahead. It's not a race. Just . . . walk normal!"

"I'm trying to walk normal, but you keep crowding me!"

He tries to push past me toward Mal, and I throw my arm across his chest, and he whirls around and shoves me, and then, somehow, in a way that is utterly not my fault, we end up in the dirt, wrestling and slapping and throwing elbows.

"Hey! You guys promised!" Mal shouts as she puts the lead on Thingy and runs back to stand over us.

"We're roughhousing!" I squeak out as I try to knee him somewhere very tender. "Roughhousing is an important part of childhood development."

"Yeah, you didn't say no tussling!" Jarro adds as he tries to strangle me.

Lenna joins Mal to stand over us, and I can tell that they both want us to feel ashamed of our behavior, but I'm not, and judging by the elbow I just took to the nose, neither is Jarro.

It's not long before we're both bruised and out of breath. My elbows grow feeble, and Jarro's lip is bleeding. We untangle, and I flop onto my back in the dirt.

"You done?" Mal asks.

"No," I say, grinning. Poppy sits between her and Lenna, her tongue out and her eyes twinkling. I lunge for Poppy and drag her down, gently and playfully tussling with her. She wriggles and tries to lick my lips, and Lenna laughs.

"Wolf!" Jarro shouts, scuttling backward. "Isn't it . . . dangerous?"

I rub Poppy's belly. "No she's not dangerous, are you? Are you, girl? You're a big ol' softy, aren't you?"

"Unless someone threatens us," Lenna warns. "Then she's not soft at all." She raises an eyebrow at Jarro as he absorbs this information.

"Can I pet her?"

Lenna nods, and Jarro creeps closer, his hand shaking as he extends it toward the big gray wolf that I now think of as a friend. Poppy sits up and sniffs him before looking to Lenna.

"It's okay," Lenna says.

After an experimental lick, Poppy wags her tail politely, and Jarro rubs her head. I remember what that felt like, the first time I touched a wolf. I thought it would be rough, but it was so soft. I still can't believe Lenna tamed her, considering Lenna used to be the scaredy-cat of the group. But here we are, in the Overworld, petting a wolf . . . with Jarro.

"She's sweet," Jarro says, like he can't quite believe it. Poppy rolls onto her back, and Jarro rubs her belly with a look of utter awe.

"As long as you're not an evoker. She loves tugging on their cloaks," I say.

"It's a great strategy," Mal explains. "Poppy distracts the monsters, and then we can hit them with our swords, or Lenna can use her bow and arrow."

Jarro looks at each of us in turn, confused. "Wait, where are your weapons? Don't tell me you're out here without any protection."

Mal whips her diamond pickaxe out of her pocket, and Jarro's eyes go as big as pumpkins. "How'd you do that?"

I pull a sword out of each pocket just to watch him gawp again. "It's a magic trick Nan taught us. I'm carrying an entire armory."

Jarro stops petting Poppy and stands. He reaches into his pocket and pulls it inside out. It's clear that it should only be able to fit an apple, maybe. "So teach me."

Mal puts her hands on her hips and stares him down.

"Try manners," Lenna reminds him.

Jarro rolls his eyes like this is the dumbest thing in the world. "*Please* teach me?"

So Lenna does, because Lenna is kind like that, and because she's really dedicated to helping spread Nan's lore. Soon Jarro is practicing putting everything from Lenna's pockets into his pockets and pulling it all back out again.

"It's so easy!" He pulls out a huge book. "I can't believe everybody doesn't know about this!" Mal and Lenna exchange a wary glance, and Jarro notices it. "What?"

"We've been teaching everybody back home. Your mom learned it weeks ago. She didn't show you?"

Jarro's face goes as red as beetroot. "She must've forgot."

Mal winces. "Well, I'm sure she meant to. She said it would come in really handy when it came time to harvest the sweet berries." She takes the huge book in Jarro's hand and hands it back to Lenna. "And the cookies."

Looking a little guilty, Jarro pulls out a dozen of Lenna's cookies, which she tucks back into her own pockets.

"I told you we can't trust him," I mutter.

"I just forgot because I was mad because—" Jarro goes quiet, frowning.

Because his mom lied to him, or at least neglected to teach him something she knew, something he would find helpful. That's got to hurt.

Good.

"It's okay," Lenna says in that Lenna-ish way that makes you feel okay about messing up. "Here. You probably need a cookie, anyway. I'm guessing whoever tied you to that tree didn't feed you."

She hands him back a cookie, and he devours it in two chomps and mutters, "Thanks. 'Sa really good cookie."

"Thanks. I made it."

"Really?"

"Yeah, it's Nan's recipe."

"She always just seemed like a crazy old kook, but she can bake."

"She's not crazy!" I snap, because I definitely don't like the way Jarro and Lenna are just talking, like he doesn't have a long-running history of bullying her.

"It's true. She's just eccentric," Lenna adds.

"And also my great-great-grandmother, so not a great target for rudeness," Mal continues.

Jarro is turning red again, but he wipes cookie crumbs from his lip and tries to play it cool. "Well, she definitely seems unusual. And bossy. So I can see how you two might be related. Still, great cookies, and fun pocket trick. Nan's cool in my book."

Mal nods, and Jarro nods, and then everyone is getting along again, except for me, because I'm still mad and I will probably be mad forever, or at least until Jarro helps us get Tok back.

"Guys, we're losing time. Thingy is getting antsy. Let's go." I take the lead back from Mal and let go so Thingy can run ahead, not caring this time what order we're in. Jarro's clearly not going to hurt the girls, but he's more than glad to get on my nerves.

My pig is still chasing his berry trail, and it takes me a while to catch up. I follow him from berry to berry, scratch his back and enjoy his happy oinks, then prepare for him to run off for the next berry. But after a while . . . he doesn't run up ahead. He cocks his chubby pink face back and forth, oinking confusedly.

"What's up?" Mal says, arriving by my side.

"Either he's full or the berry trail has run out."

Of course, Thingy is never full, so it's obviously the latter.

We spread out to look for berries, but if Thingy can't find a berry, then there is no berry. We're out in the middle of nowhere, and now the trail has run out. It would make sense if the kidnappers headed for the village or woodland mansion, but what if they didn't? What if they suddenly changed direction? The world is so much bigger than we'd ever dreamed, and we've seen only a small fraction of it. Who knows how far away Tok could be right now?

I sigh and droop, and Mal pats my shoulder. "Don't worry, Chug. We'll find him. I just know we will."

"But what if we don't?" Jarro says.

We all glare at him. If looks could kill, he would be a skid mark right now.

"We're going to find him," Mal repeats. "And that's that."

"But how?" Jarro asks.

No one has an answer for that.

As we stand around, uncertain, hopeless, Poppy sniffs the ground like she always does when we stop. She follows her nose over to a small copse of trees, the only one for what seems like miles. Whatever she's found on the ground has really caught her attention. Her ears perk up as she sniffs and wags furiously before giving a sharp, excited yip.

"Maybe Poppy found a berry?" I ask, voice cracking with hope.

Mal nods and leads us over there, and I'm surprised to find an iron ingot, of all things. I pick it up and turn it over in my hands. "It's basically a rock, Poppy, but, thanks, anyway." I angrily shove it in my pocket, reasoning that if we find Tok—no, *when* we find Tok—he can use it for his crafting. Mal puts her hand on my shoulder. She's the kind of friend who can always tell when I'm on the verge of tears.

But Poppy isn't done. She paws at the ground and rolls around in the dirt, wiggling on her back in ecstasy. I squat down and notice that there's something weird about this dirt.

It's got funny little shapes pressed into it here and there, like raindrops, all going in the same direction.

"Llamas," I murmur.

"Where?" Mal asks, perking up as she pulls a lead out of her pocket.

I shake my head and point. "No. Those are hoofprints. There were llamas here. And someone must've dropped this iron ingot." I take it out of my pocket and run my fingers over it before holding it out to Poppy. She sniffs it and yips excitedly.

"It's got to be Tok!" I nearly shout. "He must've dropped it on purpose. His pockets are always full of crafting stuff."

Mal squats beside me to inspect the prints. "Maybe he ran out of berries and had to use the next best thing."

"It makes sense," Lenna adds. "With all the loot they stole, they would need some way to carry it all."

"Come to think of it, I do remember hearing big animals when I was blindfolded," Jarro says. I hadn't noticed that he had rejoined us, and now I am significantly less happy. "I don't know what llamas are, but do they make weird sounds? Like, *meehhh* and *bleh* and *ptoo*?"

I'm honestly shocked at how well Jarro can reproduce llama sounds, possibly because he, too, is a stinky, hairy, drooling beast.

"Yeah, that's exactly what they sound like." Mal is similarly stunned.

"Then they've got some."

Following a trail of llama prints isn't nearly as pleasant as following a happy pig eating sweet berries, but we manage. When there's dirt, we can see prints, and when we enter thick grass, there's almost a trail where the grass has parted—and chunks of it have been nibbled off. As we walk, we fall back into our familiar line, with Mal in the lead, then me, then Lenna, but Jarro hangs around Lenna and starts asking her all sorts of questions. The funny thing is that the old version of Lenna, Loony Lenna, the one whose family kicked her out of the mine for being weird and dreamy—she would've been scared of Jarro and gone quiet and avoided eye contact. But since Lenna's been working with Nan, she has this new confidence. She's discovered that she really likes talking about her interests, and since Jarro is asking questions about animals and mobs, she knows exactly how to answer. She stinks at small talk, but she's great at lecturing about the stuff she loves.

Fine. At least she's keeping him occupied. And if he tries to hurt her, Poppy will bite off his arm. And then I'll bite off the other.

I hurry up ahead with Mal.

"So they're getting cozy," I say darkly.

She glances back over her shoulder. "I mean, they're walking side by side and talking, but I wouldn't call it cozy."

"He's our enemy."

"He's just another kid who can be a jerk sometimes, Chug."

"All the time."

She glances back again. "Well, he's not being a jerk now. Maybe he's only a jerk around Remy and Edd."

"He's always around Remy and Edd, back home."

"Exactly."

I stomp a little harder so she'll know I'm mad.

"We're stuck with him, you know," she finally says.

"Just because I know it doesn't mean I like it."

"Me neither. He wasn't nice to any of us. But we changed out here. Maybe he can, too."

I can't imagine Jarro being anything other than the bullying jerk who torments my brother and lives to see me get in trouble, but there's no point in arguing with Mal when she's trying to play peacekeeper. I can't believe my life right now depends on following hoofprints and playing nice with someone who treats me like poop. On our last adventure, I felt like I had everything I needed, like even when we'd been robbed, I could survive and thrive as long as I had the Bad Apples by my side. Now we're missing Tok, my brother and best friend, and in his place, we're stuck with . . . a moldy apple?

No. A moldy beetroot.

Whatever Jarro is, he's not part of the Mob Squad. He's just a jerk who's too stupid to avoid being jerknapped.

Which reminds me . . .

"Hey, Jarro?"

"What?" he shouts back.

"Why'd they jerknap you, anyway?"

Mal and I slow down—since we're not chasing Thingy's appetite anymore, my desperation to find Tok is what's really driving us—and Jarro and Lenna catch up.

"Stop calling me a jerk," he growls.

"Then stop being a jerk," I growl back.

"Boys!" Lenna and Mal say at the same time.

Jarro and I both growl in response, and it's so funny and stupid that I nearly choke trying to hold back a laugh.

"But really. Why did they take you?" Mal asks.

Jarro walks for a minute before answering. "I heard a noise last night, out in the sweet berry field. I grabbed our axe and went running out there, thinking I would scare away some lost sheep or naughty little kids trying to eat the berries. But I ran right into a bunch of adults—strangers in armor with weapons. They already had Tok tied up, bound and gagged on a lead. They were ripping the berry bushes out of the ground and stuffing the berries into chests. I tried to stop them, but one kid against six adults? I never had a chance. And their swords didn't look like the ones in Elder Stu's shop, all shiny and new. They were dirty and chipped and stained, like they'd been used a lot." Jarro shudders. "The leader was—mean, but almost like he felt sorry for me? He said they couldn't let me go because I'd seen them, but that maybe they could put me to work in the mine."

"My parents' mine?" Lenna asks, worried.

Jarro shakes his head. "How would I know? They were blind-folding me. They'd taken my axe—it was my grandmother's axe. One guy put his hand over my mouth before I could shout and wake up everybody. After that, they kept me with Tok, with some-body holding our leads, and I don't know what the rest of them did. I just know they stole all our sweet berries, and it was my fault."

Much to my surprise, Jarro is starting to tear up and trying his hardest not to cry. I know what it feels like, when you can't protect what's yours. When strange adults take what you've worked hard to collect—and when you realize for the first time that there might be people in the world who want to hurt you. And I remember how scary it was, the first time we were out here, in the Overworld for the first time. At least we had Nan's books and teachings. At least we had one another. Jarro is a jerk, but he got kidnapped from his own yard in the middle of the night and then abandoned, alone, with nothing, in the middle of nowhere.

Still, I don't trust him.

I reach into my pocket and pull out an axe.

## 7
## MAL

 Just a few hours ago, I would've sworn there was no situation involving Chug, Jarro, and an axe that could end well, but here we are. Tok made that axe, and Chug carried it in his pocket to sell to potential customers, and now he's giving it to his worst enemy.

"It's dangerous out here," Chug says. "Take this."

Jarro holds the axe like he knows what to do with it, at least; I guess he splits logs for his mom. I remember the first time Chug held a sword, when none of us knew what it was and thought it was just a really long knife. It's probably better to start Jarro off with something familiar. An axe can definitely put a hurt on a hostile mob.

I was worried they were going to bicker and shove each other all the way to—wherever we're going. But if Chug trusts Jarro enough to put the axe in his hands instead of in his back, then maybe miracles do happen. Maybe they can get along.

Lenna and I exchange a surprised glance. She's smiling a

smile that reminds me a bit of Nan, a satisfied, smug sort of smile that suggests she knew everything would be just fine. Then again, Lenna often looks to Poppy to decide how to react to something new, and if Poppy will let Jarro not only pet her head but also rub her belly, then the wolf must really see our former enemy as more of a friend.

Jarro takes the axe with a nod, stiffly says thanks, and puts it in his pocket using our trick. He's trying to cover up how upset he was, telling that story, and that's totally okay. I want to keep things this way, with Chug feeling benevolent and Jarro feeling anything but cruel. I need to get them moving, so I spot the next place in the grass up ahead where there is another iron ingot and hurry toward it. The boys will feel better rushing toward a goal than they will standing here being awkward with each other.

Chug collects the ingot, and we continue in the direction of the hoofprints. As we follow the trail, I start to notice something I can't ignore:

This is nearly the same path we took on our last adventure.

The beacon outside the village, while still far away, seems to be the way the llama prints are pointing us. I briefly wonder if it was the villagers there who took Tok—

But no. All they can say is, "Hm," and Jarro said he heard people arguing. Plus, the villagers just want to live their lives and trade for emeralds. In our time in the village, I never saw a single one of them holding a weapon. They're peaceful, whatever they are.

So the question remains: Who kidnapped Tok and Jarro and stole all of Dawna's sweet berry bushes and Elder Gabe's potions and ingredients? And where are they going?

They could be going to the village to trade, but I can't imagine those villagers trading their wares for two kids and some berries and potions. They're wild for emeralds and happy enough to accept wheat, but no one would go to the trouble of stealing from Cornucopia for such small stakes. It's the sort of thing our neighbor Krog would do, except that he's still locked up in the town jail for all the trouble he caused, and I stop by once a week just to confirm with my own eyes that he's still there. Krog is the one who started our last adventure by sending evokers and their vexes to destroy the town's crops and drive all our families away. He wanted full, selfish access to the fortress under the town and all the resources he would need to build a Nether portal, whatever that is. He wanted obscure potion ingredients, so it would make sense if he was stealing Elder Gabe's potions.

Except he can't, because he's in jail.

And then again, Elder Gabe's shop only carries simple potions, not what Krog was after. He needed strange ingredients from the Nether, which is apparently another place. Not a biome or village or town—but something else altogether. Nan told us once that her only regret in life is not journeying to the Nether and seeing if it was real, and if so, what creatures and riches could be found there.

When we stopped Krog from destroying our town, the Elders dismantled the Nether portal he was building under the Hub. It took them forever, but they were determined to keep us safe, per the town commandments. They even sealed up the entrance to the fortress down there, with its long tunnel and the rails that lead all the way to the woodland mansion we cleared while trying to beat Krog and his illagers. So whoever we're following right now knew that our town had potions and berries, and they took Jarro so he couldn't raise the alarm, but why would they take Tok? He's just a kid like any of us—

Except he isn't, is he?

Tok is incredibly skilled with his crafting table. He's invented things even Elder Stu can't re-create, things our eldest Elder has never even thought about. And now Tok's been openly attempting to add potions and explosives to his skill set. Maybe that's why they stole him right out of his bed.

Because they need his particular set of skills.

So they found out about him, and they made a plan, and they took him.

But do they want him to make weapons and armors or potions and explosives?

It doesn't really matter. In the hands of the wrong sort of people, they're all tools of war.

I speed up. I'm worried about Tok, but now I'm worried about what these people will make Tok do. And I'm not ready to tell Chug about my hypothesis yet. He feels bad enough as it is. If he starts thinking about the kidnappers forcing his brother to craft things that could hurt innocent people or pigs, he'll get even more upset.

What's more, I'm beginning to suspect we're following the kidnappers right back to that same woodland mansion, which would be the perfect hideout for bad people up to no good. Remote, big, full of resources, and the sort of place that's usually full of scary, murderous illagers. It's going to take us several days to get there, at best. The kidnappers have half a day on us at least, and we'll have to stop before dusk each day to dig out a shelter—unless we can manage to find the ones we created along the way and used last time.

I glance back at Jarro, who's lagging behind. The rest of us might be a little out of shape for life outside the wall, but he's never been out here before at all. He's not even a farm kid. His mom's sweet berry plot is right in the middle of town, a rare patch of green that she defends tooth and nail. He's probably never even walked a mile in his entire life. He's only going to slow us down.

I'm about to ask Chug if he'll let Jarro ride Thingy, but I don't bother.

Maybe he'll give Jarro an axe, but there's no way he would trust him with his pig.

"Can we slow down?" Jarro calls.

"Not until we find Tok," Chug bellows.

I look up at the sky. It's afternoon. Soon I'll have to make a shelter, because no matter what the people we're following do, we know full well we can't survive the night unprotected. There are simply too many hostile mobs, and we still need to finish healing from the skeleton horsemen. Lenna is still limping a little, and I'm pretty sure I saw her shoving her broken bow into her pocket. We're not at our best.

I look up ahead, but we're still so far from the beacon. We can't make the village tonight. We'll have to stop and rest soon, no matter how upset it makes Chug. I mark a little copse of trees, just a smudge of darker green on the horizon. If we stop there, maybe Lenna can fix her bow, and we can begin to teach Jarro how to help us survive out here. Whether we like him or not, whether we trust him or not, his axe might be what keeps us alive when the mobs strike. Which they will.

We're silent as I follow the llama prints and my friends follow me. The copse of trees isn't too far off our trail, so I dig through my pocket until I find a block of stone from the mine and drop it by the nearest prints.

"What are you doing?" Chug asks.

"Marking our trail." I point at the trees. "I need time to dig a shelter, and Lenna needs to fix her bow. Maybe you can teach Jarro how to fight while we work."

Chug looks at the sun, which is thinking about starting to set. "We can go a little farther."

I shake my head. "Maybe we could walk another half hour, but we need Lenna's bow, and we need Jarro to have some idea of what to do if a mob shows up. And shelters always take more time than we'd prefer. After what happened earlier today, we're not taking any chances."

"But every moment we spend stopped, Tok is that much farther away—"

"They have to stop, too. Whoever took him, they're not any different from us. They require rest, they require sleep, they have to get somewhere safe once the sun sets and the mobs come out. They don't even know they're being followed. It feels like a race to us, but for them, it's not."

Chug's face screws up. He hates it when our opinions differ and he knows I'm right.

"Okay, but I'm not training him. I'm going to go find something to eat. We may have cookies, but we don't have meat, and that'll help Lenna heal faster."

I give him a grateful smile. He might be scared and annoyed, but his first instinct is still to take care of us.

Jarro and Lenna catch up once we're under the trees. They're oaks, and their shade is welcome. I've already dug up a few blocks.

"Lenna, can you fix your bow?" I ask.

She picks up a stick. "I could if I had a crafting table."

We all dig through our pockets, but all we come up with are frowns.

"Tok always has one," Chug says sadly.

"But they're pretty easy to make, right?" I ask.

Lenna looks up into the oak as if wishing it would just drop a crafting table from its branches. "I always use Nan's."

"You guys know how to use a crafting table?" Jarro asks, shocked.

Chug shrugs. I know my buddy, and I know that look on his face—he doesn't feel like he's good enough for what he needs to do, but he's too stubborn and proud to let anyone else know that. "It's not that hard. Tok's really good at it, but he tried to teach me a few things." He touches the tree Lenna is looking at. "If you can chop up some planks, I can try to put a crafting table together. It won't be as nice as Nan's and Tok's," he says quickly. "But we really need to get Lenna's bow working again." He gives Jarro a dark glare. "Things get dangerous at night." When Jarro blanches, Chug grins.

I nod, trusting my friends to do their parts as I twirl my diamond pickaxe and get back to digging. It feels good, hacking into a fresh patch of rock, knowing no one has ever dug here before. Maybe I'll find nothing but boring ol' stone, but there's always the possibility of something exciting, a vein of ore or even diamonds or emeralds. I've found some treasures in my little mine back home, out behind the cow pasture, but there's just something extra thrilling about the endless possibilities of digging a hole out here in the middle of nowhere.

Jarro's axe thuds into the tree, and Lenna hums to herself as she writes in her book. Chug heads off into the plains, looking for sheep or chickens, something we can turn into dinner. I find some iron and coal, nothing unexpected, but at least we'll be able to make some torches instead of spending the night in the pitch darkness underground.

Time passes. Jarro's axe stops, and I hear Lenna droning on, hopefully teaching him useful things about life in the Overworld. Sometimes she can get very lost in her own train of thought, pursuing her more obscure interests instead of focusing on what's important. She knows so much fascinating lore now, but Jarro knowing the right things could be the difference between our survival and someone getting seriously hurt. Chug returns with four chickens, starts a campfire to cook them, and sorts through the wood Jarro chopped for the right sort of planks to make a crafting table. I manage to dig my usual chamber, then add a few extra blocks' worth of space, reckoning that while we're all fine being cozy with Tok, now that Jarro's along for the ride, everyone will be more comfortable if we're not smushed up against our least favorite person in the world.

As I'm evening out the sides of the shelter, I hear someone outside scream bloody murder. Diamond pickaxe in hand, I scramble out of the hole and search for my friends.

Chug and Lenna are nowhere to be found. Neither are Poppy and Thingy.

All I see is Jarro, frozen in place, hands thrown in front of his face as a creeper runs right at him and starts flashing.

# 8

# LENNA

 Under the dappled shade of the gently swaying oaks, I'm writing in my book. Chug is almost done with his crafting table—I think—when I hear someone screaming. I drop my broken bow and run, fingers searching my pocket for something, anything I can use as a weapon. I come up holding cookies and books, which is normally great, but in this case, not helpful at all. Chug is right behind me, though, and I know his pockets are full of sharp things.

As we run back to the fire, we see Mal sprinting toward a creeper as it starts to flash, close enough for Jarro to touch it, if he were as stupid as we always assumed. While he's backing away, hands thrown over his head, Mal hits it with her diamond pick-axe, just one solid hit—

*Boom!*

I feel the explosion in my chest as my eyes squeeze shut. My ears are ringing, and somehow I'm on my back.

"Lenna? Are you okay?"

I blink, and there's Chug, trying to help me stand up. I'm dazed, but I nod as he pulls me to my feet. Together, we run to where Mal and Jarro lie on the ground by a crater. The creeper is gone, but the explosion it made is bigger than anything Tok's managed so far. It's scary how Mal and Jarro aren't moving.

Chug goes directly to Mal, no question, and starts talking to her, touching her shoulder, begging her to be okay. She's limp and unmoving. That leaves me to help Jarro, and it occurs to me that I don't generally like being touched, and I've spent my entire life trying to stay away from this bully, to avoid being touched by him, and now I have to touch him to make sure he's not dead.

"Jarro," I say, nudging his shoulder. "Jarro, are you okay?"

He blinks up at me, skin dusted with fine black powder, hair standing up on end, eyes red, and mutters, "What was that?"

Now that I know he's alive, I say, "A creeper."

Jarro shouts, "What?" as I turn my attention to Mal.

She's not recovering as quickly, and Chug is starting to get worried. So am I. She was closer to the creeper than Jarro, and she took most of the blast, shielding him with her body.

"Do you have any Potions of Healing?" Chug asks me, desperate.

I shake my head. "Just cookies. And there's the chicken you found . . ."

Chug glances around the little clearing. We have a crafting table, a fire, a shelter, and some half-cooked chicken. No golden apples, no potions, no way to make or obtain them. I know so much more than I did on our last trip, but that doesn't mean I have access to all the wonderful things I've learned about. If we were back home, in Cornucopia, Nan and Elder Gabe would have Mal back to herself by dinner, but here . . .

"Let's get her inside," Chug says. He stands and carefully picks Mal up, cradling her to his chest like she's a baby. He walks to the shelter with careful steps, murmuring to her. Inside, we have no beds, no pillows. As if understanding our problem, Poppy curls up against the hard stone wall Mal has recently dug, making a little nest of her side. Chug nestles Mal there, and she's so pale and scorched that I don't know what to do.

"What happened?" Jarro says loudly, appearing behind us.

"You were a stupid idiot who just stood there when a creeper showed up, and Mal saved your worthless butt," Chug shouts, loud enough that Jarro can't miss it.

"You never told me weird green things would run at me and explode!" Jarro argues. "How could I know that? How could anyone know that?"

Chug falters for a moment, remembering that it wasn't too long ago that none of us knew about creepers, but his face shuts down again almost immediately. "I bet you can't even make torches, can you? Useless." Chug digs through his pocket, places our only torch on the wall, and stomps outside. "Stay with her, Jarro. Talk to her. Get her to eat. Let us know when she wakes up."

"If she wakes up," Jarro mumbles.

I have to grab Chug's arm and pull him away to keep him from beating up Jarro right there.

Outside, the air still smells of gunpowder. The chicken is half raw, and Chug fusses with it, urging it to cook faster. He paces for a moment, then stands at the crafting table he just made, looking like he's about to give up. I can see why—it's . . . not the best crafting table. The sides are all a little bit off.

"You wouldn't happen to have a recipe book, would you?" he asks me.

I pull three books out of my pockets to show him: Nan's original Mobestiary, a book on flora and fauna, and my journal, where I'm adding all the new things I'm learning daily. Crafting and food recipes aren't very interesting to me because they're always the same. I like things that change.

"Okay," Chug mutters to himself. "Okay, I can do this." He looks up at me. "I need you to drag over any coal Mal dug up." I nod and jog off.

As I bring him a few chunks of coal, Chug starts working. When Tok is at his crafting table, he has this sort of maniacal glee, like he can't believe he has so much power and can't wait to defy reality. When I'm standing at Nan's crafting table, I feel tentative and anxious, like if I don't do everything just right the whole world will fall down. But Chug seems like he's being crushed under a boulder of self-doubt and is certain he's going to fail.

"You can do it," I tell him. "I believe in you."

When he looks up at me, he's stunned. "Why'd you say that?"

"Because you look like you don't believe in yourself."

He deflates a little. "I guess I don't. This is what Tok's great at. Every time he tries to teach me, I botch something up."

I shrug. "Well, you can't really botch up a torch. It's pretty easy to burn things."

"I was going to make a bed for Mal." He's blushing now. "I snatch up puffs of wool whenever I find them for Tok to use later, so there's always some fuzz in my pockets. We need to get her up off the ground."

He goes to work, and I turn the chicken over so it'll roast evenly. It's always better when Chug takes care of the food, but I guess we're all just doing the best we can tonight. After what feels like an eternity of hammering and quiet cursing, Chug says, "Ready?" and I gather up some mostly cooked chicken before we head back to the shelter.

Jarro is sitting with his back against the wall as he watches Mal. He looks, honestly, a lot like Chug did recently—like the whole world rests on his shoulders and he can't stay standing much longer.

"No change," he says softly. "But she's still breathing. That's good, right?"

Chug ignores him as he sets up the bed in the farthest corner and carefully places Mal in it. She shifts, and the smallest smile flits across her face. We've seen Mal cut up and beaten and poisoned, but we've never seen her quite this bad. Once she's settled, Chug places his torches around the small chamber at the usual intervals.

"We should've brought the cats," he murmurs. "Then she'd be okay."

"It's not your fault," I tell him. I wish that he believed me.

When he starts waving a bit of chicken under Mal's nose, Jarro shakes his head and stands, heading back outside.

I follow him to where he leans against a tree, staring out at the blackened crater the creeper made.

"You don't want to be outside after dark," I warn him. "There are more creepers, plus zombies, skeletons, spiders, illagers. All sorts of things."

"I'm surprised you guys aren't locking me outside to get eaten."

"You're lucky we're not voting on it," I admit. "Chug would definitely tie you to a tree right now. Do you feel confident with the axe?"

Jarro pulls the axe out of his pocket and turns it over in his hands. "Against a log, yes. Against an enemy, clearly not. That thing came right at me, and I just froze." I've known Jarro all my life, but I've never seen him like this. He looks like a lost little baby, like he might cry.

"That's pretty normal," I admit. "But maybe now that you've experienced an attack, you'll respond differently the next time." I glance at the sky and walk to the crafting table, checking that I have some spare string and picking up a stick on the way. "That's why I like my bow and arrows. I don't really do well in the close-range fights, either. I do better from farther back. I guess we all just naturally found our specialties and fell into our roles, but you don't know yours yet."

Jarro looks down and kicks at a tuft of grass as I work on my bow. "I don't have a specialty. I've, uh, never really been good at anything."

"Except bullying people," I remind him, and even though the shadows have turned everything purple, I'm pretty sure he blushes.

"Well, I couldn't bully that creeper."

"Only cats can."

He shakes his head. "See, that makes no sense. They're scared of cats, but not people with weapons? Why? Are all monsters—mobs—like that?"

I inspect my bow and smile to see it repaired. I'm definitely going to need it on this journey. After I've stuck it back in my pocket, I pull out the Mobestiary and hand it to Jarro. "Read this. It'll tell you about all the creatures in the Overworld, good and bad. I know it's a lot to take in, but you just have to remember you're not alone."

"I sure do feel alone. Did you see how Chug looked at me in there? Like it's my fault."

"Well, it kind of is. You've got to be aware of your surroundings when you're beyond the wall."

Jarro cocks his head and really looks at me as if for the first time. "Do you just say whatever you think all the time?"

"Pretty much. It's easier than trying to guess what people want to hear. I usually disappoint them, either way."

"You're really weird, Lenna."

I shrug. "I know."

"But not, like, loony. Just different."

"Like I said—I know." I hand him a spear of chicken from the fire. "Here. You need to eat. Food is the cure for all ills, out here."

He takes the chicken with some suspicion but is soon wolfing it down. As soon as Chug appears, Jarro ducks back into the shelter with his chicken, wisely choosing a dank underground hole to Chug's wrath.

"What were you guys talking about?" Chug asks as he selects a few wood planks and starts making a door.

"How Jarro needs to learn about the Overworld and figure out what he's good at so he can be part of the solution instead of part of the problem."

Chug barks a laugh. "And how'd that go over?"

"Well, he admitted he isn't really good at anything, and I let him borrow the Mobestiary so the next time something runs at him, he can do something besides cower."

That gets an actual belly-shaking chuckle. "You know, I'm mad at him—but then again, I'm always mad at him—and yet it's also fun to see him struggle. I don't think I've ever frozen in the face of danger."

"I don't think you can control how you react to things the first time, but you can try to do better the next time." Chug stares at me as I nibble my chicken. "Also, I fixed my bow. Your crafting table might look a little wonky, but it works fine."

Chug blushes as he holds up his door. It's not a work of art, like Tok's doors, but it'll keep us safe through the night, and that's what matters. "Let's get down there before the zombies smell us."

I sniff near him and pinch my nose. "Before the zombies smell *you*."

He sticks out his tongue. "You know armor makes me stink!"

We're laughing as I smother the fire and collect the rest of the chicken and Chug carries his door. Once it's attached, he digs a quick little pit for Thingy and throws his pig some carrots before joining us all inside Mal's shelter. She made this one a little bigger than usual, I guess to give Jarro and Chug a little space. Chug doesn't have any more wool, so Mal gets the only bed, but that's okay. Poppy is curled up on her feet, and Jarro sits in the farthest corner, reading under a torch.

The last time we traveled, things were so much easier. We had time, we had enough beds, we had extra food, we had Tok. And, of course, there was no Jarro, and Mal was conscious. I keep going over and over in my head what we could've done differently this afternoon. Could've fixed my bow, first off. Could've brought a cat. Could've told Jarro to run if he saw a skittering green monster. Could've stuck together instead of going off in separate directions.

But none of that matters. If wishes were mine carts, illagers would ride.

I pull out my journal and continue taking notes on what I saw today. Animals, plants, mobs. I've never seen a creeper explode before, so that's new. If we're going to suffer, I'm going to do my best to record every detail to help the next person who comes along.

I fall asleep with the pen in my hand and don't wake up until I hear someone moaning in the middle of the night.

# 9

# JARRO

 I bolt awake, scrambling for my axe. I've heard that sound before. The book Lenna lent me said that zombies are the mobs that moan, and I don't know how one spawned in our shelter, but I'm ready to fight this time. I'm not going to freeze and let someone else get hurt. I'm going to stand up and—

"Lenna," the voice moans, and it's definitely not a zombie.

Lenna is across the room in a heartbeat, kneeling by Mal's bed. Since everything is so well lit for an underground hole, just like back home, I can see that Mal's eyes are open and bloodshot.

"Got any of those cookies?" she asks in a wobbly voice.

Lenna produces cookies—which she didn't offer to anyone else earlier, I notice—and helps Mal sit up to eat.

"We have chicken, too," Lenna murmurs. "That'll help you heal faster."

"But I like your cookies better."

"Mal?" Chug jerks upright and scrambles over to join Lenna

at Mal's bedside. "I was so worried. Are you okay? Can you move your arms and legs? How many fingers am I holding up? Wait, Lenna gave you cookies?"

Mal laughs weakly. "I'm okay. I can move everything a little, but I'm sore and tired. You're not holding up any fingers. And you can't have my cookies."

I'm still sitting on the floor, axe in hand, and they've all utterly forgotten that I exist. It's almost like I don't, just now. They're so happy to see one another, so happy that Mal is okay. I don't know if any of my friends would be that happy about me. My mom would, but her happiness would be tempered with anger at whatever I'd done wrong to put myself at risk and make her worry or look bad. Edd and Remy would probably just laugh at me for nearly getting blown up.

If we were back home, I'd take advantage of the chance to make fun of Mal and Lenna and Chug and call them wimps for caring so much. But out here, on my full first night beyond the town wall, I just wish I could be part of their circle.

"Is Jarro okay?" I hear Mal ask.

I look at the book in my lap like I've been reading it all along and not listening in on their private moment.

"Jarro?" Lenna prompts.

I look up. "Yeah, I'm fine. Singed off one of my eyebrows and my hearing is wobbly, but I think you took most of the blast." I fiddle with the book's binding. "Thanks for saving me. Sorry I got you blown up."

Mal chuckles, but it's a small sound. "That's what I get for not bringing a cat along. I'm just glad everyone is all right."

They all talk a bit more, and Chug nags Mal to eat some chicken, and eventually they all go back to sleep. I stay up a little later, listening to them breathing, but not in a creepy way. I'm an only child, and I've never really been this close to other people in such a vulnerable moment, when we're all exhausted and hurt and unconscious. It's always just been me and my mom. I wasn't allowed to have sleepovers—or attend sleepovers—so it's weird to me, how natural it is for the town weirdos to just curl up shoulder to shoulder and start snoring with one hand on a wolf's side.

I must eventually fall asleep, as I wake up to Chug opening the door he made last night—which, honestly, still blows my mind. Back home, Elder Stu and Tok are the only people who know how to craft things, but apparently Chug can just make a door or bed out of practically nothing. I tuck Lenna's book in my pocket— I'm not done with it, and I don't want her to take it back until I've learned everything I can. I feel so much better today. I guess they were right about food and sleep being the best cure for anything. Lenna and Mal are still asleep, but Mal looks a little less pale and frazzled, and I feel the tiniest bit less guilty.

I don't follow Chug outside, per se, but I do end up outside shortly after he does. He's squatting down, feeding his pig pota-toes and talking to it in a high-pitched, singsong voice, and as soon as he senses my presence, he stands and clears his throat.

"You better?" he asks, his voice much deeper. "Ready to walk?"

I wince. "I'm better, but my feet are definitely sore. Do you get used to it?"

He nods. "Yeah. The more you walk, the less walking hurts. But at first, it hurts a lot. I got injured pretty early on, last time we were out here, and I rode Thingy for a few days."

My jaw drops. "You . . . rode that pig?"

Chug's eyes narrow like he's one step away from bopping me in the nose, which is how he usually tries to deal with me when he doesn't like what I have to say. "Yes," he enunciates clearly, "I rode that pig. It is very good to ride a pig, when you can't walk on your own." He pulls a saddle out of his pocket, and I can't help shaking my head at what a neat trick it is. "And today Mal is going to ride the pig, and if you make fun of her, I will absolutely liberate several teeth from your face."

I hold my hands up. "No problems here. Mal can have whatever she needs." Before I really think about it, I say, "It would be pretty stupid for me to make fun of you out here when I'm the one who keeps doing stupid things, right?"

He nods. "Right."

"So what can I do to help?"

He doesn't smile, but he seems to accept my peace offering for what it is and tells me to go look for more meat. "Have your axe ready. There should be sheep, cows, and chickens out there. If you see a weird animal with an extra long neck, that's a llama, and they're not edible. If you stay away from the shade, no more creepers should be spawning." His lips twitch, and he reaches into his pocket and pulls out a helmet, which he slaps on my head. It makes it harder to see, but it also makes me feel that much safer. "Even you shouldn't be able to hurt yourself on a bright morning like this. As long as you don't drop your axe on your foot." As he walks away, he calls, "So don't drop your axe on your foot. In case that wasn't clear."

All things considered, it would be fair if he treated me a lot worse. I'd rather do work and help the group than have to listen to them sit around and talk about how I'm more trouble than I'm worth. Axe in hand, helmet tottering on my head, I venture out into the pretty green pastures. I didn't tell Chug this, but . . . I've never actually done this before. I've never killed anything. My mom trades berries for meat and eggs, so we don't have to keep any animals. I don't want to do it, but I have to do it, so I will. I refuse to give the Bad Apples good reason to make fun of me because I can't pull my weight.

I keep glancing behind me to make sure I can still locate our copse of trees. If I get lost out here, I'm the dead meat. I don't know how to make a shelter like Mal can, and even if I did, all I have is an axe, which would take forever. I can't make a crafting table or torches. I can't even light a fire. I'm like a big dumb baby. So I scan the area ahead for movement while making sure I can get back to my—

Well, no. Not friends.

My group. Our camp.

There!

Something is moving in the grass, something brown and white. A cow? I've never been near a cow before—I've never been out of the Hub back home. I don't know if cows are nice or mean. If Mal can take care of them, they can't be that bad, right? If they were really vicious, they'd escape her farm and eat the whole town.

I sneak up, axe raised, as the cow watches me. Its big brown eyes blink, long black lashes making it look curious. It stomps a foot, and I stop.

It's . . . really cute. Beautiful, even.

I can't kill it.

But I have to.

My friends—I mean, the group. They're depending on me. We need meat.

If we don't have meat, we won't survive. Mal won't be able to heal, won't be able to dig or fight. Even if we never find Tok, we still have to get back home.

I have to do this.

I have to turn this cow into food.

I take another step.

And another.

The cow shakes its head as if warning me away.

"I'm sorry," I say.

I raise the axe.

I hold it overhead until my arm starts to shake.

The cow stares at me.

Another cow walks up beside it, tail twitching.

I can't kill the cow now, not while its friend watches.

But I need to.

Two cows, twice the meat.

I hate this.

My mom would know what to do.

Even stupid old Chug would know what to do.

All I know is that the longer I stand here holding my axe, being blinked at by a cow, the less certain I am of everything in the whole world. The only thing I'm certain of now is that I can't kill it. Whatever it takes to do that kind of violence, I don't have it in me. Maybe I can threaten little stringy kids like Tok or make fun of kids like Lenna or punch jerks like Chug, but I can't actually kill anything.

I let the axe drop and shove it back in my pocket. I notice that there's still a lead in there, the one the kidnappers used to tie me to the tree. Aha! I toss it around the first cow's neck and tug, and the cow follows along behind me in a friendly enough manner. The second cow follows it, as do three more I hadn't noticed. I am bringing home the beef!

I can't stop grinning at how clever I am. Sure, I can't kill the cow, but I'll take it back to the camp, explain that I wasn't sure where to hit it and wanted to preserve the meat and leather for future use. That makes me the hero, and then the other kids can show me what to do—by actually doing it themselves. Mission accomplished, and we get beef for breakfast.

We're not too terribly far from the trees, but I'm going slowly to make sure the cows stay with me and don't get upset. I think about naming the cow, but then I realize that you probably shouldn't name things you're going to eat. I've always wanted a pet, but my mom hates noise and mess. I found a kitten once, but she gave it to my aunt Cath to patrol the alley behind her shop.

As I approach, I can hear Chug making something on his crafting table. There's a weird twanging noise, and I spot Lenna shooting arrows into a tree. Even Mal is sitting outside, eating a cookie by the fire and managing to stay upright.

"I found a cow!" I shout, and everyone turns to stare.

Mal stands, wobbling, her jaw dropping. "Oh my gosh!" she shrieks.

"What? No way! I don't believe it!" Chug screeches.

"Jarro, that's not a cow—" Lenna starts.

My smile falters. Have I brought back some sort of horrible monster that's going to kill us all? Is this another kind of creeper, something I haven't found in the Mobestiary yet? After yesterday's accident, I didn't possibly think I could mess up any worse, but . . .

"It's a horse," Mal cries, and I've never seen anyone so happy in my entire life.

# 10

# TOK

This is the longest day of my life.

They took me from my bed, blindfolded me, gagged me, and dragged me along at the end of a lead like an animal. I reached for the gag once, and a sword tip pressed deep into my belly.

"Don't even try it," someone whispered. "I can hurt you without killing you."

I listened carefully after that, because apparently whoever they are, they're more worried about being seen than heard. One of the voices is familiar, but the rest of them are strangers.

The only time they let me see anything was at Elder Gabe's shop. Someone held my head, tightly, and forced me to look only where they wanted me to look.

"Find any ingredients that can be used for potions," a stranger's voice said—a woman.

I tried to talk, to tell them that Elder Gabe had never entrusted me with that knowledge that I didn't know what any of the stuff in

Gabe's closet even was, but when I reached for the gag, the sword poked me hard enough to draw blood. If I were braver, I would've ripped the fabric away and screamed my head off, sword or no sword, knowing full well that Elder Gabe's shop is in the heart of the Hub, and dozens of people would've been asleep within shouting distance. But no—I was too scared of that sword, too scared of what they would do if I pushed my luck. Maybe I've fought illagers and hostile mobs, but that was with my friends. I've never been alone, never been helpless, never had adults willing to cut me.

I could only use my spread arms to indicate that everything in Gabe's supply closet would probably be useful for something or other. The blindfold returned, and I heard chests opening, bottles rattling, bags of powder thumping. From what I could hear, they cleaned him out. I hope no one in town gets seriously hurt, because without those potions, the healer can really only urge folks to rest and eat a lot of meat.

They led me back outside then, and the next odd sound I heard was my least favorite voice screeching, "Hey, those are my mom's berries!"

Judging by the muffled cries and scuffling that followed, I knew that I was no longer their only prisoner. Whoever these people are, they mean business, and they're willing to kidnap extraneous jerks like Jarro to accomplish their goals. I heard them arguing among themselves, and then there was a sound that reminded me of my parents' pumpkin farm back home, the crunch of a hoe and the ripping out of old vines—again and again and again. Judging by the smug chuckling, the thieves weren't satisfied to just kidnap Jarro—they took all his mom's sweet berry bushes, too.

One of the thieves—the one with the familiar voice, a man—shoved some of the berries into my hand and said, "Save these for later, kid. You're going to need all the strength you can muster." And I believed him; they weren't going to treat me well. I obediently put the berries in my pocket, my mouth watering against the gag. I couldn't eat them just then, but I know the sounds of my town, and I could tell where we were by the cobblestones, then dirt, then grass under my feet. When I was fairly certain we'd left the walled town and were walking through New Cornucopia, I dropped one of the berries, hoping my captors wouldn't notice. Maybe if I left a trail, I thought, my friends will find me.

We walked for a long time. Although they've kept me blindfolded, I could tell when night gave way to morning, just the faintest change in the light. It rained after that, a heavy, cold downpour that soaked me to the skin. There was nowhere to go, no way to take shelter. I held my arms over my head, crying into my blindfold as I slogged through the mud. My captors killed mobs during the storm, and every time I heard a moan or groan or click or clack, my heart stilled in my chest and my hands ached for a weapon. I'd never felt so helpless.

I only had ten or so berries, and I didn't know how far away they planned to take me. I dropped a berry every thousand steps, grateful that the counting gave me something to focus on. My feet grew sore as I walked and walked and walked, and then, after a time, I heard animals calling out. These thieves had planned ahead and were ready to make a quick getaway. Llamas bleated and grunted as their backs were loaded with chests, and then someone lifted me up, and I found myself precariously balanced in a saddle, sitting astride an animal I longed to see. It didn't quite smell like a cow or a sheep, so I had to deduce it was a horse.

Someone placed my hands on the horse's neck, and I held on for dear life as my mount was led away. As grateful as I was to have some relief from walking, I'm much more comfortable with cat-sized animals than horse-sized ones.

I was out of berries, but my pockets are always full of raw materials, so I chose something that hopefully no one would notice—a dull iron ingot—and dropped it as my horse carried me ever farther from home. I couldn't count a thousand steps anymore, and I knew that my pockets, like the berries, would eventually run out, so I started slowly, carefully counting to two thousand between ingots.

One axolotl, two axolotl, three axolotl.

That's how Lenna's been counting, ever since she discovered the odd little amphibians in one of Nan's books. I miss my friends so much it hurts. I miss my brother, and I hate knowing that he's surely beating himself up for letting me get kidnapped.

We rode all day, and the thieves kept rather quiet. I could hear their whispers, hear them cluck at their beasts, but no one spoke out loud or, like our old neighbor and nemesis Krog, gave a helpful explanatory evil-villain monologue that explained all the steps of their plan. As day turned to night, someone must have visually called a halt, as my horse stumbled to standing and rough hands plucked me from my saddle. I'd run out of iron ingots and started dropping coal by then.

"One word, and the gag is right back in," a voice warned as the fabric was pulled down around my neck. "Understand?" Starving, I nodded eagerly and was given mutton, dry and tasteless. I didn't have enough saliva to talk, much less yell.

As I ate and listened to my captors, hoping for clues about their identities and plans, I heard the familiar clink of multiple shovels and pickaxes and knew someone must be creating shelters for the rest of the night. Soon I was huddled against a rough-hewn wall, alone as far as my arms could reach. I knew they had Jarro, too, and I was so desperate for any kind of comfort that I would have welcomed one of his taunts, but I couldn't hear him. There was no evidence that he was with us at all—I couldn't even smell his telltale stench. I soon fell asleep, curled on the ground, miserable and far from home, wishing for the stolid sound of Chug's snores and the warm caress of my sleeping cats, laid out upon my legs.

Hands shook me awake, and I clawed my way out of dark dreams. "Get up," someone said, and I did. They gave me dry bread and more mutton, and I choked it down. I didn't even think about calling out. What would I say, and to whom? We were already so far away from Cornucopia and everyone I'd ever known. What was the point? My only hope was waiting, listening, learning, and forming my own plan. They must've taken me for a reason, must have chosen me for a reason. My best guess? They want my crafting skills. That's the only thing I can think of that makes me special, worth all this trouble. That means that sometime soon, they'll have to take off my blindfold, and that's when I'll choose my escape strategy.

Now I'm back on the horse, none the wiser, throat dry and eyes crusted with tears sopped up by my blindfold. I sway with the rhythm of the unseen beast, wondering what color it is and if it knows that it's being used for cruel purposes. Every two thousand axolotls, I drop something from my pockets . . . until I start to run out of inconspicuous things and stretch it out to three thousand axolotls. I can drop cobblestone or a compass in the tall grass tickling my feet, but I definitely can't leave shiny gold ingots and expect no one to notice.

I hope Chug is okay, but with me gone, I know he can't possibly be. He must be terrified. I'm sure the moment he discovered me missing, he took off to tell Mal and Lenna, and then they probably went to the town Elders. If, like last time, the Elders decided to do nothing, they probably went to Nan. Knowing all of them, knowing how it went last time, they have to be on our trail, following us, doing everything in their power to save me.

They have to be.

That's what I'd do for them.

And I'm sure it's what they're doing for me.

My brother has the biggest heart in the world. He would crawl over broken honey bottles to help me. Mal and Lenna would join him. That's the kind of friends they are. I have complete faith in them.

I only hope they can find us before something worse happens.

And if not, I'll have to do it myself.

I don't think of myself as brave or strong, but I'll have to figure out how to escape on my own. Since we're on horses, there's no way my friends will ever catch up on foot.

## 11

# CHUG

 So I have to say, as a big fan of pigs, that horses don't quite compare.

These horses that Jarro found—they're not cute; they don't oink. They honestly look kind of stupid. But I know Mal's been dreaming about them ever since she saw them in Nan's book, so for her sake, I hope they don't suck. At least she's standing now. It scared me, when she was so weak I had to carry her.

"So these aren't cows?" Jarro asks, holding the horse's lead.

Mal limps over to Jarro's horse and reaches up to rub its nose, a look of pure joy on her face. "No! Have you seriously never seen a cow?"

"Only when he looks in a mirror," I say with a grin.

He rounds on me, his available hand in a fist and the horse looking startled at his anger. "Shut up, Chug! Of course I've seen a cow! I just thought maybe, uh, wild cows were different."

Mal stares at him doubtfully as Lenna says, "You've never

been out of the Hub, have you? We've never seen you anywhere else. There are sheep in the Hub sometimes, and chickens and cats, but no cows. I think you're lying."

Jarro's eyes twitch back and forth like his brain is searching for something and coming up totally empty.

"It's okay," Mal says with a smirk. "We're not bullies, so we're not going to make fun of you too much, even if there are literally cows just down the road from your house. It's not your fault if your mom can be a little . . ."

"Mean? Pushy? Rude? Sour? Aggressive?" I offer.

"Strict." Mal throws me the look that means *shut your piehole, Chug, I'm working here.* So I do shut my piehole, even though I don't want to, because over many years of putting my foot in my mouth, I've learned to just trust my best friend.

Jarro is clearly upset and fighting his rage as he strokes the horse's neck. "Yeah, she . . . she doesn't like me to be too far away."

"Well, the good news is that I've seen a lot of cows, and these horses are way cooler. And we can even ride them, which will get us where we're going a lot faster." Mal looks to me. "I know Chug has a saddle, but did anyone else bring one? I know it's a long shot."

I fight the grin forming on my face as I search my pockets along with everyone else. I pretend to root around as I subtly watch everyone else look up and frown.

"Chug?" Mal asks.

"I'm so sorry, Mal," I say, chin quivering. "I wish I could help you. But . . ."

I throw four saddles on the ground and watch as Mal's eyes go as big as Nan's cookies. "All I've got are these three extra saddles."

"Chug, you magnificent genius!" she squeals.

"Oh, I wouldn't say I'm a genius." Although I'll tuck that compliment away for a rainy day. "I would just say I'm a salesman who keeps his pockets stocked with high-value items. The first time Inka went to the village, she traded a bunch of melons to a farmer for emeralds, but then she accidentally traded the emeralds to a leatherworker for saddles because she didn't quite understand how to barter and thought she couldn't say no. Inka doesn't need saddles but she does need hoes for her melons, so here we are. I thought they were pretty useless, but she threw in a free melon. Which I ate immediately," I add hastily as Jarro's eyes light up.

Mal squats down to run her hands over the saddle. It's much more elaborate than the one Nan let us use on our last trip, the one I've used exclusively for Thingy and that now smells a bit of pig. I'm trying to puzzle out the look on Mal's face when she says, "I don't think I can lift it. Lenna, do any of your books have any suggestions for taming horses?"

Lenna pulls a book out of her pocket and flips through it, nodding. "So the best way to tame a horse is to just . . . get on the horse's back and ride it out. They might throw you a few times. And some horses are easier to tame than others." She looks into the eyes of the horse on the end of Jarro's lead. "It looks nice enough, but I guess it's impossible to know what it's thinking. One of us just needs to . . . hop on up."

Lenna looks to Mal, and Mal looks to me. Lenna's leg isn't fully healed, and Mal can barely move. I'm the one who needs to hop on the horse and take my licks. But . . .

I . . . don't wanna.

The horse's back is pretty high up, and I don't know this horse, I don't know anything about horses at all. As much as I'd like to make fun of Jarro for thinking this was just a weird cow, it's not like I have any big advantages over him in animal husbandry. I can ride a pig that Tok trained, and I can distribute scraps to cats and wolves, but I absolutely have no interest in sitting on this horse, and I suspect the horse has no interest in being sat upon. I'm certain I wouldn't, if I were a horse. I love climbing trees, but . . . well, trees don't have minds of their own. If I fall out of a tree, that's my own fault. But if the horse wants to kill me, it just might try. And we don't have any Potions of Healing.

Of course, that doesn't change the fact that my friends expect me to do this. They *need* me to do it. And Tok needs it, too. If we have any hope of catching the people who kidnapped my brother, we need to be faster than we can be on foot, especially with Mal injured. I was going to let her ride Thingy, but he's not any faster than we are. We need these horses, which means I need to suck it up and hop on up there.

"I'll do it," Jarro says.

We all stare at him.

See, Jarro is taller than me. He has big jug ears and a dumb, punchable face and a ponytail. And, sure, it's got to be easier for a tall person to get on the horse's back because his legs are just flat out longer, it's just . . . well, I've never seen Jarro volunteer to do anything to help anyone else, ever. Especially not something that might be dangerous. And part of me wants to jump in front and say I'll ride the horse just so everyone knows I'm braver than he is, but most of me desperately does not want to do that. I'll fight anything that needs to be fought, but I'd rather stick to riding pigs, thanks.

"Are you sure?" Mal asks. "I mean, normally I'd do it—I want to do it—but . . ." She looks down at the black burned bits on her clothes and frowns. "I wish I could, but I was recently nearly blown up."

Jarro winces at that, which is exactly what he should do. He did almost get her killed.

"It's probably best if Jarro does it," Lenna says. "He's taller, and he's the person we need the least." His eyes bug out at her, and she shrugs. "No offense, it's just . . . we have the brains, the brawn, the bow, and . . . you."

"Bully starts with B," I remind them all.

The look Jarro shoots me is both angry and embarrassed. "I haven't bu—I mean, I haven't been mean to anybody since—"

"Since we untied you from that tree?" I ask.

"Since we were outside the wall," Lenna corrects. "Away from an audience."

Jarro looks at me. "She really tells it like it is, doesn't she?"

"When she doesn't feel threatened, yeah."

He nods and turns back to the problem at hand, running his hand down the horse's neck to its back, where the skin twitches at his touch. "Well, back up, everybody. If I get hurt, you'll heal me, right?"

"We'll feed you." Lenna holds out one of her cookies, which are quickly becoming a hot commodity. "But there are no potions out here. Hence Mal's problem."

Lenna helps Mal shuffle away from the general range of the horses. The one on the lead is watching Jarro warily, which I can relate to. The other four are alert but chill. Jarro looks like a jangling ball of nerves, and I can see him shaking from here.

"Okay, Speckles," he murmurs, running his hand down the horse's back. "I'm going to sit on you, and you're going to not kill me. Deal?"

"Promise him a carrot," I say, but I know enough about farm animals to not hold out said carrot.

"Speckles is a girl," Jarro says without looking at me. He's entirely focused on the horse, touching its—her—back and rump and legs like he's trying to get her used to being touched. Speckles twitches and watches him, curious but not, as far as I can tell, bloodthirsty.

"What do horses eat?" I ask Lenna in a whisper.

She's been scribbling in her journal, but she trades it out for Nan's book to answer me. "Wheat and apples, mainly. Sugar, if you have it."

"We've got to find some wheat, or else I'm lying to a horse."

Now Jarro has a handful of the horse's neck hair—why would an animal need neck hair?—and he's bouncing on his toes. I don't like him, and I'd love nothing more than to see him go arcing across the sky like a shooting star and land on his dumb head, but I need this to work. I need Mal and Tok to be okay more than I need Jarro to suffer.

"Come on," I whisper under my breath.

In one smooth leap, Jarro flops onto the horse's back on his belly. The horse neighs angrily and bucks around as Jarro attempts to get a leg over the horse's back. The horse wins, and Jarro lands on his face in the dirt.

And the strangest thing happens.

Nobody laughs.

I grimace, Lenna catches the horse's lead, and Mal hobbles over to Jarro and asks if he's okay.

"Nothing hurt but my pride," he grumbles as he stands, his nice town clothes stained with dirt for the first time.

"Do you need—" Mal starts, but Jarro is already back at the horse's side, one hand clutching a handful of hair, the other running over and over the horse's back. He jumps again. The horse neighs and bucks again. He eats dirt again.

I'm actually . . . kind of worried for him.

As many times as I've punched him in the gut, this is a different kind of hurt. Looking back, our relationship in the Hub was like a game little kids play, whereas this is real life. Lives are at stake here. He could get seriously hurt. And every moment we spend trying to tame these horses is a moment we're not pursuing Tok and his kidnappers. If this gambit doesn't work, we'll have three injured people and be hours behind.

"Maybe we should just walk," I say.

Jarro glares at me, looking more determined and real than I've ever seen him. "No! I can do this. I'm close. I'm sure of it. If you want to help, find some wheat or something. Distract her with food."

As much as I want to watch the Jarro Show, I head off toward a promising patch of land, glancing back whenever I hear the horse make that angry *neh-heh-heh* sound. Luckily, it's easy enough to gather a handful of wheat, and I run back and hold it out to Jarro. He nods and takes it, feeding it to the annoyed horse, whose eyes soften as it snuffles against his hand.

"Let's try it one more time. Now behave," he warns the horse, and he sounds a lot like I do when I talk to Thingy.

This time, when he leaps on the horse's back, the horse just gives a fussy little hop and settles down. He leans forward, stroking the horse's neck.

"I could kick your teeth in from here," he tells me, but he's grinning, and I don't think he really means it.

"And I could grab your foot and yank you flat on your face," I shoot back.

"Nice job!" Mal says.

Jarro smiles, and I realize that in all our years together in school and all our encounters in town, I've never heard anyone compliment him before. He's never cared about school, and he's never done anything nice or helpful, to my knowledge. Outside of bullying people, he's never exhibited any skills. But now, he's kind of glowing.

He slides down from the horse's back and selects one of the saddles—the fanciest one, of course. He takes his time, carefully arranging it on the horse and making sure it'll stay on without pinching her too badly. Speckles watches him with loving eyes, just like Thingy watched me and like Mal's llamas used to watch her, before they were stolen by brigands at a river crossing. The horse bumps his shoulder with her nose and nuzzles him, and he laughs and rubs the star between her eyes.

"Wait your turn," he tells her, turning to the next horse, which has been watching the whole thing curiously. "Now it's up to Dotty."

The final count is Jarro: 4, Horses 11.

Ten times Jarro gets tossed in the air to land in the dirt, sometimes on his belly and sometimes on his back, and once, miraculously, impressively, on his feet. Each time, he dusts himself off and stands, eyes latched onto the horse with a mix of focus, drive, and curiosity. I didn't know Jarro was capable of anything beyond tattling and bullying until today. Then again, most people thought I was only good for one-liners and gut punches before I ventured beyond the wall. Out here, I discovered that I was great at fighting mobs—and cooking. Lenna found her skills with the bow and arrow—and applied her dreamy curiosity to Nan's lore. Mal always knew she was a leader, but out here, she led us with purpose and learned how to dig shelters and mine ore. Tok, wherever he is, went from creating nonsense machines that never worked to crafting better than our town's Elder craftsman. I guess people just discover who they really are in the Overworld.

Now we have four saddled horses, a confused spare, and one very indignant, unsaddled pig staring up at them from a paddock hacked into the grass. Thingy wants to come with us, I can tell, but he can't move as fast as the horses, so he has to stay here. I hate leaving him behind. It happened accidentally on our last trip, and it's happening on purpose now. I give him all my potatoes and carrots, but I'm still nervous about leaving him alone. I borrow Mal's pickaxe and dig until I have ten stone blocks, which I stack up to form a tower.

"There. Now we'll be able to find him on our way home," I say, returning the pickaxe, as I know Mal doesn't like to have it out of her immediate area.

I squat down and rub my pig's ears. "I'll be back soon, buddy. I'll ride you all the way home." I lean in closer to whisper, "I like you better than horses, I promise." Before I turn around, I dash away the stubborn tears speckling my cheeks so Jarro won't see them.

The horses are waiting in a line, with Dotty, Bee, and Mervin saddled and ready to go and Ol' Stinkeye unsaddled and annoyed, which is why Jarro didn't even try taming him. As it turns out, Jarro isn't very good at naming things.

We've packed up our little camp, leaving the door behind but taking the bed and crafting table, as poorly constructed as they may be. Jarro and I gently hoist Mal into Mervin's saddle, as he's the shortest and calmest of the horses. I give Lenna a boost onto Dotty's back, and Jarro swings up onto Speckles like he's been doing it every day of his life. Honestly, I'm kind of jealous—of his horse skills and his height. But I'll never tell him that, not in a million years. I tell myself riding a horse can't be any harder than riding a pig and clamber up into Bee's saddle. He grunts a little but doesn't seem too annoyed. Thingy oinks like he's been betrayed, and I can't look him in the eyes.

We haven't really discussed how things will work now, because normally that would be Mal's job, but she's weak, and we all know that being in pain makes it that much harder to think a normal thought. I guess that makes me second in command. I grab a handful of Bee's neck hair and gently guide him in the direction we were headed yesterday, before we stopped in the copse to make camp. I'm nervous at first, wondering if I've chosen the right path. Mal is behind me, then Jarro, then Lenna, and they're all relying on me to get us headed in the right direction, which is not usually one of my skills. As soon as I spot a chunk of coal sitting in the grass where no chunk of coal should be, I know we're headed the right way.

I . . . kind of can't believe the most important thing in my life right now is coal.

Whoever took my brother is clever. When they grabbed him, I didn't wake up, and the animals were kept busy. In town, Jarro was the only one who saw them, and they kidnapped him, too, to make sure no one interfered. I know Tok is dropping the raw materials for us to find, which means he was probably dropping the berries, too. But his captors themselves are being very, very careful. No noise, no evidence. If they're killing mobs or building shelters along the way, they haven't left any signs of their passing behind, not even the grossest chunk of zombie meat or an arrow stuck in the ground. These people—they know exactly what they're doing. They planned for this. It sends a chill down my spine, to think that they must've been watching us in our own home, at some point, to determine exactly how to kidnap my brother.

But there's something else bothering me. Along with the llama hoofprints, I now see bigger, U-shaped tracks. Now that I've met a horse up close, I know that this means that Tok's captors are also on horseback. Which means they're just as fast as we are, now.

We've got to hurry. We've already lost too much time.

## 12

# MAL

 When I was a tiny little kid, I dreamed of what it would be like to ride a cow. As I grew up, I tried it over the years, with various amounts of success. As it turns out, cows don't particularly want to be ridden. And even when we discovered that one of the old heifers didn't mind being sat upon, she didn't want to go anywhere. She just stood in the field, chewing her cud and switching her tail, no matter how much I urged her forward. I wanted to feel wind in my hair, to feel the reckless abandon of galloping atop long, wild legs.

Yeah, cows don't do that.

But horses do, and as soon as I learned about horses, I realized what my dreams really meant. Nan tells me I have an adventurer's spirit, that I'm descended from explorers who craved the open wilds. Maybe my longing for horses is something I inherited, like my red hair and freckles. And maybe I'm too weak to kick my horse and take off at a run across the rippling prairie, but the view up here still makes my heart sing, and my body feels a lot better now that I'm not the one responsible for moving it.

That explosion yesterday was the scariest thing that's ever happened to me, and I've smelled Chug's farts. I keep thinking that if only I'd kept a better eye on Jarro or told him about creepers or brought a cat along or hit the dang monster just a little faster, just a few more times, I'd now have a swollen sense of pride instead of a swollen . . . everything. My skin is burned, my clothes are singed, and everything I have is sore. It's even hard to hear, like there's this ringing in my ears. I ate as much chicken as I could, but I need more—more meat, more food, more of those magic potions Elder Gabe charged too much for back home. As glad as I am to have the horses—and I am glad, they're a dream come true and our only way to catch up to Tok's captors—I really wish Jarro had found something we could eat, too. I'm keeping my eyes peeled as we ride, knowing we'll stumble across some sheep sooner or later.

We're still headed along the same path we traveled last time, the beacon growing closer with every clop of Mervin's hooves. I would've named him Dream, or maybe something with gravitas, like George, but instead, I guess now my majestic steed with his noble gray spots and rippling gray mane is . . . Mervin. He seems gentle, though, which is nice—I'd hate it if he hated having me on his back.

It's kind of weird that Chug is leading, but we're always learning new things, out here. The world spreads out before us as the wind ruffles my hair, and I would be truly and completely happy if I weren't severely hurt and one of my best friends hadn't been kidnapped. It's funny how it's possible to enjoy a little moment of mercy when everything else is falling apart, but I'll take what I can get.

Time stretches out, golden as honey. We pass flowers and trees, and when we see sheep grazing, Lenna steers Dotty toward them, looses a volley of arrows, and proudly brings me chunks of raw mutton. It doesn't taste as good as Chug's food, but I know we don't have time to stop and cook. If I want to heal faster I need quantity, not quality.

"I sure do miss your flaming arrows," I say, accepting several chunks of meat as she shoves wads of dropped wool in her pocket.

"Me, too. But at least we get wool this way."

She makes sure everyone has something to eat, and we chew as we ride. The trail certainly passes faster when you're on horseback, but I just wish we could go a little faster. Even though I know it's likely the kidnappers had to take shelter overnight, just like we did, I'm sure they have a head start on us, since they already had horses and didn't lose the time we did this morning. If I weren't so hurt, maybe we could gallop and go faster, but this is as fast as we can go right now. Luckily, it won't be too long until we reach the village, and maybe we can trade for something that will get everyone back to full health. And find some of their amazing pies.

We must be going twice as fast as we could on foot, as we reach the village just before sunset. The last time we were here, it was pouring rain, and we didn't know who or what we'd find in the oddly shaped houses. As we near the beacon, our horses move faster, their legs a blur as the flowers whip past us. We head straight to a small building that was empty when we were here last, and Chug looks in the window and gives me a thumbs-up.

"I'll go trade for goodies," he says. "Jarro, do you need to heal, too?"

Jarro shrugs. "I feel a little beat up, but in a good way."

"That's what hard work feels like," Lenna tells him with a grin.

Chug dismounts and stares at his horse for a moment. "I guess we don't have any more leads?" We all know by now what's in our pockets, which is not leads. With a good-natured shrug, Chug hacks a paddock in the ground, just like we did last time. We settle all of our horses safely in there and head into the empty building as he goes out to trade with the villagers. When the iron golem walks past him on his endless patrol, Chug gives him a salute and says, "Hey, Rusty! Keep up the good work!"

Once we're inside the building, I give a little sigh of relief. I'm not used to feeling weak and helpless like this. Outside of the time I got poisoned by our old nemesis Krog, I've never taken more than minor damage. It takes everything I have to slump down the wall to sit on the ground without just collapsing.

"What is this place?" Jarro asks. He's got his nose pressed up against the window. "What was that thing? These people are really weird."

"The villagers are a mystery," Lenna says. "They don't speak our language, and we can't figure out theirs, but they craft interesting things and love trading. The thing Chug called Rusty is an iron golem that patrols the village and attacks hostile mobs. Don't hit one, or it'll attack you, and believe me: You'll lose."

She hands me another piece of mutton, and I get to eating. One of the horses whinnies from outside, and I freeze.

What if the kidnappers stopped here, too?

"Lenna, do you have enough energy to take your bow and look around the village?"

She perks up. "Sure. But why? The villagers are peaceful."

"But the kidnappers aren't, and if it makes sense for us to stop here, it might make sense for them, too."

Lenna's eyes go wide as she realizes the gravity of the situation. They could already be here. They could be watching us. They might already have Chug. She bolts to her feet, nods at me, and heads out with her bow in hand and Poppy trotting along behind her.

"Want me to go, too?" Jarro asks.

I shake my head. "You've never fought a person before, not really. With her bow, Lenna can do damage from afar." *And she's not afraid to use it against enemies, and you are,* I want to say but don't.

Jarro paces around the small building, and I feel the same frantic energy. If the kidnappers are nearby, we're basically trapped here. I'm helpless, and he has no experience. Chug is taking longer than anticipated. Even if our plan is ultimately to find the kidnappers and take Tok back, we'd rather all be together, at full health, and ready to fight rather than be caught unawares and separated at nightfall.

The door flies open, and my hand goes to my pickaxe—

But it's just Chug, and he's exuberant.

"Excellent trading!" he crows. "I'm so glad my pockets are always full. I unloaded everything that we didn't really need and got the things we needed most." He holds out an arrow. "My lady, your Arrow of Healing."

I take the arrow and inspect it. It looks odd, with a glowing pink tip. "I was hoping for a potion."

Chug's brow draws down. "Yeah, me, too. But I went into every single shop and couldn't find one. I did get some steak and some rabbit stew." He guiltily wipes at his mouth. "And some pies."

"But what do I do with the arrow?"

"No idea. But it's the only thing around that has anything to do with healing, so I just handed over the emeralds. Maybe Lenna will know?" He looks around the small house. "Wait, where is she?"

"I realized that the kidnappers might be thinking the same way we did, so I asked her to scope out the village—" I start.

Chug immediately goes to the window and looks around. The sun is setting. Even if the kidnappers aren't lying in wait to ambush us, the hostile mobs will start spawning soon.

"Should I go after her? She can't fight them alone— Oh." He opens the door, and Lenna hurries inside. "All clear?"

"No sign of Tok or the kidnappers."

Chug manages to look both disappointed and relieved. "Then I guess we don't have to share all this food."

We sit down to enjoy the village cuisine. Lenna eats more steak than I've ever seen her wolf down and instantly perks up. I feel the same way, although I have to switch to rabbit stew once my jaw starts aching from chewing so much. I still feel a little singed and woozy, though, so I hand her the Arrow of Healing.

"Know how it works?" I ask.

Her mouth twitches. "Yes. I read about it in one of Nan's books . . . but you're not going to like it. I have to, uh, shoot you."

Chug's eyes fly wide in alarm. "No way! That's the opposite of healing!"

"I don't make the rules," Lenna says.

Before he can argue and before I can even raise my hands in defense, she whips out her bow and shoots the arrow directly into my belly. I gasp, but it doesn't hurt—it has that same, warm, melty feeling of a Potion of Healing. I reach for it, but it disappears.

"Oh," I say dreamily. "That's nice."

"Your eyebrows grew back!" Chug shakes his head, looking like an exhausted mother hen. "But I don't think I can take any more scares like that tonight. No more shooting anyone, even if it's ultimately helpful."

Once he's recovered from his shock, Chug pulls out his crafting table and uses the wool Lenna collected earlier to make two more beds—there's just not enough for three. The boys play bedrock-paper-sword to determine who gets the third bed, and when Jarro wins, Chug looks put out but doesn't argue. He curls up on the ground, pie stains on his cheeks.

"I'm much better at trading than I used to be, you know," he says. "And I'm really good at saying 'hm' now."

"Hm?" Jarro asks.

"Hm," Chug confirms, sounding exactly like a villager.

Lenna and I laugh, but we're interrupted by one of the worst sounds in the world. Something thumps against the door, nails scratching down the wood.

"What is that?" Jarro asks, shrinking back in his bed.

"Just a zombie," Chug says blandly.

"Can it get in?"

"Nope. My brother built that door, and it's as solid as they come." Chug gets up and walks over to it, running his fingers over the wood. "When we stopped here last time, the door was flimsy and had a window in it. But Tok made this one, and here it still stands."

"Huh. I guess that's pretty impressive," Jarro says.

Chug nods. "It really is."

I fall asleep after that, and it's like falling down a deep, dark hole. It was like that when I had a Potion of Healing too, like your body knows that it has more healing to do while you're out cold.

When I wake up, all is well, and I have to admit that the village house is much more comfortable than the holes I dig in the ground. Then again, being off the floor in a cozy bed helps, too. As I look around, I notice that the two beds Chug crafted last night are of better quality than the first one he made. Like his brother, he gets better with every item he crafts. Chug always undervalues himself, but it's clear he pays attention to what Tok does and tries to improve his skills.

As we remount our horses, our pockets packed with food and our bellies full of pie, I look to the mountains beyond the village. If I'm right, and I sense that I am, the dropped bits of coal and iron will lead us up to a pass, then down a treacherous, zigzagging trail that ends at a raging river. There was a log over the river, once, but we pushed it into the water to thwart the brigands who'd set up a trap to rob unwary travelers, including us. On the other side of that river lies a dark forest, and in that dark forest is a woodland mansion. If I were a bad guy, it's definitely where I'd be going.

I wish there were a way to get there first, because whoever does has a huge advantage over anyone attempting to storm it. There are dozens of rooms, dozens of windows, hundreds of places to hide. Even though we cleared out all the illagers and other hostile mobs, there are still plenty of dark places where zombies and skeletons can spawn. It would be much easier to defend the woodland mansion than it would be to attack it. We just have to get there first.

And that's when it hits me—

We can get there first, but we can't do it on horseback.

There's a faster way, a way that doesn't depend on crossing the river.

Before we found the village last time, I discovered something odd while digging out our nightly shelter: a hole in the ground.

That hole leads to a fortress, hiding innocently under the plains, and in that fortress, there are mine tracks that lead directly to the woodland mansion's basement.

"Hey, Chug," I call.

"Yeah, Mal?"

"Think you can craft a mine cart?"

# 13

# LENNA

 I can't believe that we finally found horses but now we have to travel underground instead. It's a good idea, though—the tunnel in the fortress is a straight shot, and mine carts are fast. The first time I stood over this open hole in the ground, I was scared and excited. Maybe it's because I'm descended from miners and was born underground, but I've always felt at home down there in the dark. Still, before our adventure, I'd never explored beneath the surface anywhere except my family's mine, where I was surrounded by people I knew and places long proven to be safe. Well, relatively safe. A mine is still a mine, after all. And then Mal was digging out a shelter and randomly found this yawning chasm.

We're lucky that Chug has a ladder in his pocket—he almost always has a ladder, now that he knows the pocket trick. He says it's because Tok's cats sometimes get caught in odd places, but if I had to guess, I would say it's because we spent most of our childhood getting in trouble and running away from angry people, and that's a whole lot easier if you can climb up a tree or a building to escape whoever's chasing you. It's not surprising that I have déjà vu as I climb down into the cavern, but I'm a lot more confident this time than I was back then. Whatever is down here, I'm ready for it.

Mal went first, because that's how we usually do things. I'm so glad she's back to normal, healthy and full of energy and always so certain about what to do. It was weird, when she was injured and mostly helpless. I've only seen her that way once before, and it was really scary. It just goes against the natural order of things, when someone you trust and look up to is suddenly fragile, like if salmon could fly or chickens could swim.

Which makes me wonder . . . if salmon could fly and chickens could swim, would they taste like each other or a mixture of both?

"Lenna?"

Chug calls up to me from the ledge down below, where he waits with Mal, both of them holding torches. It's a long way down to the bottom of this cavern, so we agreed we'd all meet on the ledge before moving the ladder down to the ground for another climb. The horses and Poppy are waiting in a little paddock Mal dug for them. I don't want to go anywhere without my wolf, but I also don't know how to get her down a ladder. I gave her a bone and told her to sit, and she's such a good girl that I'm sure she'll still be sitting there when we get back.

I look to Poppy one last time before stepping onto the ladder. As I begin to climb down, I can't help noticing Jarro, who's staring at me with bald terror written all over his face. I stop.

"What's wrong?"

He looks back at the horses. "Will they be okay?"

"They're wild animals. They're in a pit. Mobs don't care about them. And Poppy is with them, too. They'll be safer here than they would be underground. If we could get them underground. Which we can't."

He sighs, and his shoulders slump. "I guess I got kind of attached to Speckles. I hate leaving her behind."

"We all hate it. Chug hated leaving Thingy, and I hate leaving Poppy. But we have to keep moving forward. Don't worry—they'll be here when we get back. And since you know there's no way I'd leave Poppy behind, you know we won't forget them."

Jarro nods . . . maybe a little too much. He can't stop nodding. He's biting his lip and pacing and breathing too fast.

"Is something else bothering you, Jarro?"

He cranes his head to look down into the hole. "Is it safe?"

"As safe as a ladder into a hole underground can be."

"But, I mean, you guys have been telling me that everything gets dangerous when it's dark, and now we're all going into a cave. So that's got to be dangerous, right?"

I shrug. "We have weapons. We have torches. We're at full health. You haven't really seen us fight yet, but we're good at it. We took down over a dozen illagers in a woodland mansion once and didn't get hurt too badly."

Jarro looks away nervously. "Okay, but . . . I don't even know what illagers are. My mom sent me home when they attacked the town, remember? And I always thought I would be a good fighter, but it's like . . ." He angrily kicks a stone. "I'm afraid that when the time comes, I'll just freeze again, like I did with that creeper, and somebody will get hurt. Or I'll fall off the ladder, or the ladder will break and drop me, or—"

"Stop." I step off the ladder and hold my torch between us.

"You're telling yourself stories about things that haven't happened. Why don't you tell yourself a story with a happy ending?"

He looks at me like I just grew a second head. "Because I don't see anything good coming from us going underground! We should just keep riding the horses and following the trail. We know what to expect up here. We know we'll be okay."

"You think you know that, but we've had bad things happen to us up here. We don't even know if the bridge has been replaced." I cock my head. "I think you're just scared of the unknown. You're scared of what you don't know."

"Obviously!" he splutters.

"Well, here's what I know. If you go with us, we know what we're doing and we have experience and weapons. If you stay up here alone, you've got nothing."

"You wouldn't leave me here," he says, daring and smug.

I blink at him.

"Jarro, do you know that for years, I had a headache every morning because I knew you were going to bully me? But I had to go to school anyway. I tried all sorts of different timings, tried to walk by your house earlier or later or take a different route, and sometimes it worked, but most of the time it didn't. But I still went to school, knowing you were going to make my day stink. So if I can do that, you can do this. You can climb down the ladder, because fear only stops you if you let it. You just have to feel the fear and do it anyway. I'd go underground a thousand times before I went back to first grade and had to walk by your house."

With that, I swing around on the ladder and climb down. He can join us or he can stay behind, but I'm not going to sit around feeling sorry for him.

"What was that all about?" Chug asks.

"I told Jarro that if he didn't climb down, we'd leave him behind."

Chug's eyes bug out. "Whoa. You're hard-core."

I stare up at the top of the ladder and speak loud enough for my voice to carry. "He's never had real problems before. He can learn to face them, like we did, or he can hang out in that shelter and wait for us to find Tok. It'll be boring but safe. We can't waste any more time."

Chug holds out his fist, and I bump it with my own. He knows I'm not really big on hugging.

"If Jarro's not coming, can we move the ladder and head down?" Mal asks.

I steady the ladder with both my hands and wait. "Not yet."

I'm just about to give up when I feel the ladder shift under Jarro's weight. He climbs down slowly, trembling, clinging to the wood. I step back once he's near the bottom rung, and he steps off onto the ledge.

"Don't look down," I tell him. "Sit, if you need to."

He drops to his hands and knees, and Chug smirks but doesn't say anything. I know he'd love to rib Jarro for his fear, but Chug seems to understand that you don't pick fights while standing on stone ledges over a dark abyss. Chug is also not the sort of person to kick someone when they're trying. As scared as I once was of Jarro, out here, he's pretty pathetic.

Mal pulls down the ladder and lowers it until it touches the ground below. I hold the top rungs to steady it as she climbs down from the ledge with one hand, a torch in the other. Then Chug goes, leaving me with Jarro, who's still clinging to the rock.

"Almost there," I tell him. "If you did that, you can do this, too."

He nods, and I hold the ladder for him, knowing Mal is holding the bottom of it. As Jarro passes by me, he whispers, "Thanks," and I just nod. Once he's safely down, I collect the torch hanging on the cavern wall and climb down myself.

The last time I was down here, there'd been a cave-in. But now, those boulders are gone, the area cleaned up to clearly reveal rails. This track connects Cornucopia to the woodland mansion. Even if our town Elders sealed up our end of the tunnel, they didn't destroy the track this far in. If Chug really can make a mine cart, our journey will be so much faster. He puts his torch on the wall, and I walk seven blocks and attach mine. Mal keeps hers in hand.

"Okay, here we go," Chug murmurs, pulling the wonky crafting table out of his pocket.

As he gets to work, I take out my bow and arrows, and Mal has her diamond pickaxe at the ready. The cavern is utterly silent, other than Chug's crafting noises, and all of my senses are on high alert. I can smell water somewhere, and minerals, hear dripping far off and the squeak of a bat. It's colder down here but not unpleasant.

"What do we do now?" Jarro asks nervously. In the quiet, his voice is startling, and it echoes off the walls.

"For one thing, be quiet," Mal whispers. "We're listening for mobs—for groans or clacking or twanging or squeaks. Get your axe out. Be ready. Chug's our best fighter at hand-to-hand combat, and we have to defend him while he's working."

"You're not the best?" Jarro asks her.

Mal shakes her head ruefully. "Nope. I mostly distract them so

Chug can use his sword. If you see him swinging, get out of the way."

"And if you see me nock an arrow, also get out of the way," I add. "I can't shoot stuff if you're between us."

Jarro nods and pulls out his axe. "So it sounds like my job is to be quiet and stay out of the way."

"Anytime you want to jump into a fight, we can use you," Mal assures him. "Even Tok can take up a weapon, if we're in trouble."

Jarro is about to say something snappy about that, but Chug stops hammering and glares at him, so he wisely reconsiders and instead asks, "Where'd you guys learn to fight?"

"Out here. We almost lost our first fight—with four zombies. I felt like I was just flailing, like I didn't know how to swing my pickaxe or where to aim. I was sure we were going to lose," Mal admits. I appreciate that she said "lose" instead of "die," because that's a much friendlier word.

"So you guys left town, found weapons, and just started fighting zombies?" Jarro asks.

Mal nods. "Yeah, except Nan gave us the weapons."

He snorts. "My mom would never give me a weapon." He sniffles and swipes at his nose with his fist. "I mean, she won't even let me cut up my own steak."

"Why not?" I ask, and Mal shoots me a look that suggests it's not my business.

There's something about the darkness of the cave, how remote and alien and separate it feels from the world, something that makes it feel like it's okay to say things you wouldn't say in daylight. That has to be the reason that Jarro says what he does.

"Because after my dad died, I was all she had," Jarro says softly. "She had me when she was older, and my grandparents are dead, and then my dad— Well, it was an accident. He was fixing the roof and—"

He takes a big, sucking breath, and I notice that Chug has stopped his hammering to listen.

"Anyway, she always tells me it's just the two of us against the world, and it's her job to keep me safe. So I can't climb trees or leave the Hub or slice bread. So there. I'm sure you'll have something clever to say about that."

Mal and I both look to Chug, because it's true: He's never missed a chance to eviscerate Jarro with words. But Chug looks . . . sorry for Jarro.

"I didn't know about your dad," Chug says quietly.

"Yeah, well, it's not exactly something I like to talk about."

For a moment, they just stare at each other, but it feels like someone should say something, so I say, "Is that why you're so mean all the time?"

"Um—I—what? Why would you—pssh. Whatever." Jarro shakes his head. "You guys were just annoying. Are annoying. You always act like you own the town and you're better than anybody else. Like the rules don't apply to you."

Mal holds up her pickaxe. "I mean, they kind of don't. Chug, how's that mine cart coming?"

Chug sighs and slams metal down on the crafting table. "I messed this one up. I need more iron. Could you do a little mining?"

Mal hands her torch to Jarro. He takes it and looks from me to her.

"Just go against your instincts and protect Chug at all costs," she says with a smirk.

Mal runs a hand over the roughly hewn stone wall near one of our torches. That's where I'd start, too—it looks about right for a vein. As her pickaxe strikes again and again, Chug hammers and grunts and tries to salvage what he can from what was well on the way to being a very bad mine cart. "This is harder than it looks," he grumbles.

A lump of iron clumps onto the ground. "I think there are a few more—" Mal says. As she mines, she burrows deeper into the rock.

"So you can just . . . dig through rock?" Jarro asks, mesmerized.

"That's what mining is—" I start, but then I hear it.

Rattle. Rattle.

"The rattling thing," Jarro whispers, clutching his axe to his chest—luckily with the blade pointed away. "A—a skelbie!"

Chug is hammering, Mal is deep in the stone wall, and that leaves just me and Jarro.

"It's a skeleton," I tell him, nocking an arrow and listening for the next click of bone on stone. "It'll shoot arrows. I'll shoot back at it. If you can hit it from the side, it should go down without too much trouble."

"But—"

"No buts. Just use your axe. And remember: We don't have any potions. If you don't help with the fight, we might be in trouble."

Rattle.

I take aim and let loose an arrow, satisfied at the clatter of a solid hit. I get another arrow ready, but then a groan echoes around the chamber.

"Jarro, there's a zombie!" I shout. "You've got to take it down!"

"I can't!" he shouts back. "I'm not ready—"

"Tell that to the zombie."

I focus everything I have on the skeleton. I can see it now, rushing toward me by the light of the torch, and I release arrow after arrow until it falls. I spin, looking for Jarro, but I don't see him. The zombie's groans are louder now, and when Jarro cries out, I know he's taken a hit.

"Hit it, Jarro! Pretend it's a log!"

"I can't—"

"You can, you big idiot!" Chug bellows from his crafting table.

But he clearly can't. The axe forgotten in his hand, Jarro turns his back on the zombie, as if not seeing it will mean it doesn't exist.

"Jarro, you have to fight!" I shout. They're in the shadows, so I can't risk hitting Jarro with an arrow, but I grab the torch he dropped and run. The zombie is groaning and biting, and Jarro is holding it off with one arm—which has a nasty wound on it.

But he's not going to use his axe. He can't. He's frozen.

I whip my pickaxe out of my pocket. It's not much, but with the zombie focused on Jarro, I'm able to take it down without suffering any damage myself. It falls, leaving rotten flesh and, luckily, an iron ingot. Jarro frowns at the wound on his arm before scooping up the ingot and holding it out to Chug.

"I was looking for one of these," Chug says, taking the ingot and putting it into service.

Mal pops out of her hole with three more chunks of iron. "How's it going out here?"

"Jarro almost got killed by a zombie, and I took down a skeleton," I tell her.

"I didn't almost get killed," he says. "It's not that bad—"

"Speaking of not bad . . ."

We all turn to look at Chug, and he's proudly holding a mine cart.

"Nice work," I tell him.

We bump fists, and Chug puts the cart on the rails.

"Let's go get my brother," he says.

And that's the exact moment Jarro chooses to faint.

# 14

# JARRO

 I don't know what happened. Everything was fine, if mortifying, and now I'm on the ground on my back with everyone asking if I'm okay. I can't quite focus, and everything hurts, but especially—

Oh no.

When I turned my back, the zombie bit my butt, and I was in so much pain I didn't even notice. But now I do. Now that I'm lying directly on what's got to be a horrible, life-ending wound.

"Jarro? Are you okay?" Mal asks, kneeling by my side. She looks genuinely worried, which feels nice.

Nothing else does, right now.

"Zombie bite," I groan. Then it hits me. "Wait. Am I going to turn into a—?"

"We were worried about that, the first time, too," Lenna says from my other side. "But no. I can see the wound on your arm, but where else did it get you?"

My face flushes. "Uh, nowhere. Just the arm."

"Nobody passes out from one zombie bite," Chug says. "Unless maybe you're allergic?"

I shake my head and try to sit up, but that puts the place that hurts the most in direct contact with the bumpy stone floor. They all see me gasp and wince.

"Jarro . . ." Chug pins his lips, his eyes sparking with amusement. I have never wanted to punch him as badly as I do right now. "Did the zombie . . . perchance . . . bite you . . . on the rrrrump?"

He rolls the R for emphasis, and Lenna squeaks a smothered laugh. Mal's keeping it together better, but even she is fighting her giggles.

I glare at Chug, and I want to hit him and call him names, but he's the one holding all the meat that could help me heal. "Yes, Chug. That is exactly what happened."

As if on cue, all three of them burst out laughing. Their big, raucous belly laughs fill the cavern and echo back. It's like being slapped with embarrassment, and I can't take it anymore. I just can't.

"You guys are jerks!" I bellow. "You think you're the good guys, but you know what? You're mean. You leave people out of your little circle at school, always act like you're royalty while the rest of us are losers. And you're not that special, okay? Just because you know stuff I don't doesn't make you special. I'm hurt and scared, and you're laughing at me. So go ahead and be bullies, but don't pretend like you're the victims or the heroes here, because you're not. You're not heroes!"

My voice echoes through the empty cave.

*Not heroes—not heroes—not heroes.*

They all look . . . stunned.

And hurt.

And ashamed?

"Do you really feel that way?" Mal asks.

"No, I just came up with the whole speech on the fly." I shake my head. "Yes, I really feel that way, and so do a lot of people. Now that we're outside the wall, it's like sometimes you guys are nice and kind of accept me, but then you find some reason to laugh at me again."

"I don't want to be a jerk," Lenna says, thoughtful. "But that doesn't mean it's not true."

Chug says nothing, but I can hear his teeth grinding.

"I didn't know people thought of us that way." Mal blinks back tears and dashes at her eyes with her hand. "We saved the town—"

"That's not how people in the Hub see it. *They* fought the il-lagers. They saved themselves." I shrug. "You guys only see what you want to see."

"So what do we do?" Lenna asks.

"Just be nice. Stop treating me like who you think I was and start treating me like I'm an equal. I'm . . . I'm trying to be better, okay? So you guys have to try, too."

Lenna nods. "I'll try."

Mal nods, too. "So will I."

Chug says nothing, and Mal stares at him like she can tele-pathically force him to step up, but he stubbornly refuses.

"Can I please just have some meat so I can start healing?" I ask as exhaustion floods into the empty spaces left by my anger. Be-cause it's great that they're realizing that they can be jerks, too, but I'm still in bad shape.

"Well, you have to show us the wound first." Maybe Lenna and Mal heard me, but Chug is still Chug, and he's enjoying this way too much. "Because it'll probably heal fine with a good meal.

Zombie wounds aren't quiet as dire as explosion wounds. In fact, I would say when it comes to wounds, they're at the *bottom* of the pack. Don't worry—soon, this will all be *behind* you."

Mal smacks his shoulder. "Chug should behave, but he's mostly right. For real, Jarro, this is not something to be embarrassed about. We've all been wounded. We've all healed. Laughing just makes it easier to deal with . . ."

"The emptiness left over after a fight," Lenna finishes for her. "And, hey. At least we're not on horseback for the next part of the journey." She holds out a cookie, and I take it, recognizing a peace offering when I see it.

With the first bite, I already feel a little better. It's a good thing I'm on the ground, because if I could stand up, I would most likely end whatever truce I thought we'd found and beat the crud out of Chug. Mal and Lenna are smiling at me, but he is clearly still trying to think of more embarrassing puns to torture me with.

Mal holds out some chicken, which I also take, as the cookie is already gone. "Good point. The mine cart is a lot faster, and . . ." She looks up at Chug, and I realize that I don't like it when Mal looks worried. "Don't we need two mine carts?"

It's a pleasure, watching Chug's smugness disappear. "Oh. Wow. Yeah, I guess so." He sorts through the stack of stone and ore left behind by Mal's mining, and she picks through her pockets with more offerings. "I think I remember how to build a furnace. Tok said it was super easy. But then again, for Tok, pretty much anything smart is super easy."

Mal puts a hand on his arm. "I know it's hard, not having him here, but you can do it. I believe in you. We all do."

I have to look away. No one has ever spoken to me like that before. Including my mom. No wonder Chug does whatever she says.

"You can do it," Lenna agrees, and I feel like a lost little kid. Mal nudges me with her foot and raises her eyebrows expectantly. She wants me to encourage Chug, too. I don't want to, but I do want to get back home, so I have to say something.

"I guess if you can make a mine cart, you can make a furnace, whatever that is," I grumble.

Chug gets to work, and Mal looks to Lenna before she goes back to mining. "Can you two stand guard again?" she asks.

"We kind of have to," Lenna tells her.

Mal takes her torch and pickaxe back into the hole she's hewn in the rock, and Lenna stands over me while I finish my chicken. I guess the great thing about using a ranged weapon like her bow is that she's usually not close enough to a mob to take any damage. One skeleton shows up while we wait, but Lenna knocks it down easily. I can only hope nothing worse shows up. I'm clearly not going to be any help.

"I never stopped practicing, but I can feel my skills and instincts coming back. It feels good, like stretching when you've just woken up from a deep sleep," Lenna says, but more to herself than to me. She's a weird kid, but out here, away from town, she makes a little more sense.

Mal finds more iron ore, Chug pulls things in and out of his furnace and hammers on his crafting table, and then we have two mine carts. They fit perfectly on the track, and Mal and Chug help me stand and climb into the first cart. Mal hops in beside me, does something with a lever, and without a single word of warning, sends our cart careening out into the darkness. I jerk backward, my entire body rattling as we hurtle through space.

Only then does it occur to me that . . . well, there are plenty of things that could go wrong. There could be another cave-in like the one that Lenna said once covered these tracks, making them dangerous and unusable. There could be mobs. There could be pretty much any horrible thing that spawns in darkness—or hides there. Things I've never seen—things I've never even heard of.

But it's too late now. The cart is going, and there's nothing I can do but hold on.

After a few minutes, I realize that it's actually not terrible. I like this feeling—the wind in my hair, even when I know perfectly well there's no actual wind underground. I like the smells, the glimmer of ore and stone as Mal's torch briefly illuminates the sparkling wall. I've never gone this fast in my entire life, and I'm scared, but there's nothing I can do about it. I can either enjoy it or be terrified, and maybe it's the zombie bite talking, but I'm just going to try to enjoy it.

"Are you feeling any better?" Mal asks.

I do not like girls asking me about my wounded butt.

"I'll be fine."

"I have some more chicken—"

"I'm getting a little sick of chicken. Do we have anything else?"

She rummages in her pocket. "Nope. We already ate all the steak. That's how it goes, beyond the wall—you take what you can get. Chicken is better than starving. And it really does heal you."

She holds out another strip of chicken, and I take it and chew. "I miss potions."

"Yeah, me, too. The woodland mansion—we don't know what we'll find there. Last time, we found a few potions in random chests, but it was full of mobs. We almost lost, tons of times. We don't know if it's full of illagers again."

"Or just the regular kind of bad guys who kidnap kids."

I think back to what it felt like, being grabbed roughly by adults and shoved around. Realizing that my mom couldn't save me. Being marched farther and farther away from home. I shudder before I can stop myself.

"Sounds scary," Mal says.

"It was," I admit, because it's just us. No one else can hear us. It's like we're all alone in the world. "It's like I had no control. There was nothing I could do. I just felt so helpless."

There's a pause. Maybe I said too much and she's going to make fun of me now? I brace myself for the worst.

"It sucks, feeling weak and helpless, doesn't it?" she finally says.

"Yup."

"I used to feel that way when you and Remy and Edd stole my lunch at school."

My jaw drops. She remembers that? "I mean . . . we were just little kids. That's what little kids do. It's no big deal."

"It was a big deal to me. I started having stomachaches every day."

I would rather jump out of this mine cart than continue this conversation, but she's right there, and her shoulders are hunched up like she's about to cry. "You were probably drinking too much milk, Mal. You always brought twice as much milk as anybody else."

"It wasn't the milk, Jarro. You made me feel terrible. You made me hate school."

For a moment, there's no sound but the whoosh of air and a distant rumble that must be the other mine cart. I realize that there is nowhere to go, nowhere to hide. My mom's not here, Edd and Remy aren't here. It's just me, Mal, and things that used to make me feel tough but now make me feel like kind of an idiot. I can't even remember all the times I used to mess with people — or why I did it.

"I'm sorry." It comes out almost a whisper.

"Say it louder."

I clear my throat. "I'm sorry. That was dumb."

Mal looks back over her shoulder at me, her profile lit by her torch. "Are you really sorry, or are you just saying that because you don't know how to survive out here alone and you understand that I — or any of my friends — could abandon you at any moment?"

I take a deep breath. "Can't it be both?"

Mal turns around, and her face is ghoulishly lit by the torch as she glares at me. "Okay, then, real talk. Maybe we were snooty, but you were really horrible to us back home, and yet we've still saved your life multiple times. We have real weapons. Real skills. You can't ever bully us again. You get that?"

I nod. "But you guys can't bully me, either. Chug needs to cool it."

"He does. He will. I'll talk to him."

"Because if he keeps on taunting me, I'm going to defend myself. You get that, right?"

"I get it, Jarro, I do, but someone has to be the bigger person. Someone has to take the first step. So get on our team and don't be a jerk."

"But Chug was making fun of — of my wound!" I splutter. "You all were!"

Mal snorts. "Because friends laugh together! Can't you admit that it's kind of funny? Like, if that happened to Chug, wouldn't you laugh?"

I chuckle. "Oh, yeah. I'd never let him forget it."

"What if it was Remy or Edd?"

"Same thing."

Mal shrugs. "So learn to laugh at yourself. Just drop the ego, laugh along, and get over it."

"But then Chug wins," I say before I can stop myself.

She looks at me like I'm an idiot. "You know that no one's keeping score, right? This isn't the Hub. No one cares. If you survive out here, you're winning."

And I kind of hate it, but I guess maybe she's right? Back home, it's like there was always an audience, always someone watching and judging. But here, now, it's just us against the world. And, yeah, okay, fine, maybe getting bit in the butt by a zombie is kind of funny. If it was anyone else, at least.

She hands me more chicken. "Here. Keep eating."

"Because I can't talk smack when I'm eating?"

"Because you can't talk smack when you're eating. And because you need to be as healed as possible for what happens next."

I spend the rest of the ride eating while Mal fills me in on what we might find in the woodland mansion—other than the humans that I'm already perfectly scared of. Evokers and vexes, vindicators, zombies, skeletons, spiders, skeletons riding spiders.

"And you guys emptied this place out last time?" I ask.

"Yep."

"But it might be completely full again?"

"Yep."

"And we're going anyway?"

"Yep." She turns back to pin me with a glare. "We're going back for Tok, and if they took you, we'd go back for you. That's what friends do."

I want to say *that's what idiots do*, but I told her I'd stop smart-ing off, and I definitely don't want to get sent back in this cart alone, so I don't say anything.

And then it hits me . . .

She said "friends."

Like I'm one of their friends now.

It's funny—back home, I saw these four kids as losers who stuck together because nobody else wanted anything to do with them. But now I'm seeing that they care about one another in a way that Edd and Remy and me . . . just don't. We don't talk about feelings or encourage one another. We talk about how much we hate school and how stupid other people are and what we could do that wouldn't be boring. We don't even get one an-other birthday gifts, because we're always trying to act grown-up and tough, but it sure does make birthdays lonely. Maybe the Bad Apples are on to something.

Honestly, it would be hard to think of a reason to make fun of any of them right now. They're just so . . . capable. It's annoying.

I want to find stuff I'm good at, too.

Finally I've eaten so much chicken that I feel like I'm proba-bly going to sprout feathers, and my butt doesn't hurt anymore. Neither does my arm. I guess they were right—food really can heal anything. I'm about to ask Mal for some pointers on taking down evokers when the cart comes to an abrupt halt.

Mal jumps out, and before she can try to help me, I jump out, too. I feel much better, and I immediately reach into my pocket for my axe. If there's one thing I've noticed about this crew, it's that they're always ready, and I don't want to be the only person who isn't contributing.

The cavern around us is ginormous and almost looks like a

fancy house someone built underground, with walls and stairs and torches everywhere. I don't see any bad guys, at least—or mobs.

"This is the underground fortress," Mal tells me, her voice low. "The woodland mansion is overhead."

The other mine cart zips into view and jerks to a halt. Chug and Lenna hop out.

"Mal, you doing okay, or did being that close to Jarro for so long make you barf?" Chug shouts.

Mal bumps her shoulder against mine. "We've declared a truce on barfing. I think we're all gonna get along fine from now on, right?"

They all look at me. The pushy jerk in me feels like I'm being ganged up on and forced to agree, but there's this new part of me that thinks that's just so pointless. Mal's right—I've always thought of life as winning or losing, but there's no one keeping score. Being a jerk suddenly seems like such a waste of energy.

"No barfing," I agree. "But I'm still allowed to retch a little, every now and then."

With a measuring, testing look, Chug holds out his fist, and I bump it.

"Where to first?" Mal says, all business now. "Upstairs?"

Chug looks around and shivers. "Yeah, given a choice, nobody would hang out down here." He looks to Lenna. "Do you remember which stairwell?"

Lenna spins in place. "I wish we had Poppy. It was so much easier with her nose leading the way." She points at an unpleasantly dark doorway. "Maybe that one."

We walk up and down stairs, finding dead ends and ledges aplenty. Up until this moment, I had a lot of confidence in this crew, but now it looks like they've run up against something they can't quite figure out.

"So you guys don't know how to get up to the building?" I ask.

Chug bristles. "There was a lot going on last time."

"Why not just get to the highest point you can and mine up, then? Mal's pretty good with the pickaxe, right?"

They're looking at me like I'm either the dumbest person ever—or the smartest.

"Yeah, why not?" Mal finally says. "It's not like this is someone's house and they're going to get mad." She charges up the nearest spiraling stairwell, and we follow. When she reaches a dead end, she hangs her torch on the wall and starts tunneling upward.

"Good call," Chug says.

I can't help grinning.

I finally did something right.

# 15

# TOK

 They must have used one of Elder Gabe's potions on the horses for this part of the journey, as it feels like we've been traveling at an unnatural speed. Or maybe we stopped at the village earlier—we definitely stopped for something, but my captors keep quiet around me. I wish I could see even a peek of what's passing, but the blindfold is way too tight.

It must be evening—I'm so tired, and my posterior is one giant bruise. They've given me food, but nothing good, and all eaten on the road. Now that we're away from people, I guess, they leave my gag out. The air is the tiniest bit cooler. My horse slows to a normal speed, and I exhale; it was pretty bumpy for a while there.

When we stop, I brace myself for the familiar feeling of strange hands grabbing me and unceremoniously dropping me on the ground. I stumble every time, my feet numb and my senses thrown off by the blindfold. This time, a hand reaches out to steady me.

"Easy there," says a familiar voice, the one I know but can't quite place. "Not used to horseback, eh?"

I steady myself and stand tall. "There are no horses in Cornucopia. Surely you know that, considering you must've spent time spying on me before planning your heist?"

The man laughs and smacks me on the back in a way that his cronies probably find friendly, but since I can't see and I'm exhausted, I stumble, and he has to catch me so I don't fall.

"That's true enough. Odd people in your town, behind that big, silly wall. No horses, no dogs, no pigs. Well, that one pet pig that I nearly stole, just so I could have my delicious revenge."

All the pieces snap into place, and I realize exactly who he is, why I know his voice.

"You're the leader of the brigands who stole our llamas at the river crossing."

He barks a laugh. "The very one! Took you long enough to figure it out."

"Well, you've kept me blindfolded and gagged and threatened to impale me on a sword if I spoke, so pardon me if I kept to myself."

He laughs again, like I'm the funniest person he's ever met. "You're an odd one—you and your friends. How'd you come to be outside the wall in the first place? Our mutual friend Krog said no one had left for a hundred years or more—besides him, of course."

I lick my lips, sensing some bargaining power. This man—this brigand—this *kidnapper*—wants knowledge that only I currently hold. "Take off my blindfold, and I'll tell you."

There's a long pause, and I can imagine him looking around, surveilling the falling night.

"Fine, then. But the lead stays on."

"I'd expect no less."

It's funny. After a few days of captivity, I feel a new sense of recklessness. The situation can't possibly get any worse, so I might as well push back, right? I'm scared, but they obviously need me for something, so they're not going to hurt me. Too much. Probably.

I'm right, and he pushes the blindfold down around my neck.

Night is falling, and we're surrounded by horses, which look just like they did in Nan's book. Two people cook meat over a campfire while three people keep watch for the hostile mobs that constantly spawn when it's this dark. Everyone is bristling with weapons. No one is digging a shelter.

"Are we not sleeping?"

The leader shakes his head. He's holding a torch, and he looks the same as he did the last time we saw him: burly beard, armor, cocky smile with a gold tooth. His hand rests comfortably on his sword hilt. "Not here. We're only stopping for a quick bite. We'll reach the woodland mansion soon, and then we'll sleep. You'll need sleep, where we're going."

"Where's that?"

He grins, tooth glinting. "You'll see."

"Did Krog put you up to this?"

His mouth twists up in a sneer. "Krog? That self-important blowhard? He's still in your town jail, as far as I know. His plan was a bit overcomplicated for our needs. He wanted to make everyone leave Cornucopia so he would have access to the fortress. We don't need anyone to leave to accomplish our goals." He prods me in the chest with a finger. "We just need you."

"Why?"

He shakes his head. "Doesn't matter, does it? Because we've

got you. Thing is, when people build high walls, they start to think they're safe. They get comfortable. Then Krog left, and then you lot left, and then your town decided to open up. Ha!"

In response, the other brigands throw back their heads and shout, "Ha!"

"The only thing worse than walling yourself off is being completely open. One gate with one guard—who falls asleep at a reliable time? There's a middle ground between complete distrust and complete trust. Bunch of fools, those Elders of yours. Forget that people weren't entirely altruistic. Never faced a threat, so how could they possibly know how to prepare for a threat?"

I'd like to argue, but I can't.

He's right.

As much as we needed to open the wall, we messed up. We left ourselves vulnerable.

"Once we beat you, we'll know better," I growl.

"Beat me? Who's going to beat me? You?" He plucks at my arm, raises it up and drops it. It falls to my side, limp as a flower stem.

"My friends," I say with confidence I almost feel.

At that, he nods. "True enough, true enough. You bested us once before, didn't you? Four kids, outside for the first time ever, and you managed to surprise me." He leans in. "I admire that, you know? You lot are brave, I'll give you that. But your friends can't save you. Not where we're going. And they don't have horses or potions—thanks to your help, we made sure of that last part. There's no way they could catch us before we're beyond their reach."

"Where are we going?"

He bops my nose with a finger. "So many questions. You're

curious, Tok. I like that. Don't worry—you'll find out soon enough."

He reaches for my blindfold, and I start to panic. I don't want to be relegated to darkness again. "But where's Jarro?" I blurt. "I heard you take him."

The blindfold slides back into place. "The sweet berry kid? We dumped him way back. Didn't have enough horses. And let's face it—that kid was dead weight. We only took him so he wouldn't sound the alarm." He pulls down the blindfold, just enough for me to see him. "Why? He a friend of yours?"

I snort. "The opposite. He's a bully. He deserves whatever he gets."

The brigand looks into my eyes. "Yeah, I had bullies, too. Might've been a bit of a bully myself in response to it. Never found a group of friends like yours. You're lucky, you know?"

I stare directly into his eyes, unblinking. "My brother and my friends will find me."

The blindfold snaps back into place.

"Not soon enough," he says. "Now let's get you back in the saddle for the last leg of our journey. You do your job, and you'll be back in your own bed one day, and that's a promise."

I want to ask what good a promise from a kidnapper might be, but I don't test my luck.

This time, when hands drop me back onto my horse, I know it's him. He's not gentle, but he's not cruel. It's businesslike. And I think about who this brigand must be, that he can steal me from my bed and my family so callously and yet talk to me like I'm some friendly acquaintance. He's stern but not mean, friendly but aloof, almost paternal. I want to ask him how he became this way, a dangerous outlaw roaming the Overworld and taking whatever he wants, but the brief openness we shared is over. I'm just bag-gage again.

I hear everyone else mount up, and then we're on the move. The path changes, a downward slope that makes me lean back. We zig and zag, and I understand where we are: the mountain pass right before the river. I can hear it now, the rush of water, the way the air goes cool and moist. They must've replaced the log bridge we toppled with something wider, as my horse clips and clops slowly through the mist. Nausea rises as I think of the waters raging below, but there's nothing I can do but hold on. Finally we're back on dirt, and my horse sags with relief.

"Almost there," someone says, and a cry of victory goes up.

Raindrops plink on my head, but only for a few moments. Then we're under the cover of the dark forest, its canopy so dense that it blocks the sky. I hear a rattle, then several twangs followed by the clatter of a collapsing skeleton. My captors are competent in the wilderness. That's a point against my escape—they've got at least one good shot among them, if not more.

There are more groans and rattles, more arrows loosed, more clatters and grunts. Finally my horse stops, and someone grabs me and drags me to the ground.

"Walk," the leader says, punctuated by a prod in the back.

So I walk, and I mentally map where we must be—the wood-land mansion. Up the stairs, then up more stairs to the top floor. I throw out all my senses, waiting for the grunt of an evoker or vindicator, but the brigands must be keeping this place empty of mobs and illagers.

As I walk, led from before and prodded from behind, I realize something that makes me grin.

My friends know how to get here. They know this place.

There's a good chance they really will find me—at least, a better chance than if they were wandering out in the middle of nowhere. The leader said they won't find me in time, but he's probably underestimating how far the Mob Squad would go to bring me home. And he also doesn't know about the trail of iron ingots and coal I've been leaving all along.

"Stop," the leader says, and I do. "Climb up this ladder. No funny business."

"Yes, sir," I say.

He places my hands on a ladder, and I climb until I run out of rungs. Someone else lifts me to stand on the floor above.

My blindfold is untied and—

I'm stunned.

Now I know why they needed me.

## 16

# CHUG

 It's dark by the time we climb up out of Mal's tunnel and into a room with a giant chicken statue, and the woodland mansion is quiet. We're ready, weapons out, but no foes appear. Mal fits in a stone block, and you can't even tell there was ever a hole there. I yawn so big that my jaw cracks, and that makes Lenna and Mal and Jarro yawn, too.

"We have to sleep," Mal whispers. She jerks her head toward the stairwell, which has a nifty hidden spot behind it. We slept there last time with no trouble, so it looks like we're going to do that again.

"But Tok," I protest, and she's already shaking her head.

"When we don't sleep, we get stupid and clumsy, and when we get stupid and clumsy, we get hurt. If they're here, they're sleeping, too. If they're not here, we'll be ready when they arrive."

I know she's right, but I hate that she's right. "Can we at least visit the room full of food?"

Mal shakes her head sadly. "We're too beat. If we walked into a room filled with enemies, they'd destroy us." She looks to Jarro. "How many of them did you see, back when they kidnapped you?"

He thinks back. "Six or seven? I don't really know. It was dark. Between five and ten."

"Four of us against five to ten adults is not great odds." She doesn't say it, but her eyes shoot to Jarro. He was pretty good with the horses, but otherwise, he hasn't proven to be a real asset. He barely managed to take down a zombie, and if he had to face an actual human, I know he'd freeze up. If we got in a fight right now, we'd probably be better off if he just hid behind the stairs.

They put out their beds, all in a row because there's not much room, and I curl against the wall, resigned to discomfort. There might be beds somewhere in the mansion, although we took several during our last visit, but we're just too tired to fight. As I toss and turn, wishing for a blanket or anything other than cold, hard stone, Mal stands up and roots through her pockets. She saved a lot of the stone she found mining earlier, and she uses a few blocks to wall us off. I sigh in relief. It's funny how when you're constantly in danger, you forget how exhausting it is to be constantly in danger. I hang my torch on the wall, and the light is back to what I think of as Cornucopia Normal. I never knew true darkness until we ventured beyond our town's walls. There are so many torches in Cornucopia that no mobs can ever spawn. It's more comfy like this, with the torchlight flickering.

Jarro is the first one asleep, and I'm forced to stare at him, which is not something I would choose. He looks different out here. Smaller. It's almost like he's a different person, and even if I have a lifetime of grudges against him, I don't feel that familiar tightening in my chest I get every time I see him back home, my jaw grinding, my hands in fists. Out here, he's just another kid, and even if he isn't one of us, a member of our Mob Squad, he's still on our side. I need to work on seeing him differently and stop wasting my energy on hating him. In my mind, he's this towering monster, but out here, he's just a tall but frightened child. It's easier to think kindly of him when he's asleep and drooling a little.

Which makes me think of Tok, because the last time I saw him, he was asleep. There at bedtime, gone by dawn. My poor little brother must be so scared. Whoever grabbed him must have pulled him right out of bed, a hand over his mouth to keep him from calling out. They dragged him out and forced him to leave his home, to leave me. I know he didn't want to. He didn't have a choice. I wish I weren't such a heavy sleeper. If only I'd heard them, I would've been there to protect him, to save him. I'm usually glad that I can fall asleep anywhere, anytime, and that I can sleep through a rooster fighting a cow, but this time . . . well, I failed my brother.

"Don't worry," Lenna whispers. She looks smaller now, too, probably because Poppy's not with her. "We'll get him back."

It's what I needed to hear. "Yeah, we will," I whisper back. And then, satisfied, reassured, I fall sleep.


"Chug, wake up," Mal says, shaking my shoulder, and I open my eyes to . . . well, not daylight, because we're in the shadowy area behind some stairs in a woodland mansion. But I can tell it's morning because I have eye boogers and my mouth tastes like dead fish. I keep my mouth closed for Mal's benefit and sit up.

Lenna is already up—they all are—and she hands everyone a cookie. "We're almost out of cookies," she warns us. "And after that, we've got nothing but chicken."

"Look at the bright side." I grin. "If we find any mobs, we're bound to get some potatoes."

As we eat our cookies, the mood is solemn and quiet. Everyone is getting ready for what has to be a fight, because whoever took Tok isn't just going to say, *Oh, you wanted him? Sorry, my bad, you can have him.* No one goes to this much trouble—infiltrating a town, stealing, kidnapping—just to give in to some angry kids.

I reach into my pockets and pull out all the armor and weapons I have. It's a mishmash of pieces, styles, and material. I'm the only one who wears armor most of the time because let's face it—armor is pinchy and clunky and uncomfortable. I've gotten used to it because I'm the most likely to do something stupid and take damage, but the others will just have to join me in discomfort as we run headfirst into danger.

Mal's lips twitch, and then she goes around assigning us pieces. I keep the diamond helmet, because, let's be honest, I'm the most likely to end up with a concussion, but we have enough helmets for everyone. Jarro gets the diamond chest plate—again, because he's the most likely to get hurt in a vital place. We're short a chest plate, so Lenna goes without, since she's able to fight from far off. Everyone gets something gold, and it's pretty, how it shines, even if it's pretty useless. We're mostly covered. Lenna is glad to take the arrows in my stash, and I offer Mal a sword, in case her pickaxe is out of commission. Jarro looks pretty lost, standing there in calico armor, holding his axe, so I offer him my only shield. His face scrunches up, but he accepts it without a fight. I wish I'd brought more. I just need more magic pockets, I guess.

"We ready?" Mal asks.

She meets my eyes, then Lenna's, then Jarro's. Everyone nods. Looking determined, Mal mines the stone blocks she used to barricade us in last night and stores the stones back in her pockets for later. She leads us down the exact same path we followed the last time we were here, and I notice a bunch of horses milling around outside the front door in a small paddock.

"Looks like Tok's kidnappers are already here," I say softly, pointing at them.

Jarro stops in the open doors. "They're still wearing their saddles."

"So? Maybe they don't like being naked," I say.

"But if we take the saddles . . . then they can't use the horses to escape."

My jaw drops. Did Jarro just . . . say something useful?

"Good call," Mal agrees. She and Jarro hurry outside and divest the horses of their saddles while Lenna keeps watch for threats outside and I guard our backs from the inside.

Mal and Jarro rejoin us, and we go through the woodland mansion room by room, taking everything useful we can find. Like last time, the chests contain random loot, some of which we can use—like apples and one lone golden apple—as well as stuff we don't need, like flowerpots. In the third room, a zombie lunges at us, and Mal and I take it down easily without absorbing any damage.

"Nice," Jarro murmurs. He stayed out of the fight, which

might have once given me reason to call him a coward, but honestly, it's just smart. Mal and I work best as a team, and we're definitely getting back in sync.

We clear the first floor, finding only a few skeletons, a zombie, and a spider. There are no illagers, which is great, but we haven't seen any sign of Tok or his captors. In one room, we find the open trapdoor to the fortress below, its rug rumpled to the side. I don't remember exactly what it looked like, the last time we were here. Maybe we left it that way, or maybe the kidnappers did. Maybe they're down in the basement, or maybe they're just around the corner. We know they're here because the horses are here, but that's all we know.

On the second floor, I pick up the pace, headed for the room I remember best. Last time, it held a feast, big bowls of food heaped and waiting for our nemesis, Krog, to stuff himself. This time, there's far less food, but we're able to load our pockets with apples, potatoes, mutton, and bread.

"No cookies," I mumble through a mouthful of meat.

"I'll be sure to complain to the chef," Jarro shoots back, and I grin.

We clear the second floor, disposing of a few skeletons and zombies like they're old hat. With each room, I grow more and more anxious. We've been through every part of the mansion I remember from last time, but there's no sign of Tok or his captors. I'm disappointed as we head back downstairs to stare at the horses outside.

"They have to be here," Mal says, reading my mind. "Maybe down in the cavern?"

"We didn't hear them, though." Lenna frowns. "I wish Poppy was here."

"And Tok," I add. "He always knows what to do."

With a shrug, Lenna says, "Then just think like Tok."

Huh.

That's an interesting idea. If I know Tok super well, then I should know what Tok would do right now.

I consider where we're standing and what we know about this place. "They could be in the cavern, but . . . it was just so quiet. Maybe . . . they're on the roof?"

I can't tell if it's a stupid idea or not. Compared to my friends and especially my brother, I always feel like the least intelligent one, but maybe spending so much time around Tok has had an effect. If not . . . well, I guess we'll get some sunshine.

Outside, I back away from the mansion to get some perspective. I can't really see the roof from here, so I pull the ladder out of my pocket and stare at it for a moment before pulling out my crafting table, grabbing some sticks from the forest, and crafting a bunch of ladders.

"What's he doing?" Jarro asks.

"Building ladders." Mal grins. "So we can get to the roof."

"Shouldn't there be stairs inside or something?"

"If so, then they'll be guarded," Mal reminds him. "Just trust Chug."

I practically glow at that compliment.

Once I'm done crafting, I attach my first ladder to the mansion's outer wall and start climbing. Maybe I should be scared, but all I can think about is that Tok is nearby and might be in more trouble with every passing moment. Up and up I climb, adding ladders as I go, grateful to know that the creaking of the ladder below me is Mal, always at my side—or a few feet below me. Lenna will be on the ground with her bow in hand, ready to protect us, and Jarro will be just standing there, I guess, hopefully with his axe out.

We reach the roof, and I step out onto the flat surface and immediately have a sword in hand. But . . .

Well, the roof is empty. It's just a big, flat area with nothing on it.

"So that was a bust," I mutter.

"Now we know they're not on the roof. That's valuable knowledge," Mal says.

"I just wish Tok was here!" I wail, taking advantage of the fact that we're alone and away from Jarro. "He would know what to do. He's so smart, and he would figure this out, and then he'd . . . uh . . . find himself. Ugh!"

Mal pats my shoulder. "As smart as Tok is, he'd still have five wrong answers before he found the right one. I mean, how often does he set something on fire or cause an explosion? Every success starts as a bunch of failures."

"Whoa." I shake my head. "That's deep."

"So let's keep failing until we find him."

We stand there for just a moment, looking out.

"This is the first time someone from our village has seen a view like this," I say. "So high up. It's kind of pretty, for a dark forest." We can see so far in every direction, and on the far side, the opposite one from our home, very far away, something twinkles on the horizon like a ribbon of light.

"What's that?" I ask.

Mal shields her eyes and looks. "I can't tell. It's shiny. And bright."

"Maybe it's gold?"

"Maybe. But I don't think that's how gold works."

"We'll have to ask Nan."

Mal grins. "If anyone knows, she will. And if she doesn't, we'll have to go find out for ourselves."

I head for the ladder and motion for Mal to go first on the way back down. I note that Jarro is on the ground looking up with his hands held out, like maybe he would catch her if she fell. My estimation of him goes up just a smidge. Considering it was bedrock level before this adventure, it's risen quite a bit.

As I'm climbing down past the second floor, something catches my eye. The ladder is near a window, and what I'm seeing inside doesn't match any of the rooms I've seen before. I stop and lean in. The room is dominated by a mass of black stone—the blackest stone I've ever seen. And there's something purple . . .

"Hey, Lenna," I call. "Come check this out. There's a new kind of stone."

Mal hops off the ladder and Lenna clambers up. I move up a few rungs to give her room.

"This room doesn't exist." She touches the window. "We've been through the entire woodland mansion twice, and we've never seen it."

"So it must be a secret room. I don't see a door, do you?"

"Nope. No door." She reaches into her pocket and pulls out a pickaxe. With a few hits, the window shatters, and she carefully steps inside.

"Wait for me!" I shout, hurrying to join her. She's a great fighter, but she shouldn't be in a new room alone without someone to help her fight any mobs that might show up.

Soon I'm standing in a small, square room with no doors. At least there are no mobs. The floor is lighter than the walls, and a block of diamond sits in the corner like someone accidentally left it behind. I grab it and stash it in my pocket for later as Lenna calls down for Mal and Jarro to join us.

"So what is that?" Jarro says with appropriate awe.

In the center of the room is something I've never seen before. It's a big rectangle of the odd black stone blocks, and the space in between them is . . . weird. It's not window glass, but it's purple and shimmery, waving almost like water.

"I think it's a—" Lenna starts.

But she doesn't get to finish, because someone pops out of a trapdoor in the floor that I didn't notice before.

It's an adult, and he looks vaguely familiar.

"Get away from the portal!" he barks, whipping out a sword.

Mal and I lock eyes, but we don't get away from the portal.

We take our own weapons in hand and prepare to fight.

# 17

# MAL

 Other than Krog, we've never been in a fight with actual humans before, but I'm not about to start taking orders from this guy. He's got to be one of the people who kidnapped Tok, which means he doesn't have our best interests at heart. Whatever this "portal" is, it's important.

"How about no?" Chug replies.

The man's sword looks old and worn and stained—by blood?— and that's when it hits me—

The brigands.

The ones who once stopped us on our way to this very woodland mansion, who ambushed us at the river crossing and stole my llamas and all our loot and tried to take Chug's pig. We found out later that they were working with Krog, but they abandoned him when he decided to attack our town directly. I guess we thought they would go back to roaming the wilds without Krog's leadership, but instead, it looks like they took advantage of our town's newly opened walls.

This isn't the brigands' leader, but he's definitely one of the minions. I recognize his braided beard and potbelly and the vacant, stupid sneer on his face.

He doesn't look any nicer than he did back then, but at least he's alone.

I glance at Jarro, hoping he takes the hint and stays out of our way, because we're not about to trust this guy.

"I don't want to hurt you," the brigand warns us, but he's grinning.

"We don't mind hurting you," Chug snarks back. "What's with the portal?"

The brigand's eyes shoot to the portal and back as he aims his sword at Chug and shuffles forward menacingly. "Nothing you need to worry about, kid. Just drop your weapons, and we'll get all this sorted out."

Chug holds up his sword, mirroring the brigand. Lenna has her arrow nocked, and I have my sword in one hand and my pickaxe in the other. Jarro has sort of backed into the corner nearest the window, hiding behind his shield, which is fine. We don't need to get him involved. This is a very small room, and things could get nasty.

"Put the sword down before you get hurt," the brigand says, more sharply than before, pointing his sword toward Chug's chest.

Chug smacks the sword away easily. "Here's a hint: If you say you don't want to hurt people, maybe don't point weapons at their tender bits."

The brigand smacks Chug's sword back, and the tension in the room goes up a notch. Lenna's bow creaks as she pulls back her arrow.

"I'm serious. You kids don't know what you're getting tangled up in. You could really get hurt. Drop the weapons and I'll get you somewhere safe. Just stay away from the portal. It's dangerous."

"Says the guy threatening us with a sword," I say, drawing his attention away from Chug. "What kind of person does that? Who threatens kids?"

"You're trespassing. This is none of your business."

"If you took my brother, it's my business," Chug barks.

The brigand chuckles. "The little skinny one in the cat pajamas?"

Chug meets my gaze, furious, and his eyes flick to the floor. I immediately know what he has in mind, and I stand by his side, facing the brigand. We both take a step forward, and the man has no choice but to take a step back.

"You kids really think you can fight an adult and win?"

"It wouldn't be the first time," Chug says. I can tell he's doing his absolute best to hold back his anger, now that we know for certain that they have Tok. He takes an experimental slash with his sword, causing the brigand to defend himself as Lenna edges around behind him.

The brigand slashes back, and then they're fighting, almost halfheartedly. This guy doesn't actually want to hurt us, it seems, but he's also not willing to let us take control. Chug is being very careful, not really aiming for eyes or heart, and I have my sword up, too, should the man suddenly go berserk and decide he's done playing around.

"Look, I'm warning you for the last time. This is serious business. If Orlok finds out—"

We don't get to learn what happens if Orlok finds out, because Lenna sticks out her leg and Chug advances and the brigand has to shuffle away, and he trips and falls backward through the trap-door.

Chug is ready, diamond block in hand, and he fits it to the hole in the floor, making it that much harder for the brigand to mine his way back into the room.

"We're going through the portal, right?" Chug asks me.

I can see the desperation in his eyes, hear the begging in his voice.

Because I know he's thinking the same thing I'm thinking: These brigands took Tok, and if they're working this hard to keep us from going through the portal, it's because Tok is on the other side.

"I'm surprised we're not already through the portal," I respond with a grin.

Lenna frowns at the diamond block in the floor. "I wish we knew where it leads."

But something is scratching at the back of my brain. We've heard the word "portal" recently, although it didn't make sense at the time . . .

"A Nether portal?" I say. "That's what Krog was trying to build. He had one almost finished under the town, but the Elders dismantled it. It was made of these same black blocks, remember?"

Lenna nods. "Right! I asked Nan about it, and she said it led to a horrible place filled with riches. Which didn't make sense to me, because how can it be both horrible and full of riches? But she wouldn't say anything else except . . ." Lenna's brow rumples, her lips jutting out just like Nan as she speaks with a gruff tone. "'You stay away from the Nether, you hear? It's not safe.'" Her face goes from Nan-grouch to normal. "I asked her if she'd ever been there, and she said no. Two of the town founders were experts on it, and it was so dangerous that they didn't risk going often. One of them died there." She looks to Jarro. "Your great-great-great-grandfather, I think. Anyway, I guess Nan used to have a book about it, but she lost it." Her whole face brightens. "So maybe I can write a new book about it! If that's where we're going."

"Just keep your bow ready," I warn. "We don't know anything about this place."

"We know Tok is probably there," Chug says.

"But why?" It's the first time Jarro has spoken in quite some time. "Why would someone go to the trouble of kidnapping your brother, just to drag him to some weird place?"

The thing is . . . I think I understand now. "Krog wanted to go to the Nether to get potion ingredients. The brigands knew his plan, because they were working with him for a while. So they must know what's so valuable on the other side of the portal. It has to be potion ingredients. They took Tok because he's really good at making things, and he's been trying to figure out potions."

"That's why Elder Gabe was so upset," Lenna says as all the pieces come together. "He said without his potions and ingredients, we were doomed. The town founders must have left behind a stockpile of ingredients from the Nether for his potions, and when the brigands stole them, there was no way to replace them. The Nether must be the only place you can get certain things. Our Elders probably don't even know it exists. And Elder Gabe is too old and grumpy to kidnap. So they took Tok to make their potions."

Chug's shoulders sag in relief. "So that means the brigands must be treating Tok well, right? Because when you need someone, you're good to them."

I shrug. "It would make sense. He couldn't craft if he was hungry and hurt. And potions are really valuable."

Emotions flash over Chug's face at the thought of his brother suffering—rage, worry, determination. "So we know that on the other side of this portal is a horrible place that Nan—who encouraged us to go out into the Overworld alone—is scared of. And my brother is there with the brigands who threatened us and wanted to eat my pig. And we know literally nothing about it. Fantastic."

I look at my friends—and Jarro. Lenna looks ready, maybe even a little eager, now that she realizes she'll get to take notes on a new place. Jarro looks just as scared and doubtful as he has been all along. But Chug is in the Chug Zone, when he's like a shaken bottle full of emotions and he needs someone to either settle him down or point him in the right direction and pop the top.

"We're so close," I tell my best friend. "Tok is on the other side of this portal. Think of how far we've come, and how much our skills have progressed since last time. If this Nether place is new to us, it's got to be new to the brigands, too. I bet they needed Tok's help to build the portal in the first place. I mean, what even is this stone? So they're going to be just as unsteady as we are. And they're not expecting us. If Beardo down there didn't call for help when he saw us, it's because there wasn't any help."

Chug nods, warming to my words. "Yeah. They don't know we're here."

"So we're armed, we're ready, and we're unexpected. And we're together."

I put my hand out. "Mob Squad?"

Chug puts his hand on mine, and Lenna puts her hand on his. I look over to Jarro, who has crept out of his corner and is staring at us like a starving cow looking at a big pile of wheat. "Come on, Jarro. Are you in or are you out?"

It's a tense moment. It could go either way. Jarro could stay here, alone, knowing Beardo might come back, possibly with reinforcements. He's not a great fighter, and an experienced adult with a sword would definitely have an advantage over a scared kid with an axe, even if Jarro is taller than that adult, which he is. I'm guessing Jarro doesn't know much about mining, but he has to understand that Beardo can hack into this room pretty easily and overpower him. If he stays here, he stays here alone and with the knowledge that sooner or later, an enemy is going to take advantage of that fact.

On the other hand, if he goes with us, he has no idea what he'll find. The Overworld isn't all that different from the town inside Cornucopia's walls—there are new animals, villagers, mobs, and illagers, but the terrain is pretty similar. Judging by the swirling purple miasma within this portal and the sinister black blocks framing it, whatever's in the Nether is going to be drastically different. We've never seen it before, either. I mean, this kid thought a horse was a cow; how's he going to handle something so new he can't even imagine it?

He's inexperienced and scared, and I realize that he can't get through this moment alone, much less what comes after.

"You should come with us," I say, and Chug's eyes shoot to me, doubtful, so I push on. "If you stay here, that guy is coming back, and you're going to be blindfolded and gagged and tied to a tree again. And if you try to go home, you could get lost and wander forever or come up against all kinds of enemies. But if you come with us, you won't be alone. Whatever is on the other side of that portal, we can face it together. We have weapons, we have food, we have one another. So do you want to be alone, or do you want to be part of something bigger?"

Jarro's mouth is open, his eyes flicking back and forth as he runs the calculations. I always thought he was stupid, but I'm beginning to understand that he just has a different kind of intelligence. When he's not scared, he's steady. Maybe he's not great in a fight, but he tamed those horses, and he's had other little victories along the way. I've felt incomplete without Tok—we all have. And Jarro can't complete that circle. But maybe he's ready to try.

"But what if—we don't know—" He exhales, and in a smaller voice than I've ever heard out of him, Jarro says two words I never thought I'd hear. "I'm scared."

Chug snorts, and I'm about to interrupt him before he can get into trouble, but then he, too, surprises me.

"Yeah, bud. I'm scared, too. Like, all the time. The world is straight-up scary, even when you have my rugged good looks and muscly sword arm. But you just have to get used to the idea of doing it anyway. Believe me: It's a lot easier with friends. Real friends, not toadies who agree with everything you say. Because real friends tell the truth, and the truth is that we're probably all on the verge of peeing ourselves when it comes to going through the scary purple portal, but we're going to do it anyway."

"I'm scared, too," Lenna admits. "I hate being hurt. I hate knowing we don't have any Potions of Healing. I hate fighting adults. I hate not having Poppy with me. But more than that, I hate that Tok is in trouble and probably a lot more scared than I am." Her mouth quirks up. "And, hey. We're about to see something no one in town has ever seen before."

"Think of the bragging rights, Jarro," I add. "No one back home will be able to say a word against you if you go on a successful rescue mission through the Overworld to the Nether."

"That's not true," he starts. "When you guys came home, people still made fun of you—"

"Well, you did," Chug reminds him, stepping close and poking him in the chest.

Jarro grimaces. "Okay, good point."

And then Chug does the unthinkable: He slings his arm around Jarro's neck.

"And if anyone tries to make fun of you, they'll have to face us, too. If you're with us, you're with us."

"So I'm a Bad Apple?" Jarro asks.

"No way," I tell him. "We're the Mob Squad."

I put my hand back in the center. Chug and Lenna pile on. Jarro takes his time, considering. My arm is starting to hurt. I can tell that Chug is nervous about how much time is passing. Down below us, we hear someone start hacking away at the diamond block we've used to plug the trap door.

I look Jarro dead in the eyes. "Do you want to be a hero or not, Jarro? It's now or never."

Jarro stands tall, nods, and puts his hand on top of the pile.

## 18

# LENNA

 Usually, I'm the last one in our group. I trail a bit behind, my bow and arrow ready for dangers coming from any direction. But this time, since we're going to a new place and we don't know what it will be like on the other side of the portal, I go first. That way, I can defend my friends as they come through. I should probably be more scared, but I'm also really excited. Since I started working with Nan, I've grown to love my role as her assistant, especially regarding any jobs that contribute to the lore she's collecting for our town. I love discovering new things and writing them down in my journal. I love reporting back with new findings and seeing Nan cock her head and try to hide her surprise. I never really felt important before—my family made sure of that—but now I have a job, and I'm buzzing with excitement as I think about bringing Nan a book full of my notes and drawings of the Nether.

That's not our main goal, of course. We're here to rescue Tok.

But along the way, I plan to document whatever I can. I'll press flowers and leaves and grasses in the pages of my journal, name new things I find, and sketch pictures of any unknown animals and mobs. I'll be contributing something valuable to my town's understanding of the world. People will go to the town library and pick up this book with my name on it and gaze in wonder at things they never even knew existed.

"Lenna?"

My head jerks up. Mal has a very familiar look on her face, the one that suggests that I've been daydreaming when I was supposed to be doing something important. It's not quite as harsh as the looks my family used to give me when they assigned me jobs around the mine that I promptly abandoned, and at least my friends never call me by the cruel nicknames batted about by my nine siblings—and parents. Loony Lenna was the main one, and no one has called me that in quite some time, probably because after our last adventure, I moved out to Nan's cabin and stopped trying to fit in with my family. We're all happier that way.

"Are you ready?" Mal prompts.

I shake my head like it's full of wool and ready my bow and arrow. I step up to the portal, noting that it smells a little like sweet berries and fresh rain with a touch of . . . is that fire? Odd. I step up and poke the purple swirlies with my foot, and then it's like I'm walking into a wall of wiggling violet water, except it doesn't feel cold and wet, it feels warm and dry, almost like smoke, and then . . .

I'm somewhere else.

I'm in the Nether.

It takes a moment for my eyes to focus and make sense of what's around me. This place is . . .

Whoa.

It's like a giant cavern, the biggest cavern I've ever seen, but everything is in shades of burgundy and red and purple. There are stone blocks I've never seen before, fires and fungi and glowing things, all completely unfamiliar. I immediately want to start sketching, but the portal wavers and Chug steps out beside me, sword at the ready.

"Bad guys?" he growls.

"I haven't seen anything move yet."

His sword arm drops. "I thought we'd be walking into a villain party, but this place is just—a blood cave?"

The portal swirls again, and Jarro stumbles out.

"What the huh?" he murmurs, axe dangling from his fingertips like he's forgotten it exists.

"Blood cave," Chug says with authority. "You get used to it."

The portal shimmers one more time as Mal comes through. We've all moved away to make room, and I have my bow and arrow ready, even if I haven't needed it so far. This place is so hard to understand, the colors so similar and everything encased as if underground. There's plenty of room between me and the ceiling, but there is most definitely a ceiling, no sign of sun or moon or sky. I don't feel the usual comfort I feel in cool, cozy caves. I feel like this place . . .

It wants to hurt me.

Maybe it's the lava waterfall dripping on the edge of my vision, maybe it's the randomly burning fires, maybe it's the way everything seems more vertical than horizontal, but the Nether just feels malevolent, like being in the belly of a giant, angry beast.

"So this is the Nether," Mal says wonderingly. "It's . . . not what I expected."

"Nice place for a vacation." Chug jabs his sword at the ground. "If you wanted to vacation inside a place that looks like meat rock. Anybody see Tok? Or brigands? Or anything that isn't red?"

I spin in place, looking in every direction. There's no sign of anything even remotely human—no buildings, no drops, no sign that anyone other than us has ever set foot here.

"Maybe Tok's back in the woodland mansion?" Chug asks with what we all know is false hope.

"He has to be here," Mal says. "Otherwise, why hide the portal in a secret room, and why have some tough guy guarding it? Tok is definitely here. But the group he's with must either have a base somewhere or be looking for something specific." She mines a block of the red . . . stuff . . . and looks at it before shoving it in her pocket. "Huh. It's pretty soft."

Something moves toward us, and I nock an arrow and gesture at it silently. Mal follows my gaze and holds her pickaxe in a more threatening manner.

"What is that?" Jarro asks.

"We don't know," Chug whispers back. "We've never been here before, either."

The figure approaching us reminds me a little of the villagers— it's vertical and bipedal and seems to be going about its business, not really reacting to our presence. As it gets closer, it doesn't charge us or yell at us, but it does make a curious sound.

"Did that guy just . . . snort?" Chug asks.

"Like a pig," I reply.

"I'm going to go talk to it." Chug has his sword in hand, but not up in a threatening position.

I can tell Mal wants to stop him, but . . . well, no one really knows what's going on, so why not let the most dangerous one of us go talk to the first creature we see? When Mal gives me the look, I draw my arrow and aim, just in case things go badly.

"Hi," Chug says, waving at the creature, which I can now see has a piglike face with tusks and a sword of their own. "My name is Chug. What's your name?"

The pig man, who isn't quite a pig or a man, snorts curiously. Their eyes seem drawn to Chug's gold boots.

"You like the boots, huh? Yeah, my brother can make pretty much anything. Do you want some boots, too?" Chug reaches into his pocket and pulls out a pair of leather boots, but the pig man—well, let's call them a piglin, since they don't really seem to be male or female—the piglin seems uninterested.

"How about some food? I've got some nice apples." Chug holds out a shiny red apple, but again, the piglin doesn't really care. They just keep staring at Chug's boots.

"Give them your boots," Mal suggests.

But I feel like that's a bad idea. If we give the piglin Chug's boots, what if they expect us to give up all our armor? And what if the ground burns Chug's exposed feet? "No, keep your boots on," I say. "I think they just like gold. They keep looking at my helmet and Mal's chest plate and Jarro's leggings. Do you have any gold that you're not currently wearing?"

"You just don't want to smell my feet," Chug murmurs as he digs in his pockets and produces a gold ingot, which we often use as money back home. "How about this? Do you want some yummy delicious gold?"

He tosses the ingot at the piglin, who catches it and just stares at it for a long moment, eyes shining. Then they toss something at Chug, and Chug turns to us, holding a shiny purple bottle of potion. He looks dumbfounded. "I've never seen this potion before. How'd this dude get a potion?"

"Who cares where they got it," Jarro says. "Do more trading."

Chug nods excitedly. "Yeah. Why not? I've got tons of gold ingots." He throws another one to the piglin, and this time they gleefully toss me eight arrows. "This is like hitting a piñata. You never know what you're going to get!"

By the time Chug is done trading, we have a pair of iron boots, two more mysterious potions, three weird green pearls, some string, a brick, five hunks of black rock that looks like cobblestone, and a black-and-purple block of the strangest stone I've ever seen.

The piglin wanders off once Chug stops throwing gold at them, and Chug stands before his pile of loot. "I can't tell if this is great or useless." He rolls one of the green pearls between his hands. "But I'm pretty sure this is going to look great in our garden. The bees are gonna love it."

I pick up one of the other pearls and turn it over, noting how smooth and iridescent it is. I want to draw it, write about it in my book, and take it back to the library. "Can I have this?" I ask.

Chug shrugs. "Why not? My pockets are getting pretty full."

We stash all the goodies and shuffle around in silence as we realize that we're right where we started: in a strange place with no idea what to do next. Even if they didn't try to hurt us, the piglin still wasn't particularly helpful. I guess this place is like the village—we just have to figure it out ourselves.

"That looks pretty interesting." Chug is pointing at a weird area where the red wasteland seems to transition into a red forest. There are plants, or maybe giant fungi, that look like someone described trees to a confused, nearsighted artist and they just did their best. We walk toward it, and as we get closer, we begin to see odd animals moving around, eating the fungus. They look like pigs, but big, wild, brutal pigs with mohawks and tusks.

"Pigs!" Chug shouts, hurrying forward like he's just spotted someone he hasn't seen in ages.

"Slow down!" Mal calls. "We don't know if they're friendly!"

"Thingy is a pig and he's friendly, and the pig dude was—well, not friendly, but fun to trade with, so why would something just randomly attack me?" Chug is close to the hog-thing now, and he takes a potato out of his pocket and holds it out, crooning, "Here, hoggy hoggy!"

Because it's Chug, and because this place is weird, we hurry to join him. I have an arrow ready, and Mal has her pickaxe out. The hog-thing—let's call them a hoglin—looks up at Chug with beady little eyes and gives a deep, annoyed grunt.

And then they run right for him.

Chug backs up a few steps, hands up. "Sorry. I'll back off. You seem like you're, uh, busy—"

He cuts off mid-sentence as the hoglin rams him and tosses him in the air. We're close enough now to see that there's no way this thing is nice.

"Should I—" I start, right as Mal says, "Lenna, can you hit it?"

I loose my arrow, and it punches into the hoglin's side. The creature gives a furious grunt before swinging over to focus on us.

"Don't hurt them!" Chug calls.

But he's wrong this time—this creature will straight up kill us. Just because they look a little bit like a pig doesn't mean they *are* a pig.

Something grunts behind me, and I spin to find another hoglin preparing to charge. I hit the second with an arrow and have the next arrow ready before I spin to handle the hoglin that attacked Chug. Mal is running toward them with her sword out as Chug struggles up from the ground. Assuming they have that one under control, I focus on the angry hoglin that's decided I'm the enemy. Two more arrows and they fall, leaving fresh meat and a chunk of leather.

"But maybe they're just scared," I hear Chug say.

"They're trying to murder me!" Mal shoots back. She hits the hoglin with her sword again and again, and they fall.

Poor Chug has his head in his hands as he stares at Mal. "You killed them! You just killed them!"

"Chug, these things are not nice! They attacked you! That other one attacked Lenna. We all love animals and want to let nature run its course, but you've got to accept that not every animal wants to be your friend!"

"You're not the boss of me!" Chug hurls back. "I know I usually do what you say, but you're not always right. You shouldn't have killed them."

But Chug is so busy shouting that he isn't paying attention to his surroundings.

"Look out!" Jarro shouts, but not fast enough.

A hoglin barrels into Chug from behind, throwing him in the air. Chug lands in a broken heap. Before anyone can get there, they root under him with their tusks and toss him again. Chug slams into a red rock wall and slumps to the ground. I hit the hoglin with two arrows, but Mal finishes them off with her sword before kneeling at Chug's side.

"Chug? You there, buddy? You okay?"

I hurry to join them with Jarro at my side. He had his axe in hand for the entire fight but didn't do anything. He does look worried about Chug, though, so my anger at him lessens.

"I just wanted . . . to be friends," Chug whispers.

He's as beat up as I've ever seen him, pummeled black-and-blue, his nose smeared with blood. Mal helps him sit up as I keep watch for more of the hoglins. Jarro collects all the meat and leather, but he doesn't put any of it in his pockets—he places it near Chug like an offering.

"Food's not going to fix this fast enough, is it?" Mal asks me.

I nibble on my lip; questions like this always take me longer than most people. "It might take all our food, and I don't know how easy it is to find more food here. But I do know there could be more hoglins, and we're vulnerable right now. Might as well give him the golden apple. We don't know what those potions are, and we don't know what else is around here. Maybe worse stuff than that, and we need Chug to be able to fight."

She nods and pulls our only golden apple out of her pocket. It's a sad, serious moment, as we all know that sometime soon, the gleaming golden fruit could be the only thing standing between any of us and . . . well, death. Potions were rare enough back home, where Elder Gabe demanded outrageous trades, but down here, it's just us and a hostile, red-tinged world without a single potion to be had. When Chug coughs wetly, Mal puts the apple to his lips. Luckily, even a half-dead Chug is still Chug, and he tentatively takes a bite and starts chewing.

It only takes a few moments before he's sitting up, grinning as the bruises recede. "I'm still one hundred percent Team Potion, but I can be Team Golden Apple, too," he says, voice a little raspy but on the mend.

"And hopefully you're no longer one hundred percent Team Hoglin?" I say darkly.

Chug's head droops. "If that thing—those things—are hoglins, then yeah, I'm no longer on their side. I, uh, I thought I might be permanently broken there for a minute. Like, all my bones felt like they were made out of mush." He looks into Mal's eyes. "Thanks. Sorry. Thanks."

She nods and holds out her hand to pull him up. "Let's make a deal. In the Overworld, we assume everything is a friend until it's a foe. In the Nether, we assume everything is a foe until it's a friend."

"But the piglin was an okay dude," Chug argues weakly.

"That one was. But if one looks like they're going to attack, you've got to promise me you'll hit first."

"But they make such cute little oinky noises—"

"Chug, that was our only golden apple."

At that thought, the color drains out of Chug's face. He nods. "I'll be more careful."

"Now, let's look for a trail. Clues. Something." Mal flaps her hand at him. "No petting monsters."

We fan out, and although I normally act as lookout, I'm too curious about this place to just stand in one place with my bow ready. I take out my own pickaxe and take samples of all the new things I find—fungi, stone, glowy things, vinelike whatchama-callits. I scribble a quick sketch of everything I find in my book and give them names, just the first words that pop into my head.

Nylium.

Netherrack.

Glowstone.

"Lenna! A little help?" Mal calls, and I drop my book and nock an arrow.

*Thwack thwack thwack!*

I take the hoglin down before it can do any damage and return to my explorations.

It doesn't take long before we're huddled up again without any clues to Tok's whereabouts. Everyone looks glum, so I try not to seem so happy. Yes, I still need to find Tok, but this place—it's amazing. My pockets are full of things I never knew existed, things that even Nan doesn't know about. I could study this place for the rest of my life and never learn everything. It's kind of hard to concentrate on anything else.

"Anybody find anything even vaguely human?" Mal asks.

We all shake our heads.

"I found a sea of lava over there," Chug mutters, pointing. "Not particularly helpful."

"I found red stuff," Jarro says. "Like, lots of red stuff."

That earns a chuckle from Chug, but Mal doesn't laugh. I can tell by her rumpled eyebrows and frown that she's frustrated.

"The brigands must be here somewhere. They must know things we don't know. But where did they go? We have to keep looking for clues." And it feels pointless, but I trust Mal, even if she doesn't currently trust herself, so I go back to looking around.

Jarro has walked over to where Chug pointed at his sea of lava. The red fungus of the forest ceiling dangles down like tree branches, obscuring the view, but Jarro pushes past and disappears.

"Found something!" he shouts.

We hurry to his side, and he's holding up something that really, really doesn't belong here:

A sweet berry.

## 19

# JARRO

It feels good, to finally do something helpful. They're all too nice to say it, but the fact that I freeze up in every fight and am utterly useless for anything but taming horses is super embarrassing. If the tables were turned, I would probably be making fun of anyone who behaved that way. But now that I look back, the stakes back home were just really, really low. It was easy, making fun of people or chasing them down an alley. No one was ever in real danger. There was nothing to really fear.

But here? Everything is scary.

I hold out the sweet berry, thinking about how weird it is that just a few days ago, both this berry and I were in my backyard in the Hub, living our normal lives, and now we're down here in the scariest place I've ever seen.

It's funny how I think of the Nether as "down here," like we're just underground and things got weird, when really we're in an entire other dimension. Or something. Not that I've ever been allowed to go underground. I've been trying not to think about it, but the more I see of the world—and other worlds—the angrier I am at my mom. She never let me try anything new, go anywhere interesting, do anything other than what she thought best. I'm in no way prepared for this adventure, and I feel like a little baby sometimes. I'm pretty sure I wouldn't have walked through that portal if Mal hadn't been behind me, which is probably why Mal waited to go last. All I know is that I feel useless and I hate this place and I want to leave and never come back. Chug nearly died, Mal is freaking out, and Lenna . . . well, it looks like Loony Lenna has found a place that makes her happy, which isn't even the most bizarre thing about her.

I shouldn't think of her as Loony Lenna, though—she's weird, but that doesn't have to be a bad thing. I feel guilty every time I call her that in my head now.

I just have to make sure I don't accidentally say it out loud, or I'm pretty sure Chug will punch me in the teeth, even if we've been getting along okay. He's actually—ugh, I can't believe I'm saying this—a good guy. He's brave and loyal and funny, and if I didn't hate him, I would like him. Maybe I'm starting to like him anyway. It's hard to change the way you've been thinking your whole entire life. It's a lot of work. But it makes things easier, and it makes me feel a little lighter, too.

And I can't help noticing that even Chug froze up in that last fight. It makes me feel a little less alone, to know that I'm not the only one.

Mal takes the berry from my outstretched palm, probably to keep Chug from eating it.

"Okay, so this means they must've gone this way, because there are definitely no sweet berry bushes down here," she says.

"But there's something over that way—kind of bluish?" Lenna is pointing, and I squint to follow. Maybe something over there is the tiniest bit blue or green? Lenna has the best eyesight among us, and the area she's pointing at is in the same direction as the patch of red ground where I found the berry, so it would make sense to keep exploring in that direction.

"Bluish sounds funner than reddish, at this point," Chug says.

"Bluish it is." Mal puts the berry in her pocket and starts walking.

I'm just standing there, but Chug gives my shoulder a little shove. "You next, bud."

I nod and follow Mal, with Chug behind me, which would've made me super nervous just a few days ago. But now, it makes me feel safer. Nothing can sneak up behind me with Chug and his sword there.

The going is tough, as the bluish area is on the other side of a big valley with a river of lava and several fiery waterfalls in between. Mal hacks stairs into the ground, but it's still pretty steep, and I'm very aware that I could fall at any moment and break every bone in my body. They were quick to use that golden apple on Chug after the hoglins mauled him, but it was our only one, and I don't know how much of our quickly disappearing food they'd be willing to use to heal a useless guy like me.

It takes everything I have just to keep up, hopping down, down, down as Mal grunts and mines and collects the soft red rocks hewn away from her steps down to the valley floor.

"What is this stuff?" I ask, a hand clamped down on the wall beside me as Mal works.

"Netherrack," Lenna answers.

"How do you know?"

"Because that's what I decided to call it."

"You can't just name things whatever you want, Lenna."

She shrugs. "Why not? Nobody else is, and we have to call it something."

And I hate to say it, but I can't argue with her logic. "Nether-rack it is," I murmur. One point to Lenna.

When I finally step down onto the floor of the valley, it's a huge relief. I've been holding my breath this whole time—I'm not really a big fan of heights. I thought I was okay with them, back home, but the tallest building in the hub is only four stories, and we've just climbed down what must be twenty stories. The bluish place is within view now, and I can see that it's another, different sort of forest. Still dominated by fungus, because I guess everything is fungus here, but it's actually kind of beautiful, the vibrant teal against the deep burgundy. The crimson forest we've just passed through towers over the valley, and I can't believe how far we've come.

And how very far I am from home.

I feel tiny and helpless and hopeless, and then Chug slugs me on the back. "Ready to cross the lava river, bud?"

He's grinning, but I have no idea why. There is indeed a lava river flowing between us and the blue-green forest. But—and I guess this is another sign that we're going the right way—there's a cobblestone bridge stretched over it. Nothing fancy, but wide enough that I won't freak out and clearly built by human hands. Nothing else in the Nether is that normal, boring shade of gray that I see every day back home.

Mal approaches the bridge first and tests it with her weight. "Seems pretty solid," she says. The orange lava reflects back on her face, almost making it match her hair, and I guess I really am changing because back home I would have had something to say about that. "Everyone ready?"

Lenna and Chug nod, but I don't, because I'm pretty sure nobody here cares about my thoughts on crossing the lava bridge.

"Jarro?" Mal asks, surprising me.

I nod, too. I kind of have to. I begin to see how things work, outside of Cornucopia: Even when it's not fun, even when it's scary, you press on because that's the only option. You can move forward toward your goal or you can go home like a coward. I guess that's how they learned everything they did on their last trip. They knew that if they gave up, everyone in our town would leave. So instead, they got tougher. They got better.

Mal steps up onto the bridge for real now, just a few blocks from a huge river of lava. I've never seen lava before, not until we got here, and I never imagined there could be so much of it. She holds out her hand, but I can do this on my own. The bridge is two blocks wide, and there are no handrails, but I should be okay. I step up and feel the heat rising through my boots. The lava makes a gentle, glugging sound underneath me. It would almost sound cheerful if it weren't molten death. I focus on Mal's back as I inch forward, sure to give her plenty of room. Behind me, Chug's boots shuffle onto the bridge. It doesn't shift under his weight, at least—it's sturdy.

"Don't look down," he murmurs to me. "It's always worse when you look down. Once, I had to run across a log over a raging river carrying my pig, and I don't think I looked down a single time."

"You got lucky," Mal calls over her shoulder.

"I'm always lucky," Chug assures her.

*Pop!*

A bubble of lava startles me, and I jump—

But Chug's hand is on my shoulder, steadying me.

"Just keep walking. Don't look down. That's the only way to make it through."

I'm pretty sure this bridge is longer than our entire town, because it's taking me forever to get across it. I want to look down, but I don't, because I know Chug's right. I want to look to my left and right, but I don't do that either. I focus on Mal's braid, as orange as the lava, and shuffle across, inch by inch, bit by bit, step by step.

Finally I hop off onto the spongy red blocks. I notice that I'm shaking and shove my hands into my pockets as I watch Chug and Lenna finish crossing the bridge.

"Everyone good?" Mal asks, and this time I go ahead and nod along with them.

She leads us toward the blue-green forest, and looking at it makes my chest swell and my eyes tear up. It's so pretty, with the dark burgundy against the blue-green and bright pops of flower-like fungi and dripping spirals of emerald vines. A soft blue mist floats here and there, making everything seem magical.

"What do you call this one?" I ask Lenna.

She considers it for a moment. "A warped forest. Because it's like a regular forest, but . . . warped."

It's a pretty satisfactory answer. "Warped forest," I say to myself. "Nice."

As we approach, Lenna collects all the flobby flowers she passes, shoving the warped fungi into her pockets. I see her try to press one between the pages of her book, but it just goes wet and squishy, and she dumps that one back onto the ground with a sick splatter, muttering, "Bleh." Mal takes out her pickaxe and collects samples of the stone and treelike fungi we pass. Chug is on the lookout for animals, but I haven't seen any yet. At least there aren't more hoglins—I definitely don't want to get tossed in the air and trampled like that.

I keep hearing this weird noise, almost like someone crying, but far off and wavering. It echoes off the stone, haunting and sad. Mal catches me listening. "I hear it, too. We need to be on the lookout." She shakes her head and goes back to investigating the area and hunting for clues.

My first thought was that maybe that sound is Tok, but . . . I've made Tok cry before, and it doesn't sound like that at all.

"Hey, buddy! What's up? How's things in the Nether today?"

I turn to look at Chug, and he's waving at . . . something. Like a person, but much taller and thinner, all black with big purple eyes and long, graceful arms. Beautiful violet sparkles drift around it like leaves falling. It has a peculiar gait and doesn't seem to be responding to Chug's overtures of friendship. It's just ignoring him entirely, which is a tough thing to do.

"Be careful," Mal warns him. "Remember the hoglins . . ."

"I saw one of those things before," Lenna says, her voice low. "It was carrying a flower, and then it disappeared. I've been thinking of him as Mr. S. L. Enderman. Because he's a slender man." She shrugs. "It made more sense in my head, now that I say it out loud."

Chug takes a few steps toward it. "Don't run away, Mr. Enderman. We wanna be friends." He pulls a gold ingot out of his pocket. "Do you like gold as much as the piglins?"

But the tall thing—the Enderman, I guess—locks eyes with Chug. Its mouth opens and it begins to shake violently while making a terrible grinding growl that builds until I have to put my hands over my ears.

Chug glances back at us and sticks out his thumb. "What's up with this guy, huh?"

There's a weird popping sound, and the Enderman disappears . . . and reappears right by Chug. "Hey, pal!" he starts.

But the Enderman screeches and hits him with those long arms. Chug, again, goes flying. Lenna has already released an arrow, but the Enderman disappears and reappears a few feet to the side, and the arrow zings off into the forest. Mal hurries to stand protectively over Chug, and when the Enderman runs to attack him again, she hits it with her sword, making it squawk with anger and pop out of existence. Lenna puts away her bow and pulls out her pickaxe, running to help Mal. I pull out my axe and join them, standing directly over Chug so they're free to swing at the furious creature.

"I just wanted to be friends," he groans.

The creature reappears on Chug's other side—right in front of me. I'm between Mal and Lenna and the Enderman now, and it's about to hit Chug, and that makes me really angry because Chug just wanted to be friends, and there's nowhere for me to hide, no way to avoid it except fighting back, and it's like my arm swings of its own accord and my axe lands a hit that makes my arm shudder. With a cry of pain, the Enderman pops out of existence again.

"Good shot," Chug says.

"Thanks."

*Pop!*

It reappears on Mal's side, and she hits it, hard, with her sword, and then it falls over like a tree, screeching, leaving behind a shiny green pearl that almost looks like an animal's eyeball.

I reach down and help Chug stand. "You hurt?"

Chug shakes his left arm. "Naw. My left arm is pretty useless, anyway. A few of those hoglin chops will fix me right up. We just need to build a fire."

I honk a laugh, and he gives me a look. "What?"

I gesture to, well, everything. "There's fire everywhere here."

Chug nods, chuckling. "Good call, bud."

He pulls some hoglin chops out of his pocket and hands me one, and I realize that no one has ever called me "bud" in a genuinely friendly way before. And I kind of like it.

# 20

## TOK

The Nether would be fascinating if I were here of my own free will and able to control my own experience. But no. I was blindfolded, and instead of seeing a new world for the first time, I could only smell it and use my imagination. Judging by the scent—and the tickle of smoke in my nose—I've decided the Nether is dominated by fire and mushrooms, and not like the delicious mushroom soup my brother makes.

Even though my captors kept me from seeing anything, I knew the smell of the woodland mansion the moment they dragged me inside. I recognized the plushness of that particular carpet under my feet, remembered the feel of the steps and the odors of stone, wood, and food. When they marched me past the library, I nearly drooled.

Funny, how those books are what I wanted the most in the world, and now I'm here and have no way to access them.

Instead, they made me climb up a ladder, shoved me through

some weird smoke, marched me over a squishy sort of stone, and . . . well, it wasn't a fun trip. It all felt impossibly dangerous and like I might die at any moment. Funny how I could feel even less safe when I'd already been kidnapped. And now they're whispering together while I just stand here, unable to see, unable to move, kept on the end of a lead like I'm someone's pet pig. It's mortifying and infuriating, and there's nothing I can do.

I've never felt so alone.

I've never missed Chug so much.

For a long time, I waited to be rescued, whether by Chug, Mal, and Lenna or, if they'd finally learned to believe and trust kids, the adults of our town. I dropped berries, and then inconspicuous materials, and then berries again when the leader gave me another handful. But as I spent more time with my kidnappers, I began to hope that my brother and friends wouldn't risk it. I've heard these brigands kill tons of mobs, and they're ruthless and efficient. If they're the kind of people who will steal a kid out of his bed, maybe they're the kind of people who will do worse to a kid they don't need quite as much. They've already abandoned Jarro to his fate, after all.

"No funny business," the leader reminds me, which is the same thing they said when they whipped off my blindfold in Elder Gabe's potion workshop.

"What's the point?" I mutter. "Where am I going to go?"

"Smart kid."

The blindfold is finally off, and it takes my eyes a moment to adjust. We're in a room with a relatively low ceiling. All the walls are a rich, meaty, speckled red, and the floors are dark wood planks. There's one big window, and through it, I see . . .

A sea of lava.

Like we're in an inexplicably ginormous red cavern, with odd towers and waterfalls of lava and no sky in sight. Everything glows in shades of red.

"Go on and look. Get it out of your system," the leader says. When I look around, I realize we're alone in the room. I walk to the window, put my hands on the cold stone sill and look out.

We're at least two stories up, almost like we're floating. Down below is so much lava that I can't really contemplate it. It reminds me of the first time I saw beyond the wall back home, looking out through Nan's secret window. There was so much grass, so much green, that it was incomprehensible. But this is lava, and it doesn't give me that rippling joy of awe and discovery. It just makes me realize how very flammable I am.

"That's the only way out, and I think you can guess what happens if you hit the lava," the lead brigand says. "So if you had any ideas about escaping, forget 'em. If you do what we say and don't do anything stupid, you can earn your way back home."

Which reminds me of the question I forgot to ask the first time we talked and that I've been regretting not asking ever since. "Is my brother okay?"

"We left him sleeping in his own bed. Whatever he did after that is his own business. We're not monsters, kid."

I'm sick of him calling me "kid" like uncles do. My uncles are nice and friendly and care about me. Whatever this guy says, only a monster would do what he's done.

"My name is Tok."

"And my name is Orlok. Mr. Orlok, to you. Hey, we rhyme! I'm sure you remember my friends, too. Fellas, come say hi!"

Four more brigands appear in the open door, the same ones who stood against us at the river crossing on our last adventure.

Only one has a weapon out, the biggest one among them. They must really know, bone deep, that there's nowhere I can go, nothing I can do. They don't see me as a threat at all.

They're wrong, though. These may be my pajamas and not my work clothes, but I'm the kind of person who's always working on something, always has something up my sleeve. Even if I've been dropping stuff every few thousand footsteps, my pockets are still decently full. If these guys were smart, they would've checked, but I guess they figure no one keeps weapons in their jammies. Last time, we had unloaded all of our loot into easily stolen chests, but these days, I always have full pockets.

"What do you want from me?"

Orlok gestures across the room. I'm intrigued despite my fear, rage, and bone-deep exhaustion. They've set up a really nice workshop. There's a crafting table, a smithing table, a brewing stand, a forge, a furnace, a desk. Torches light the area nicely, and shelves hold rows of water bottles, piles of powder, collections of ingredients I know well and objects I'm eager to test. I'm guessing the chests are full, too. Most importantly, there are several books piled up on the desk, and the top one is called simply: *Potions*.

I'd be in heaven if I weren't in . . . the Nether.

That's got to be where we are. This can't be our world. I'd be excited—

If I weren't separated from my brother, my friends, my family, my town. And my freedom.

"Can you be more specific?" I say, because I'm pretty sure Orlok and his cronies didn't bring me here for my own good.

"Did you know about Krog's plan to secure the town for himself and access the Nether?"

I nod. "Yeah, we heard his evil villain speech. He's in jail back home now."

Orlok throws back his head and laughs. "Good. That's where he belongs—out of our way. See, we decided that his plan was too complicated. Run off the town, then keep the fortress and get to the Nether to benefit from all the rare ingredients and drops. We realized we could skip the town and just go to the Nether, start up a farm and workshop, and profit. And then we heard there was this kid just outside town who could craft anything and wasn't afraid to mix up potions." He pokes a finger in my chest. "That's you. So you're gonna eat up and start crafting."

"Can't I sleep?" My fingers twitch toward my pockets and what I could do if left alone and out of sight.

Orlok shakes his head. "No sleep in the Nether. You don't want to know what happens if you put down a bed here. Or maybe you do, judging by your singed eyebrows. Anyway, there're no maps here, no clocks, no escape, so you'd better get brewing."

"Just like that? Just start making potions?"

"I marked a few pages in the book—the most valuable items. We still need to find some more ingredients, but you can start with something easy. And when you run out of what you need for the high-value potions, make armor and weapons. We can always sell those." He leans in so close I can smell the sweet berries and fish on his rancid breath. "But again: No funny business."

He hands me, of all things, a cookie, and I eat it and move to the desk, sitting down and cracking open the book.

Orlok nods his approval. "I've got business to attend to. Rex, stay here and watch him. If he does anything that looks sneaky, stop him."

The big guy turns to me, his giant, droopy mustache quivering. "Stop him how, boss?"

"With a weapon of your choice."

Rex smiles, and it's like looking at a murderous jack-o'-lantern.

Waving, Orlok leaves. His other three minions follow him, leaving just me and Rex, who settles down in the doorway like a chicken sitting on an egg.

"I'll be reading," he proclaims, pulling out, to my surprise, a thick leather tome. "Don't bother me. And don't explode yourself. I don't like loud noises." As soon as the book is open, it's like he's in his own little world, his muscular shoulders blocking the doorway.

Finally alone, or as alone as I'm going to get, I sit at the desk and look at each dog-eared page. There are helpful potions, like the Potions of Healing and Regeneration that Elder Gabe knows, and there are also harmful potions, like the Potions of Weakness and Harming that Krog threw at Mal and Chug last year. My eyes light up when I see the recipe for a Potion of Fire Resistance. It's not dog-eared, but that's the one I've been struggling with back home, and it turns out there was a good reason for that. I'd been using slimeballs, whereas I actually need something called magma cream. I go directly to the shelf and find a bowl labeled MAGMA CREAM, which is full of iridescent spheres that look halfway between a slimeball and fire. I'm not sure what magma is or where the spheres might come from, but if they're the key to that elusive potion, I'm all for them. I've been trying so hard to make my potions work, and now the answer seems so obvious.

But I need to make sure my captors are happy with me. I focus on the first potion Orlok wants, the Potion of Invisibility. Knowing these brigands, he's going to use it to steal things—or sell it to people who want to steal things. I study all the steps—because there are many—and turn to the shelves and chests of ingredients.

I don't like being here. I don't like being kidnapped. I don't like helping bad guys.

But I really, really love making things, especially when there's some expectation that they'll actually work. Maybe if I get good enough, and if Rex gets deep enough into his book coma, I can figure out how to escape.

## 21

# CHUG

I do not like being smacked around by Endermen, and I don't really want to make eye contact with anybody ever again. The Nether is a tricky place. It's hard to determine friend from foe here—or, more accurately, friend from fiend. I just wanted to pet the hoglins, and they nearly finished me off. I don't feel so bad eating the tasty chops they dropped. I tell myself that Thingy would taste very different, and this is just an entirely different animal.

"Let's take five to look for more berries while Chug fills up," Mal says, pickaxe over her shoulder. Lenna nods and pulls out her book, and I stop trying to hold myself upright like I didn't just get the mashed potatoes beaten out of me. I don't want to be the one to slow us down, because I know Tok needs us, but I also know enough about adventuring these days to recognize the value of a quick break and a big pile of food when someone just got pulverized.

Jarro and I roast some chops, and then I eat while my friends explore this weird new biome. I sit on the ground, marveling at how it can be both stony and spongy, warm and moist. I see another Enderman appear, but I look away. The last one didn't seem to notice us at all until I locked eyes with it, and then it got super mad. Maybe if I ignore them, they'll leave me alone. This one is carrying a block of fungus, and it looks pretty happy to just do its thing. I notice that Lenna is sketching it in her book, while Jarro has automatically moved away from it.

He did pretty well in that fight. That was the first time I've seen him actually hit something—well, except me, with his fist, back home. I guess it takes a different kind of nerve to hit a monster with an axe than to trade punches with a kid you've known since you were a baby. He's not so bad here. I wonder if he'll go back to being a jerk if we manage to rescue Tok and get back home. Maybe travel is like a potion with a limited impact, and the moment we return, he'll go right back to acting like we're not friends. Because right now . . . we're friends.

Not that I'm going to mention it. Something tells me Jarro's not one of those people who's really good at talking about his feelings. That makes me feel a little sorry for him. My parents might not understand me, but I've always had my brother and Mal and Lenna. When something is bothering me, it helps to talk it out with them, and then I feel better. Maybe that's why Jarro is so mean—he doesn't have anyone to talk to.

Somewhere in the warped forest, I can hear Mal's pickaxe. It must be neat, to discover stone and ore no one in our town has ever seen before. I never would have guessed that mining would kind of become Mal's thing. Lenna's family runs the mine back home, but they're boring people who like stone and number crunching more than they like Lenna, so I've always thought of mining as a bad thing. But now that Mal's into it, I can see its value. Well, outside of the value all that raw material has to crafting.

Which I can do now, apparently, much to my surprise. Not as well as Tok, of course, and not as well as Elder Stu or Nan, but decently enough to help us on the road. I guess I absorbed more from working with Tok than I really knew. I'm proud of myself, which, again, is not something I usually felt before we began our adventuring. I look down at my hands, now glistening with chop grease. I can cook, too. Who knew I was capable of so many things?

"Chug, you still flat?" Mal calls.

I stand up and wiggle around to determine if anything still hurts. "Nope. Good as new!"

I still kind of expect Jarro to say something snarky about that sort of thing, but he remains silent. Much to my surprise, he's using Lenna's pickaxe to collect the pretty fungi.

"What are you doing?" I ask him.

I think he blushes, but when the whole world is red, it's hard to tell.

"I was just wondering if this fungus would grow back home. I know a lot about growing sweet berry bushes, so maybe there's a use for this stuff. Maybe it's edible, or maybe it goes in potions, or maybe it's just pretty in pots." He shrugs, looking very self-conscious. "It would be cool to have a job, you know? Like, all of you guys have jobs now. Every family back home has their own niche. This would be a new thing, so I wouldn't be stepping on anyone's toes."

"I get that. Your mom's pretty protective of her farm, huh?"

He nods. "Yeah. She likes being the only source of sweet berries. But if I can find something new, something nobody's ever done before—"

"It would be just for you."

Jarro grins. "Exactly."

"You could be the horse master. Or the fungus king!"

His eyebrows rumple up. "Are you making fun of me?"

I hasten to assure him, "No way. I love mushrooms. I have some really good stew recipes. I would totally buy fungi from you."

"You cook?"

"I'm a great cook."

He looks contemplative at receiving this information, which is the sort of thing he'd make fun of me for back home. "Then it's a deal," he finally says.

We walk over to Mal, who's sweaty but radiating excitement. "Lenna!" she calls, and Lenna reluctantly closes her book to join us.

"Look what I found while I was mining." Mal grins as she holds up a single sweet berry. "I hate to say it, Jarro, but I'm really glad these guys robbed your mom. Shall we keep heading in that direction?" She points to where she's hacked a messy mine into the ground, but it's hard to see what lies beyond the warped forest, thanks to the hanging fungi, twisting vines, and gently floating fog.

"Always follow the berries," I say, pulling out my sword. I briefly ache that Thingy isn't here to help us find the trail, but I'm glad he stayed home. This place is too dangerous for pig-shaped things.

Mal goes first, then Jarro, then me, then Lenna. The forest feels both huge and intimate. The way the gigantic fungi float and drip and the vines swirl on all sides make it seem like we're in a small room, but then it just keeps on going. We hear that odd, sad crying sound again and again, echoing back from somewhere far off. Endermen pop in and out, busily carrying blocks and minding their own weird business.

"Remember not to look them in the eye," I remind everyone. They probably know that already, but sometimes I just need to say something out loud so I can stop worrying about it.

The ground goes up and up like we're headed up a mountain, then slopes back down. The forest begins to feel like more of the same, and I wonder how far the Nether can really go. It feels like a cavern, and caverns have to have limits, but what if this place has no limit? What if it just keeps on going forever, and we can never catch the people who took Tok?

But that makes no sense. Whoever they are, they have a plan. They need him, and they need something only the Nether can provide, and eventually, they have to stop to put their plan into place.

The forest falls away to reveal a far less pretty place. The ground is brownish, wreathed in cyan mist and interrupted by tall black towers of stone. The forests were kind of friendly, with pretty colors and promising plant life, but this place is just . . . dead. There are even curved white things poking out of the ground that look like the bones of monsters that were once as big as houses.

"It's some kind of desert," Lenna says. When we all look to her for further information, she adds, "A desert is a biome in the overworld where there's no dirt or grass, just sand. It's very dry. This is like a desert, but . . ."

"Worse?" I offer.

She shrugs. "Maybe. In Overworld deserts, the sun can be punishing, but here . . . well, there's no sun."

"But there is . . . that thing."

Jarro is pointing at—well, definitely not the sun, but it's the biggest living thing we've seen here so far. It's floating toward us, a monstrous gray beast with wavering tentacles that remind me of a squid. As we watch it, hoping it's friendly or at least chill, it opens its mouth and lets out that eerie, creaking cry we've been hearing.

"That's one mystery solved," Mal mutters.

The thing is moving toward us now, and everyone readies their weapons, even Jarro.

I wave my sword, making sure I'm all healed up. "Maybe it's nice?"

"It looks ghastly," Lenna replies.

The next time it opens its mouth, it releases a ball of fire, which flies straight toward us—but not with particular speed.

"Not nice," I amend. "Definitely ghastly. Let me try something." I step up, carefully tracking the fireball, and the moment it's about to hit me, I swing my sword and lob the fireball right back at the ghastly thing. A direct hit! "Take that, ghast!" I shout.

It screeches and releases another fireball. I get in position to return fire. "Lenna, see if you can take it down with arrows. I don't think this guy wants to chat."

Lenna dutifully sends over a volley of arrows as I smack the fireballs, and with our combined efforts, the big gray monster soon makes a hissing screech and falls, leaving behind an odd, glimmering jewel.

"Well, I felt pretty useless in that fight," Mal says to Jarro. "How about you?"

"I guess I feel pretty useless in most fights down here," he admits.

I hurry over to grab the jewel, which looks like a giant tear. "Uh, was that thing crying? Because this is weird."

"A ghost tear," Lenna murmurs, furiously sketching in her book. "Fascinating. And now we know what the noise is."

"And we know they're relatively easy to kill." I toss the tear up in the air and catch it, thinking about how cool it felt, smacking those fireballs. "Maybe we should invent a game where somebody throws a ball, and somebody else hits it with a stick?"

Mal laughs. "That makes no sense."

"You've got to try it next time. It was super fun!"

She looks worriedly off into the teal fog writhing among the black towers. "I hope there's not a next time. If there were two of those at the same time, or fewer of us, or multiple mobs, I think it would feel less like a game."

As if on cue, an arrow zips past her ear, and Lenna drops her book and spins to shoot back at a skeleton. This is a good reminder: Just because the warped forest felt safe doesn't mean everything else here is. This desert doesn't look friendly, and we don't have any of our usual tricks for quick healing.

Mal picks back up on the trail she's chosen, and we follow her. As I pass under one of the big, white, bonelike structures, I run a hand over the smooth, solid curve. Whatever beast died here long ago, it was massive, bigger than most of the structures in Cornucopia. Only then does it occur to me that just because there are bones doesn't mean they're all dead. They could still be here, lurking. Waiting. Hungry.

My stomach growls, right on cue, and I pull out another hoglin chop and nibble. This is not a great place to forget about your health.

We walk and walk and walk, and it feels like it's taking forever.

I struggle forward, straining, but it's like when you're in a dream and you can't move. I look down, and my legs are halfway sunk into the ground.

"Uh, guys?" I try to pull up my foot and fail. "This sand is . . ."

"I'm sinking!" Jarro squawks.

"It's sucking us down," Lenna notes without nearly enough emotion. "But only to the knees?"

"Then we have to keep going. Stopping will only make it worse. Come on!" Mal redoubles her effort, flailing forward, and we follow, because we'd follow Mal anywhere. I think she's right, though—I can see something, way up ahead, that isn't sand. It almost looks like a shadow made of blocks, a looming, sharp-cornered form poking up from the ground.

I focus on that goal, slogging forward, throwing my arms to help propel my legs. Ahead of me, Mal and Jarro similarly flounder, grunting and groaning as they fight against the sucking sand. Behind me, Lenna struggles along, and I wonder if she'll be able to cover us from behind if we're attacked. If we hold still, will we be sucked under?

We can't find out. We have to keep fighting.

This is the longest day—night? Nightmare?—of my life. No matter how hard I push, I'm still twice as slow as usual. My armor weighs me down, makes me feel thick and clumsy. My legs are covered in sand, scratchy grains pouring into my boots. It's coarse and rough and irritating, and it gets everywhere—and I mean everywhere. I have my sword out, because if something that can actually walk on this sand attacks us, we'll be at a disadvantage. When an arrow whistles past, Lenna takes down the skeleton in six shots instead of her usual three, and I realize that the sand is making us exhausted.

I can see now that the form ahead is some kind of structure, and my heart lifts. A structure means people, and people means my brother might be there. Whatever it is, it's not a neat, well-planned construction. Maybe it's a shelter they've hastily thrown up.

Maybe they're waiting for us, weapons at the ready.

It doesn't matter.

We're going to get to that bastion, and if Tok is there, we're going to save him.

# 22

# MAL

 We're almost there, almost out of this horrible, soul-sucking sand. I've never really thought about dirt or grass or stone before because I didn't know there were places without them, places where the ground wasn't solid and dependable and boring. Now I long for the most basic plot of land, for a dull, quiet place where I can see my feet and every step isn't a battle.

Finally I lurch up onto the red, spongy stone that seems to dominate this place, sword at the ready. We're back in the same sort of biome we started in, and it feels pleasantly familiar by comparison. I'd like to stop and shake the sand out of my boots, but we don't know what's inside this structure up ahead, and I'm currently the only person with the ability to move quickly with a weapon or do more than flail around. Once Jarro and Chug are up, I leave them to cover Lenna and head toward the tall, black wall. I can't see any doors or any way in, so when everyone is safely out of the sand, I lead them along the edge around to the left. As we near the corner, I'm stunned: The sandy valley has fallen away to show a huge lake of lava surrounded by the spongy red blocks. We're out of the valley, I guess, and into a new sort of place.

"What is this?" Chug asks.

"I don't know, but it's promising. It looks like people made it."

"Not recently," he says nervously, and I can tell he's worried about Tok.

"Just because it's not a hastily made structure doesn't mean he's not here. They're probably taking shelter anywhere they can, just like we are. Even if you're here on purpose, it's not particularly pleasant." That seems to calm him down, and I keep exploring.

I can't find a door on the ground level, so I reach into my pocket for some leftover stone and build a staircase up to an opening high up in the side of the looming stone wall.

Up close, the whole place is beginning to look like some ancient remnant that's fallen to ruin. Towers of lava flow from high overhead, plunging into the glowing orange sea below. Glittering globs of stone hang down from the stone ceiling like chandeliers, and I can begin to see human touches among the crumbling architecture, and—

Well, maybe they're not *human* touches, because I can see inside the bastion now. A piglin with a gold sword trots down a narrow hallway as if on some kind of important business. Maybe this is where the piglins live, their form of a village? Still, just as we took shelter in the empty building in the village, maybe Tok's kidnappers are taking shelter within this bastion remnant. The piglins didn't bother us last time, so maybe they won't bother us now.

I look at my friends and hold a finger to my lips before darting in the open doorway. It's cramped and narrow and dark inside and definitely doesn't have the familiar architecture of a woodland mansion. There's no rhyme or reason to its structure, or maybe there once was and it's fallen into disrepair over time. As my friends follow me, tiptoeing, weapons drawn, my heart speeds up. I wish I understood this place better. I wish it made sense. I wish I knew how to lead them. But it's twisty and dusty inside, and I have to hunch over to navigate around corners, sidle past peculiar cascades of lava, and wobble down winding, awkward stairs. I have no idea what I'm doing or where I'm going, but I have to act like I do or my friends will start to freak out, and then we'll be in trouble.

Whenever I see a piglin, I hold my breath until we're past. None of them seem to care that we're here, thank goodness, and there aren't that many around, and Chug does a great job of restraining himself instead of trying to befriend every one we pass. I think the hoglin encounter hurt his feelings, and now he's not as confident. I'm just glad we had that golden apple, or he'd be in big trouble. That was the most hurt he's ever been, and I'll never tell him this, but I was scared for him. I'm glad that the piglins seem to clear out as we get deeper inside the structure. It feels empty—almost haunted.

"Where are we going?" Chug whispers.

"I'm trying to get us to the ground floor," I whisper back. "I think that's where business is most likely to happen."

On the next hallway, we find our first open door, and I stop and glance inside. It's empty except for a chest sitting in the corner. We hurry over and open it as Lenna stands guard at the door. The chest is deliciously full of loot, some of which we've never even seen before. I pocket the golden apple right off, exhaling in relief. Chug collects the various ingots of gold and iron and scraps of some mysterious new ore. It might look like he's being selfish, but I know Chug, and I therefore know that he's thinking about all the cool things his brother can make out of raw materials.

Jarro looks kind of lost, so I jerk my chin at the chest and ask, "See anything you like?"

He points at the gold boots. "Those look like they might fit, if nobody else wants them."

I hand him the boots, and he trades them out for his leather boots and grins. "My old boots were made for town, I think. And you probably won't believe this, but they were full of sand."

Chug chuckles. "Oh, man, I should've taken them then!"

"Too late! You settled for a measly bunch of scrap metal!"

Lenna grabs the disc labeled, oddly, Pigstep, probably to add to the library she and Nan are compiling back home. We're not sure what the glowing sphere is, and we don't have a use for the blocks of weird rock, but at this point, we're going to take everything we can get. Satisfied, we close the chest, and I lead everyone back into the hallway.

It's a strange structure, and I definitely don't feel at home here. Whoever built it must have had a fever, or maybe they just closed their eyes and drew the plans without looking. It makes no sense. It's not comfortable or pretty, and even though it feels like an old building, it doesn't seem grand or fancy or like a place anyone would want to live. It's dark, barely lit, and we end up pulling out our torches so we don't trip and fall down the stairs.

We find a few random gold blocks just sticking out of the walls and ceiling, which I mine—after making sure there are no piglins around to get annoyed about it. With each turn of a spiral staircase, we expect to find the bottom story of the structure, but it's bigger than it looks. In a regular cavern, mining, I would expect it to get colder the deeper we got, but here, it's getting warmer.

When our next stairwell spits us out in an open hallway, I see why.

We're facing a bridge, and under that bridge is lava.

"Whoever designed this place makes bad decisions," Chug says.

"Not if you like lava. Or cooking over an open flame," Jarro replies, and Chug chuckles. They're actually pretty funny when they're on the same team.

The bridge, at least, seems solid. It's wide, with decorative edges and gold blocks placed like lanterns. Unlike the hastily built, two-block bridge we crossed earlier on our journey, this one is wide and sturdy and looks older than Nan. I lead my friends across it, waiting for a stone to shift or crumble underfoot, but everything stays in place. A piglin passes us on their way to the other side without so much as a grunt. I think about mining the gold blocks, but we're out in the open, and I don't want to make anyone mad.

An even bigger black stone structure awaits us at the end of the bridge, and as we step inside, my jaw drops.

The Nether is huge, much bigger than it has any right to be. And the first part of the bastion was big. But this place . . . it's enormous. One giant room, but filled with mismatched, misplaced chunks of stone that make ill-fitting stairs and rooms and hallways. It's like someone took a big house and just randomly knocked out blocks until it was full of holes. The floor, which is far below us, even lower than when we started out, is mostly lava with black stone blocks placed at intervals that will make them difficult to cross. I reach into my pocket to make sure I still have plenty of loose stone in there. We're going to need it, because in the center of the floor is an open room full of huge gold blocks and a treasure chest.

"I bet that's where they keep the good stuff," Jarro says.

I look to Chug for his pithy addition, but he's nervously scanning all the parts of the giant room we can see. I know he's looking for some sign of Tok, for a flash of anything vaguely human, but he's going to be disappointed. This place is full of piglins and lava, and that's pretty much it. There might be a few hidden rooms where people could hide, but the vast majority of the structure is visible from where we stand.

"We don't have time for the treasure," he says. "We've got to keep going and find Tok."

He's in that nervous mood where he makes decisions without thinking, and I know I need to talk him down.

"Let's think about it, bud," I say. "First of all, if his kidnappers are here, they're going to be hiding in a room, not out in the open. So we need to search those rooms." He nods glumly, and I continue. "And we need all the loot we can find. There could be potions, more golden apples, even diamond armor. There are no trees for arrows here. Not many sources of food. We need all the advantages we can get."

"I know." His big shoulders slump. "Let's go raid the dumb chest and steal all the dumb gold."

"That's the Chug I know."

I lead my friends through the open door and choose to take the path along the left wall. It's an open hallway that makes it all too clear how far down that lava is, but it's not like there are any better options. I use a spare block to bridge the gap to the next platform, and then we're passing a piglin as we scurry up the stairs. This place is like something out of a dream where nothing makes sense, and even though I was trying to lead us downward to that pile of treasure, somehow the path I've chosen is leading us upward.

"Hey, wait," Lenna calls.

I stop and look back to where she has a hand against one of the many identical black rock walls.

"I think there might be a room here," she says. "I noticed it on the way up. See how it pokes out more than it should?"

I pull out my pickaxe and mine the block she's pointing at. I shouldn't be surprised that Lenna is right, but I'm definitely pleased. Through the hole I've made, I can see a closed chest just waiting for us to pillage it. I mine another block to make a door and step inside. Before I've made sense of the room, a furious squeal rends the air as a big shape charges for me. I don't have time to get my sword, so I lash out with my diamond pickaxe. When my attacker is knocked away, I'm surprised to see that it's a piglin—but a bigger, meaner, downright brutal version of a piglin.

"How about some gold?" Chug says, throwing an ingot at him, but the piglin brute just shakes his head, squeals again, and runs at me, his golden axe raised.

I dart around him, landing a hit on his back and getting out of the way of Chug's sword and Lenna's arrows. Chug takes a swing, and as the furious brute focuses on him, I land another hit. I'm shocked to see Jarro wielding his axe. The space is so crowded that Lenna can't get a solid shot, so I shout, "We've got to take him down close range. Don't stop!"

The piglin brute lands a hit on Jarro's arm, which makes

Chug's next strike all the more severe. The small room is a riot of squeals and grunts and the heavy thud of weapons. Finally, with one last thrust of Chug's sword, our attacker goes down, dropping an enchanted golden axe.

"I think you've earned this," I say, handing it to Jarro. "It looks a lot sharper than your old one."

His eyes light up—I never really noticed them before, but they're kind of a honey gold. He gives the axe an experimental swing and puts his old iron axe in his pocket.

With the piglin brute no longer a threat, I head for the chest as Chug hands Jarro a hoglin chop to help him heal from that unlucky axe hit. The loot, again, makes stopping worth it. I take the diamond pickaxe for myself, because I know that if I break my great-great-great-grandmother's diamond pickaxe, I'll regret it forever. I offer the chain, string, and iron ingots to Chug, as well as an enchanted book he'll want to give to Tok. I let Jarro have the golden carrot, and I keep another golden apple. But, possibly best of all, we finally have a weapon we've heard of but never seen before. I hold it out to Lenna, and she smiles the biggest smile I've ever seen.

"A crossbow!" she crows, cradling it like it's a kitten.

"And arrows." I hand her all sixteen, and she shoves them in her pocket, but she's only got eyes for the crossbow.

We squeeze back out our door and continue down the strange hallway. Whenever there's a gap in the floor, I place a block so no one will be in danger. Slowly but surely, we get closer and closer to the lava—and that pile of gold blocks. We clear another room, which thankfully doesn't contain a piglin brute . . . but also doesn't contain a chest. There's no sign of Tok or any other humans. No one in their right mind would leave the kind of loot we're finding in a chest if they came across it out here. The people we're following must've hurried on to somewhere else.

Finally we're on the ground floor, and I'm studying the field of lava and the black blocks sunk deep into that shimmering orange sea. There's a walkway that reaches almost to the gold . . . but not quite. Luckily, I have plenty of blocks still, and I place enough in the lava to make sure there's no chance anyone could fall in. I lead the way and stand on the platform over the lava. Sweat drips down my nose and soaks my hair under my helmet.

With shaking, sweaty hands, I open the chest.

## 23

# LENNA

When Mal opens the chest, I'm floored. This has got to be the grandmother of all loot chests, and I can't believe our luck. There's a diamond sword, a diamond chest plate, and diamond leggings, enough diamond to be rich back home. There are several ingots of gold and iron, plus an ingot of some metal I've never seen before—and I grew up in a mine. There are two iridescent spheres like the one in the first chest that are warm to the touch and look a little like fancy slimeballs, plus blocks of peculiar stone. Mal gives Chug the diamond sword and chest plate, which means I get his gold one. Chug carries the ingots, and Mal keeps the stone. I get to carry the spheres, and I like how they glow from deep in my pocket. There's not really anything for Jarro here, but he doesn't seem like he needs anything.

That's the thing about travel—it teaches you about yourself. When we began our first journey, I didn't know what was impor- tant to me, really, or what I was passionate about. Now I know that the things I care about the most are my friends, bows and arrows, and collecting exciting new things to show to Nan and display in our library. She's going to be so excited about everything we've found here. I wish I could stop and sketch everything I see along the way, but we have to find Tok first. Maybe once he's safely home, we can come back here together and really spend our time exploring.

Then again, the adults haven't let us venture out at all. Sure, they cut a door in the wall around Cornucopia, but then they told us not to go outside, or at least not past New Cornucopia. And because we're good kids, we obeyed them.

Until now.

This time, we had no choice. And each time we break their rules and venture out into the bigger world, the harder it is to go back to being compliant.

What are they going to do—lock us up again?

We know how to get out. We can mine holes in their wall, tunnel under it, build a staircase over it. The more we know, the harder it is to contain us.

I yawn, my jaw cracking, and Mal looks at me, concerned.

"Sleepy?" she asks.

I nod. "I think it's been two days since we slept."

"No time for sleep." Chug yawns, too. "We have to find Tok."

"But if we get too sleepy, we fall into lava or get surprised by another piglin brute," Mal argues. "Tok's captors have to sleep, too. No one can stay awake forever. They'll get clumsy, too."

Chug exhales sadly. "Fine. But just a catnap."

Mal mines all the gold around the chest while we keep watch, then leads us back to the nearest room. It's not big, but it's definitely cozy. We don't have wood for a door like Tok used to make, so she just fits two blocks of stone in the open space—after Chug hangs torches on every wall.

"I still wish we had a fourth bed," Mal says as I pull a bed out of my pocket and—

*Boom!*

I'm flung backward by the force of the bed—exploding?

My back hits the wall, and I slump down to sitting, staring at the flaming planks that are all that remain of my bed. My ears are ringing, and I think my face got singed. My head jerks up as I remember that my friends were nearby for the explosion, but they all hurry to stand over me looking decently unexploded. Their voices sound far away as their hands worriedly pat me. I'm glad none of them are hurt.

"Eat," Chug says, loudly, handing me a hoglin chop.

I start eating, because I don't like this feeling. I need all my senses. Unable to hear, I feel like anything could sneak up on me at any moment, or one of my friends might need me and I wouldn't hear them calling. I choke the chop down and reach into my pocket for the very last cookie, which I've been saving for desperate times.

"A cookie? No fair!" Chug moans, and I'm so happy that I can hear him again, even if he's whiny.

"She's the one who baked them," Mal points out, patting at one of the puffs of my hair. "And she's still kinda smoking."

I hand Chug a little chunk of my cookie. Even if he's not wounded, his feelings will be if I don't share.

Once I've eaten enough, I try to stand . . . and can't. My ears are ringing, and everything hurts. The hand that held the cookie has fallen to my side, useless. Gentle wisps of smoke rise from my shirt, and I can't do anything about it.

Mal holds out one of our two golden apples, and I shake my head feebly. I don't want to waste it on me, but . . . I don't think regular food can fix this fast enough. We need to be at full health when we find Tok. Plus, we're running out of food. I'm pretty sure there's nothing left but hoglin chops and a few potatoes. She holds out the apple, and I bite it, and the golden flesh explodes with flavor in my mouth. It's like eating a sweetened sunbeam. I want to keep eating this apple forever, want to feel it pouring health into me like I'm a bottle that needed filling.

When it's all gone, my ears stop ringing and I'm able to stand. "So no beds, then," I say.

Mal shakes her head sadly. "I'm worried about what will happen if we try to sleep here. The Nether is so bizarre. I guess we can sit down for a few minutes to rest our bodies, but we have to keep one another from falling asleep.

We each pick a wall and sit down, but no one attempts to close their eyes. I realize how very hard it is to rest when you're scared of going to sleep and every twitch makes your armor clank and press into some tender part of your body.

My eyes go unfocused, and the world gets blurry. It's like I'm drifting in and out of the mist in my own mind, which feels as topsy-turvy as the building we're in. I called it a bastion remnant in my book. Naming things, as it turns out, is a new pleasure. When I tamed Poppy, I had to name her immediately before Chug called her something stupid, but I'll admit the first thing that came to mind was perfect for her. Now I can't imagine calling her anything else. Maybe naming things, like archery and baking, is a new skill, one I never would have discovered if I hadn't set foot outside the wall.

After a while, because time makes no sense here, with no sun or moon, Mal sighs heavily and stands.

"Does anyone feel more rested?"

We all shake our heads. Everyone looks exhausted and frazzled.

"Lenna, are you all healed up?"

I stand and test my body, which responds as it should. "Yeah. You guys don't sound like you're talking underwater anymore, and I'm pretty sure I'm not still on fire."

Jarro stands, too. "I can't believe you guys like this."

"The Nether?" Mal asks.

"No, just . . . leaving home. This place is exhausting. And scary."

"It's not usually like this," I tell him. "The Nether is new for us, too. Everything made a lot more sense when we were just in the Overworld."

"Except the brigands," Chug reminds us.

"And the illagers," I add.

"But the more we experience, the more we learn, and the more we can deal with," Mal argues. "If I could rewind time to that day Lenna first saw a vex and had the option to ignore it instead of doing something about it, I would still do everything exactly as we did. Yeah, it's a little scary and dangerous. But it's also interesting and fun and exciting."

"And we've all found new skills, new things we're good at," I say. "I wasn't good at anything before."

Jarro hunches over. "When do I get to find new skills?"

Chug smacks him on the back. "Bud, you already found a bunch! Remember when you, I don't know, *tamed horses*?"

"Yeah, but that's not really useful back home."

"Not yet it isn't. But if you bring horses home with you, it'll change things. You could start a horse farm outside the wall. Be the only source of horses. Anyone who wants to travel will be happy to trade with you."

Jarro's face lights up. I've never seen him look like this before—hopeful, happy. He always looks mean or angry back home. It suits him, this hopefulness.

"I guess I thought I'd have to live with my mom forever, but . . . I don't have to."

"It feels good, escaping the people who don't believe in you," I say.

The small room is getting way too full of emotion, and Chug has apparently reached his limit, as he clears his throat and points at the blocks Mal fitted into the open doorway. "So are we ready to get back on the lava-filled, murderous road?"

He gives each of us a hoglin chop as we leave. Mal leads us back through the bastion, over the bridge and down the torturous stairs until we're standing on the spongy red blocks, looking out over the lava sea. It was so cramped and dark inside that it actually feels good to be in the bigger cavern, surrounded by looming red blocks, towering rivulets of steaming lava, and mysteriously haunting pillars of stone. Strange two-legged creatures stride by occasionally, walking right on top of the lava like it's the most normal thing in the world, but they don't pay us the least bit of attention, so we all just ignore them, too. Chug has learned his lesson about looking new creatures in the eye or approaching them with overtures of friendship. I long to sketch these peculiar striders in my book, but I'm also afraid I'll drop it in the boiling magma, plus I have to struggle to keep up at this pace. It's tough going, thanks to the lava sea that interrupts all the walking paths, and Mal has to keep placing random stone blocks out of her pocket.

"You guys, I'm almost out of blocks," she says, looking utterly stretched to her limit.

Jarro points to the walls. "So just mine some of whatever that is and use it."

Mal's eyes boggle, and I understand why she's shocked. Jarro, our enemy, has just said something kind of genius that none of us thought of. It's as weird as a cow walking on its hind legs. She nods and hurries to the nearest wall. Thanks to her diamond pickaxe, she soon has pockets stuffed with the spongy burgundy stone and is able to bridge us across a narrow bit of sea so we can stand in the crimson forest on the opposite shore.

"I don't get it," she says, shielding her eyes with her hand. "If Tok's kidnappers came this way, how'd they get across? They left a bridge behind earlier, but not now? I'm worried we're not on the right track."

Chug is frowning at this possibility. "But it feels right. He's got to be this way. If they'd bridged anywhere, we would've seen it."

Ah, but they've forgotten something. They keep seeing this place like the Overworld. Like all the major business happens on the ground. I look up and grin.

"We were just looking in the wrong place." I point up and up and up, where a red-block bridge is suspended in the air, linking the walls of the cavern and the rock formations hanging from the ceiling.

"We've got to get up there," Chug says, hands in fists like he's just going to start climbing.

"No!" Jarro yelps before clearing his throat. "I mean, there are other options."

"I can't believe I'm saying this, but Jarro's right." We all turn to Mal. "If we can see their bridges, we can follow them down here. Less chance of falling. And if we run out of blocks or land, then we can tower up and use their bridges. If we stay down here, they're less likely to notice us."

And that's how we continue. Mal builds bridges over the lava, mines more blocks, builds more bridges. We follow the zigging, zagging red lines crisscrossing the ceiling overhead. While we're in the crimson forest, we know well enough that we have to take down the hoglins before they take us down, and we're also becoming increasingly aware that these wild pig-monsters are the only source of food down here . . . and we're running out. I hit each hoglin with several arrows, Mal finishes them off, Chug collects the chops, I collect the arrows. He still can't bring himself to hurt anything that looks even vaguely like Thingy, and that's okay. The nice thing about having friends is that you can lean on them when there's something you can't do, and when they're in a tight spot, you get to return the favor.

But then the crimson forest opens up to another sweeping lava sea, and this one seems to go on as far as we can see with no shores or islands, just lava from vertical red wall to vertical red wall with an occasional creature striding across it. The sea goes on for so long that it seems to dissolve into solid shadow, somewhere far away. I look up at the bridge, and it's so high that it feels impossible that we might ever reach it—or not fall off it, once we were up there.

"Please don't make me go up there," Jarro says quietly. "I'm just . . . really scared of heights, okay?" He looks sharply at Chug as if waiting for cruel words, but none come.

"Yeah, I'm not a big fan, either," Chug admits. "I'll do it for Tok, but I doubt anything else could make me willing to risk it. There's got to be another way."

Mal has purple rings under her eyes, and her braid is coming undone, and her red hair stands out around her face in a frizzy halo. I've never seen her this unnerved, this unsure, but as she looks up at the bridge, she scrunches her eyes shut and pulls herself together. It makes me want to cry, but I think I'm too tired and hot and dried out to make tears in the middle of a lava sea.

"There's no other way," she says firmly. "Come on. You can do it. We can all do it."

She and I take out our pickaxes and mine as much netherrack as we can carry. Her diamond pickaxe is far more effective than my iron one, but I'd rather toil away doing something useful than pace around looking nervous like Chug and Jarro. Once we're completely out of room in our pockets, Mal starts building a steep, narrow staircase. It's not elegant or well made, but it seems sturdy enough. As she steps up to the next level, Chug follows her, and I'm waiting for Jarro to go next, but he won't.

"You can do it," I repeat. "It's not that high."

He shoots me a furious glare. "I didn't think you were the kind of person who would lie to me."

"I'm not lying. Since it feels like we're underground, it doesn't feel that high for me. And I like being underground, so I'm not worried. And we still have a golden apple. This is the only way forward, so we might as well get started."

"No way, Lenna. No one can make me. I've done everything you guys have asked, even when it made no sense, and we've gotten this far, but I'm not going to climb up this rickety staircase and fall to my death for you."

I look up. Mal and Chug are doing fine. It just doesn't seem that bad to me. "Well, we're going to keep going, so if you can't, I guess you can wait for us here. You can go back to that room and block yourself in. But Tok needs us, so we're going."

"Fine," he barks. "You know, I thought you guys were different. I was finally starting to think of you as friends. But if you'll leave me behind, you're not worth my time."

"We're not leaving you behind," I try to explain. "We have to keep going so we won't leave Tok behind. From our point of view, you're the one who's not being a very good friend."

"Tok's not my friend!"

"But he could be. We just have to find him first. And Chug is your friend, and you're letting him down."

Jarro looks up to where Chug is standing on the step behind Mal. Chug sees him looking and gives a big, exaggerated wave that makes Jarro shudder and then sag. "It's not that I don't want to. It's that I can't."

"Lenna! I need your stone!" Mal calls.

I reach into my pocket and pull out a hoglin chop. "Then good luck, Jarro. Be careful. Remember to eat. I hope we'll see you soon."

I start climbing and I don't look back.

# 24

# JARRO

 I can't believe they're just leaving me behind like this. I've had no choice but to watch them for years, to see them laugh and smile together and have fun together. It always made me mad, I guess because I secretly wanted to be in their group, but there was never any way in. Even in our first year of school, when we were all tiny, they sat at a table for four and never really let anyone else play with them. It was actually really nice, feeling like a part of their group on this grand adventure. But here they are again, leaving me behind like I'm nothing. I can't believe I fell for it, that I let myself believe I might have real, actual friends.

Part of me wants to start hacking away at their stupid stairs with my axe, but . . . even I'm not that cruel. And if something were to attack me, I guess I could use the stairs to escape—but just to get out of reach, not to climb all the way up to the stupid ceiling.

I sit down and stare at the hoglin chop Lenna gave me. I wish it was one of her cookies. The last one she gave me was so good that I've been thinking about it all this time. She's halfway up to reach Chug and Mal now, and Chug is staring down at me like he doesn't understand what's going on. He waves his arm like a question, and I shake my head and point at the ground. I'm sure Lenna will fill him in, once she reaches them.

I look around, taking note of my surroundings. I'm in the middle of nowhere, on a spongy red shore by a boiling orange lava sea. There are no plants, no trees, no living things. Every now and then, I hear the haunting cry of a—I think Lenna called them ghasts?—and I decide that if one sees me, I'll have to hide. I don't have arrows, and I'm not a very good fighter, and something like that would straight up kill me. I don't have a pickaxe, but I do have my axe, so I hack into a block and . . . it's exhausting. I definitely have the wrong tool for the job, and I know absolutely nothing about building. It'll take me hours to make even the most pathetic little shelter.

I look into my pockets, and it's pretty bleak. I have a shield, some interesting bits of fungus, a few hoglin chops, the horses' saddles, some iridescent spheres, a bunch of little odds and ends that nobody else wanted. They've left me here with practically nothing. How am I supposed to survive until they get back? And what will happen to me if they fail and never return?

Even surrounded by lava, I shiver. That's a dark line of thinking.

I might never see my mom again, which I have mixed feelings about. I love my mom, but I'm starting to see that . . . well, I don't think I agree with all her choices. She tried to keep me close to her, to keep me safe, but now I'm scared of everything and get mad all the time. Traveling with the Bad Apples, or the Mob Squad, as they call themselves, has been the most fun, calm, happy time of my life, even if I was constantly having near-death experiences. They're nice, and I don't have to pretend to be tough around them. I can just be . . . me.

Of course, I can't be me if I die down here. I've got to find a better plan.

As I stare out into the sea of lava, contemplating my own doom, I see one of those weird strider creatures plodding along. It walks on the lava like it can't even feel the burn, its goofy eyes straight ahead and its hair?—tentacles?—whatever blowing in the wind. Its head is so weirdly flat. It kind of reminds me of a table.

Or a two-legged horse.

I have an idea.

If I'm wrong, I'll probably get really hurt, because I will never forget what that hoglin did to Chug. But if I'm right, it might solve all our problems.

I reach into my pocket and pull out some of the wheat left over from taming the horses.

"Here, strider!" I call. "Want some yummy wheat?"

It veers toward me a little bit as if smelling the wheat, then veers away. I rummage in my pockets and hold out everything that might be considered food for an animal.

"Want something else? Some nice fungus?"

The strider gives a cheerful chirp and ambles over to me, and I'm scared but also excited, and it looks kind of sweet as it chirps to itself. It reaches over with surprising gentleness and nibbles on a bit of fungus from the warped forest.

"You like warped fungus. Got it."

I shove everything else in my pockets and pull out this weird stick I found downtown once, which has string attached to it. I used to use it to dangle sweet berries down allies and then pull them up before little kids could eat them and then laugh when they cried. When I think about it now, that's just embarrassing, as is the fact that I never looked around for the stick's owner; but it might just be what saves us.

See, Chug told me about how he was able to ride his pig, and I'm going to ride this strider. And then me and my strider are going to go find three more striders, and we're all going to walk across the lava sea instead of climbing miles overhead and balancing on narrow little blocks, and then maybe I'll get to be the hero again. It felt pretty good, with the horses.

I attach a piece of warped fungus to the string and brace myself. I've definitely got the strider's attention, so I use the fungus to lure it up onto the beach. It turns a pathetic shade of purple and starts shivering.

"Don't worry, buddy, we'll be back on the lava in no time," I say, offering him a little bit of fungus to keep him happy.

I pull out my saddle and gently place it on his head, and he doesn't seem to mind at all. Then all I have to do is swing up, which is oddly easier than it looks. And now I'm sitting on top of my strider, holding out the fungus to lead him back onto the lava. I hold my breath as he takes his first steps off the shore, but he feels remarkably sturdy, and I'm high enough up that the heat isn't too horrible. The strider makes sweet, hopeful little chirps as he follows wherever the fungus goes. I've never been so proud of myself in my entire life.

"Hey, Mob Squad!" I shout as loudly as possible, my voice echoing throughout the cavern.

"What?" Mal calls from far overhead. I think I can see them, just three smudges on a towering stairwell, almost to the bridge.

"Wanna go for a ride?" I swing my warped fungus on a stick

around, and my strider takes off, zooming across the lava. It's actually pretty fun despite the ongoing threat of being boiled alive.

It's hard to watch them and control the strider, so I focus on keeping my seat. We stay near the shore, but I don't make Smokey—that's the strider's name, because Lenna told me once to always be sure to name things before Chug can—I don't make him go on land, because he probably hates being cold. It's a long wait, and I wonder if maybe Mal, Chug, and Lenna just quietly kept going on their overhead bridge, glad to leave me behind.

"Whoa," Chug says, hopping down off the stairs. "Can you ride *anything*?"

"Probably not a hoglin," I admit, grinning. "Or a chicken."

He gets very serious. "Remind me to tell you about chicken jockeys some other time."

As it turns out, the string on a stick I've been carrying around all this time is a fishing rod, and Chug has enough materials in his pockets to make three more. Lenna has plenty of samples of warped fungus, so I take Smokey out on the lava to lure in more striders. It takes longer than I'd like, but at least they don't buck like horses or fight like hoglins. Everyone mounts up, and Chug keeps telling his strider that she's beautiful.

He named her Miss Twolegs. I begin to see Lenna's point about names.

I show them how to steer with the fungus, and Chug says, "It's just like riding a pig!"

"Except it smells a lot better," Mal reminds him.

"I can't smell anything at all." Chug sniffs at his armpit. "Thank goodness. Everything here just smells like fire."

Mal moves into her usual position, leading us across the vast sea of lava, following the route of the bridge overhead. I'm so relieved I could cry. I didn't want to be left behind, but I didn't want to attempt crossing that bridge. But I found a third choice, and it's actually pretty cool. I was the first person from our town to ride horses—except Nan, probably—and I'm definitely the first person to ride a strider. It's pleasant, with their steady, rocking gait. I could almost fall asleep, if I weren't constantly assailed by the sound of bubbling lava and the occasional crying ghast. As if anyone could fall asleep in the Nether.

A ghast comes into view, and Mal swerves us over behind a tower of stone. As the ghast moves past, we edge around the stone, always staying as out of sight as possible. Once it's turned its back to us, we head right back onto our path. The striders are the only creatures that can cross the lava, so we don't run into any hoglins or piglin brutes or skeletons. The ghasts are pretty easy to avoid. I'm beginning to think we can actually do this, that we can take whatever the Nether throws at us.

But then I see something, a form looming in the darkness ahead. It's a little like the bastion remnant, but so, so much bigger. The blocks are the deep, dark color of dried blood, a color that seems to absorb what little light there is, and the structure appears to be growing through the rock, half sunken and yet so big that it sprawls overhead and stretches in all directions, bigger than all of Cornucopia. It's the most intimidating place I've ever seen in my life, and just as I know that I absolutely don't want to go there, I also know that this is where we'll find Tok.

"He's in there," Chug says, echoing my thoughts. "I just know it."

"Then let's go get him," I reply.

## 25

# TOK

 I love crafting. I love brewing. I love books full of new things to learn. But I've been here for at least a day now, and I'm exhausted, and no one will give me a bed. I've tried to sleep leaning up against the wall, then Rex shouts at me until I go back to brewing. This place feels like a permanent twilight, and it's unsettling. I've made dozens of potions and dozens of weapons, and I've made mistakes that blew up in my face and successes that I'd be crowing about all over town, if I was back home. But it's just me and Rex, and Rex doesn't care. Rex doesn't even care if I'm alive or dead—he takes half the food he's supposed to give me and slowly chews while he reads his stupid book. I'm so desperate for sleep and food that I keep looking at the weird ingredients on the shelf, wondering if any of them are edible.

Probably not. So many of them are based on spider's eyes.

I've just completed a gold sword, just to break up the monotony of making potions—the monotony of making potions! Who am I?!—when Orlok walks in.

"Show me what you've made," he says with no preamble. He stands before my work area, chewing on a piece of meat, and I have to suck some drool back in.

"If I show you, will you feed me?"

He bristles. "I fed you! You were fed."

My eyes slide to Rex, who's doing his best to loom innocently against the wall. His mustache is bespeckled with breadcrumbs.

Orlok's eyes narrow, and he barks, "Rex, go get the boy some food. He's no good to us if his health gets too low. You know that."

Rex sneers at me and leaves. It takes effort not to stare at Orlok's food, but I can sense he's feeling impatient and jumpy. I think the Nether just does that to people. Since Rex hasn't slept and won't let me sleep, there must be something here that prevents rest.

"I've got all the potions you asked for—five of each. Except the Potion of Fire Resistance. That one's tricky."

Orlok picks up a Potion of Invisibility and holds it up to the nearest torch, inspecting it. I don't know if he knows potions well enough to be able to distinguish its particular shade of purple from all the other shades of purple, but he grunts and sets it back down.

"Good work. Do you need any more ingredients?"

I look at the shelf. Several of the bowls that once held spider's eyes and magma creams are empty now, and my blaze rods are running low. "How long do you plan to keep me here? I'm going to need sleep if you don't want me to blow myself up. I already feel like I'm becoming . . ." I'm not sure of the right word, and that's part of the problem. "Unstable."

He shakes his head, showing no pity. "A bit longer. Got to make it count. Then we'll head back to the Overworld, get some rest, and come right back here. Until then, just keep your eyes open and hope you don't accidentally fall asleep, yeah? Not even a catnap.

The word "cat" makes me tear up. I miss Candor and Clarity so much.

"When do I get to go home again?"

Orlok gives a one-shoulder shrug that shows how little he cares about me. "This is your job now. So do your job. You're one of us."

At that, I step toward him, my hands in fists. "I'm not one of you! I'm a—a—captive! I'm a child. You kidnapped me. My family will be worried about me. You need to take me home."

He steps toward me, not cowed by my fury. "You may be a kid in years, but you're a business owner. You don't live with your parents. Yeah, that's right—I did my research. So if you're going to live an adult's life, you can get treated like an adult."

I shake my head, tears burning my eyes. "You once told Krog you weren't willing to attack a town. I thought that meant you had morals."

At that, he barks a laugh. "I don't have morals; I have a code. I don't want to hurt people, especially people who don't challenge me, and therefore I'm not hurting you. You're safe. Protected. Fed. You might be uncomfortable, but we all are. The rest of the crew is out gathering more ingredients. Fighting blazes and magma cubes. For you. Maybe once I'm rich enough to buy my own castle you'll have earned your freedom. Now, I'll ask again: What do you need?"

Food. Friendship. Cats. My brother. The blue sky. My mom's pumpkin pie.

"More nether wart. More blaze rods. More spider's eyes. And more magma creams. I keep breaking them."

I slump to sitting right there. It just feels so hopeless. I know I heard the brigands whispering once about how maps and compasses don't work in the Nether, so it's not like my friends could find me, even if they managed to figure out how to get here. There's no helpful beacon, no cartographer's X that marks this spot. When Orlok gave me another handful of sweet berries, I dropped them to mark our path through the Nether, but maybe something ate them, or maybe they just straight-up melted. Or maybe my friends are still at home, worried. Maybe they never found the berry trail at all.

I'm in another world, in the middle of nowhere, and with every passing moment that I can't get any sleep, I feel less able to cope with everything that's happening.

And, yeah, I feel sorry for myself, but I wasn't lying—potions are tricky, and if they push me too far, I'm going to cause a bigger explosion than I ever did back home. These ingredients are powerful, more powerful than what I was fiddling with back at my shop, and someone is going to get hurt.

Rex returns with a piece of meat for me, and I wolf it down so fast that Orlok makes his minion give me the meat he brought for himself. It's not chicken or mutton or beef, and considering what I can see of the Nether from my window, I probably don't want to know what it is.

I've stolen a few glances outside, while Rex was deep in his book. I guess they feel it's safe to leave the window open because, well, there's nowhere to go except straight downward into an endless sea of lava. There are no bridges, no ladders, few beaches, and those so far away that there's no way I could jump to them. It's just the flat, dark red side of this building, the slightly lighter red walls of the enormous cavern we're in, and the lava. There's nowhere for me to go. No way to escape. Even if I crafted a pickaxe, and even if I could mine a hole in the floor without three goons running in to stop me, where would I go?

I finish my meat, wipe my mouth, and stumble back to my workstation, where I pull a fresh water bottle off the shelf.

"Good boy," Orlok says with a grin. "My little potion cow."

The greedy, knowing way he says it makes the meat rise back up in my throat.

Even if he seems kind or wise sometimes, Orlok, like Krog, is not a good dude.

He leaves, and Rex pulls out his book, and I make Potions of Harming. I saved these potions for last, hoping that they'd be happy enough with the more harmless concoctions. But until someone replenishes my nether wart, I'm kind of stuck. I guess that's why they brought me here: There's bound to be more nether wart in the Nether. And also because no one will ever find me.

I finish my potion and place it on the shelf with all the others. They're so pretty, lined up like this, swirling masterpieces of blue and pink and purple. It's funny how a few days ago, if someone had promised me I'd have unlimited potion ingredients in a tricked-out workshop, several books on the topic, and all the time in the world to brew, I would have been ecstatic.

But only because I would have been free, and because I would have had Chug with me.

I stumble over to the window, put my elbows on the sill, and cry.

## 26

# CHUG

Miss Twolegs is a pretty good mount, but a strider just can't compare to a pig. Pigs are cute, chubby, huggable, and make adorable grunts. Striders are just weird, and their skin feels kind of like mold growing on a very warm rock. Not that I would tell Miss Twolegs that. It's not her fault that she can't hold a torch to Thingy.

She's fast, at least. We're making great time, striding across the lava sea, and it's a lot more fun than climbing a million steps and then walking on a skinny bridge thousands of feet over a boiling ocean of molten rock. I guess if the striders wanted to toss us, we'd be in trouble, but they are very motivated by fungus and haven't given us a single bit of trouble.

Time seems to slow down as we race toward the giant fortress because even though I can feel the weirdly warm wind in my hair, nothing around us changes. It's the same lava sea held by the same red walls. Every now and then, there's a cluster of glowing crystal on the ceiling, but it mainly just makes me miss the sun.

And the moon. And rain. And clouds and grass and flowers and cats and wolves and chickens and pumpkin pie. I'm starting to get sick of hoglin meat, and I didn't like it that much to begin with.

It feels like it's taking forever, but maybe that's just because I'm so desperate to find my brother—or maybe the fortress is just really, really big. It has bridges and square bits and fancy bits and corners, growing right out of the rock and looming over the lava. Torchlight shines out the windows, giving us proof that someone is inside. Sure, it could just be more piglins, but I hear a very familiar sound: mining. And, farther off, someone fighting a mob of some sort.

Mal leads us to a bit of secluded beach under an overhanging corner of the fortress where we won't be seen. There's a tiny bit of red rock reaching out of the lava, barely enough for us all to dismount. She places several more blocks from her pockets so we're not too crowded. My rump aches from hours or maybe days of riding my strider, but I pat Miss Twolegs on the side of her face, and she chirps sweetly.

"We all think they're in this fortress, right?" Mal says.

Everyone nods.

"So what's the plan?" I ask.

Mal grins that grin she reserves for strategizing. This whole trip, she's seemed less sure of herself, maybe because there's just so much about this place that we don't know. But now, planning to capture this castle, she's finally back in her element.

"I'd love to just tunnel upward, but I'm worried they'll hear us mining. I've still got a bunch of redstone, so I'll build a tower up and then bridge around to that window and peek in. If we can find an empty room, we sneak in there. Whatever these guys are doing, this place is huge, and Jarro said there couldn't be more than six of them. Plenty of rooms will be empty." But then she frowns grimly and looks each of us in the eyes. "These are adults, and we're probably going to have to fight them. You have to be ready."

Jarro looks especially worried, and Mal puts a hand on his arm. "Jarro, would you be willing to stay down here with the striders and try to catch another one? Once we've got Tok, we need to be able to get back to the portal ahead of these guys."

Jarro looks immensely relieved at this possibility. "Yeah. Just give me all the warped fungus we've got, and I'll make that happen. Although we'll need another fishing rod and saddle."

Mal looks to me. "Can you make that happen, Chug?"

I glance nervously up at the stone building overhead. "I have two more saddles, and I can make another fishing rod, but you have to wait for me. I have to go with you. I have to see Tok."

"I'll start the staircase, you start crafting that fungus on a stick. The faster we find him, the better."

I know what she's not saying. The longer we stand here doing nothing, the more likely they are to notice us, and our plan hinges on the element of surprise. If we can find Tok and whisk him away before anyone realizes we're even here, we won't have to fight the brigands at all. And not only do we not want to fight other people, but they've overpowered us once before, and they might definitely best us again. Maybe our skills and weapons are special back home, but these adults have probably been training since before we were born. We only have one chance to get Tok out, and it requires speed and stealth.

Both of which . . . yeah, okay, are maybe not my finest qualities.

"Get building," I tell her, and the way she pats my shoulder tells me she knows what I'm not saying, which is, *I trust you to do this because you're my best friend, but I'm really scared.*

Mal starts placing blocks in a winding, tight sort of spiral staircase, and Lenna hops up behind her, step by step, her bow and arrow drawn. I watch for a moment before realizing that the faster I make that fishing rod, the faster I can join them. I pull out my crafting table and supplies and work quietly. Jarro considers the striders, and they all look kinda sad to be off the lava. They're slightly purplish and shivering, but they still seem pretty healthy. He murmurs to them, talking to them like Mal does when milking her cows, as he pulls various weird blocks out of his pockets and places them along the edge of the jagged shoreline to make a small paddock. He rubs their foreheads, but they're shivering too much to chirp.

Finally, I hold out a fishing rod and saddle, and Jarro takes them.

"Be careful up there," he says.

I grin. "Be careful down here. Pick out a good strider for my brother."

I hold out my fist, and he bumps it. "You got it, bud."

Taking out my sword, I start up the stairs as stealthily as I can, considering the fact that I'm me and also wearing a mishmash of metal and diamond armor. Mal has built her tower almost all the way up to the ceiling made by the bottom of the fortress and is now building a bridge out toward the wall that has the window. I take my place behind Lenna, which feels kind of weird, as usually she's behind me. We're definitely not going to try to switch places on this narrow little bridge. It's not like anything can sneak up on us, anyway.

It's a little tricky as Mal places stone blocks along the fortress wall, right up to the window. We all creep forward, and before Mal can motion me to stay down, I peek over the edge, and—

My heart nearly bursts.

There's Tok!

He's working at a brewing stand, and he looks . . . happy?

Seriously, he's lit up like a torch, grinning ear to ear as he holds a bottle of potion.

I look closer, and now I can see that under his joy, he's caught in the same sleepless stupor as the rest of us. His eyes are red, like he's been crying, and there are black smudges underneath them, and one of his eyebrows is pretty much fried off, and his pajamas are scorched. Before I pop back down, I look all around the room to make sure I can describe it to Mal.

She raises her eyebrows, communicating that she's annoyed with me but wants to know what I know. I motion to Lenna's pockets and mime opening a book, which honestly I'm not sure any of them have ever seen me do on my own. Lenna pulls out her journal and hands me her pen, and I write, "Tok hr, mkgn poshun, 1 gard rding boook."

Spelling and handwriting are definitely not my strong points. My muscles are my strong points.

Mal nods and pops up to look for herself. She takes the pen and writes, "Lenna, shoot the guard, Chug defend, I'll get Tok out. Ready?"

We both nod. Lenna puts her journal back in her pocket and pulls out her bow and arrows. I wonder why she's not using her crossbow, but then I realize that Lenna is the thoughtful kind of person who is going to use the weapon she knows she's mastered rather than risk trying something new in a fight this important.

Mal holds up three fingers, then two, then one, and she and I stand and leap through the window. Tok looks up, and his eyes fly wide.

"Come on, Tok," she whispers. "We have to hurry. Out the window—"

"Am I hallucinating?" Tok replies at full volume, sounding dazed.

Mal holds a finger to her lips and points at the guard, but he's already standing up and turning to run. Lenna's shot hits him in the back, and the big guy stumbles and shouts, "Orlok! We're under attack!"

I run over to him and raise my sword, but . . . I can't do it. I can't bring myself to hit an unarmed man lying on his belly. Instead of appreciating my mercy, the brigand snatches his sword off the ground and swings it at me, and I have to dance back and parry his slash.

Anger rises up, my ears burn, and I fight back in earnest. I can hear Tok in the background, telling Mal that he can't leave until he has all his things. I groan—of course my brother doesn't want to leave his potions and ingredients behind. I saw some books on a work desk, and there's no way he would leave without them.

"We have to go now!" Mal says. "They're going to be here any—"

"Minute?"

The figure that steps through the door, sword drawn, is all too familiar. It's the brigand who stole our llamas and chests at the river crossing on the way to the woodland mansion on our last adventure. He looks about the same as he did then, including his smug smile, which suggests he's already won. Two more brigands follow him through the door, crossbows trained on Mal's and Lenna's chest plates.

"You kids again," the head brigand starts.

"You stole my brother. Did you really think we were just going to sit at home and be like, *Oh, well, maybe he'll turn up in the washing?*" I say.

"I could've killed you in your bed," he snarls. "But I was kind enough to leave you behind."

"Yeah, super kind! You're the kindest thief and kidnapper I've ever met! Thank you so much for that!"

Mal is pleading with me to be quiet using just her eyes, but that's never stopped me before. I'm furious, and it's all because of this guy right here. This whole stupid adventure, traipsing through the Nether, desperate, hungry, sleepless, hurt, is all because this same dude just won't leave us alone. It's not like being nice to him is going to make him let us all go.

"You're outnumbered, kid." He smacks his sword against the top of my helmet. "Now let's do this just like last time. I want all your gear in a nice, big pile on the floor. No funny business. No sudden moves."

"Or else what? What are you gonna do? You're not going to kill us."

The sword tip rests against my throat. "Don't tempt me."

"What would it take to let Tok go?" Mal asks in a trembling voice. One of the other brigands has his sword against her chest plate.

"More than three kids can accomplish," the leader admits. "Look, we're not hurting him. He's fed and safe. He's just doing a little job for us."

"It's not a job if you don't pay people," Lenna says softly.

"So I'll give him a shiny emerald!" the brigand shouts, gesturing with his hands. "Point being, he works for me now, and he'll continue to work for me until I say he's done. He'll be fed, he'll be safe, he'll just be . . . elsewhere."

"He doesn't look safe," Lenna shoots back. She nods at the crossbow pointed at her face. "I know I don't feel safe. Tok, are you happy here?"

But Tok has the strangest look on his face, like a trapped animal desperate for a way out. He's sleepless and shaky and breathing weird, and something about him just looks off. He keeps glancing at the window and then back at the brigand leader like he's running calculations in his head.

I don't like it.

I think he's going to do something stupid.

Because, funnily enough, sometimes the smartest people do the stupidest things, especially when they're put under unbelievable pressure.

"No," Tok says in the smallest voice.

"Well, unfortunately, kid, there's no way out," the brigand says with a ferocious grin.

"There's always a way," Tok says quietly.

And then he runs to the window and jumps out.

## 27

# MAL

I can't believe what Tok just did.

Nobody can.

"Tok, no!" Chug screams, shredding his throat.

As if everyone has forgotten all the weapons in the room, we run to the window. Chug is already sobbing, and I can feel every heartbeat banging in my chest. I've known Tok since he was born, and—

Oh.

*Oh.*

I look down, and he's *standing in the lava.*

He's not on fire, he's not dying, he's not screaming.

He's alive and fine, and he's laughing.

"Potion of Fire Resistance!" he shouts up at us. "I finally got it to work!"

But we're so focused on Tok that we've neglected the brigands, and cold metal jabs into my kidney.

"Drop your weapons," the lead brigand says. "We've got you surrounded."

Chug sighs heavily beside me. "At least Tok got out. He and Jarro can head for home."

I don't immediately drop my weapon as commanded, and the sword point digs in deeper. My diamond pickaxe clatters on the ground, and Lenna and Chug follow my lead. The brigand roughly grabs my shoulder and spins me around to face him. "Any of you kids good with potions?"

"I'd like to throw a Potion of Harming at your face right now," Chug growls, and I put a hand on his wrist to remind him not to push these adults too far.

"No," Lenna says simply.

The lead brigand saunters over to the worktable and slams his fist down. "Little brat took the books, too." He focuses on us. "Maybe if I dangle the brother out the window he'll come back?" The other brigands snicker as the leader grabs the back of Chug's shirt and herds him toward the window. "Wait, where'd he go?"

"Tok's smart. Probably already long gone." Chug's confidence is in full force, but he's bluffing. He knows as well as I do that Tok is under the ledge with Jarro, waiting for us. After all, that's what we'd do for him, and even if Tok is as tired and sleep deprived as we are, he's loyal.

But the brigands don't know that—they probably don't even know about the ledge.

"Then to the dungeon we go," the leader says.

He herds us toward the door, but we're not bound or otherwise restrained. He made us drop our weapons, but that doesn't mean we're without resources. Again, Chug and I lock eyes. He grins, and it's a grin I know well, a grin that suggests I have no idea what he's going to do next, but it's going to be fun and get someone in a load of trouble. I subtly slip my hand into my pocket, trying to guess what he's up to. When I meet Lenna's eyes, she gives the tiniest shrug. She's ready, too, hand in her own pocket.

Suddenly, with a roar of rage, Chug lunges for the worktable and tries to leap over it, aiming for the potions.

He fails.

But that's not necessarily a bad thing. He lands hard on the far edge of the table, and it tumbles over with him—right into the gleaming row of potion-filled bottles. For a moment, the fully stocked shelf wobbles on its edge, but then it begins to fall. Chug leaps away, barely avoiding having the whole thing land on him.

Glass bottles break, and curious liquids spill out in rivulets of pink and blue and purple. Some might be Potions of Healing or Regeneration, but if these brigands kidnapped Tok to force him to make potions, then it's likely some of these bottles contain poisons and other concoctions that would mess us up for a long time. The last time Chug and I got poisoned, Nan told us milk was the only antidote. But I haven't seen milk here in the Nether and I definitely don't want to figure out how to milk a ghast.

The head brigand, however, is not as fast as Chug. The wave of potions splashes over his legs, and he falls to the ground, writhing.

"Help!" he screeches, and when his minions rush to help him, we all run for the door. I get there first, pull my iron sword out of my pocket, and slide into the hall. I could go left or right, but my instincts tell me right, as that direction leads back toward home.

I take off at a run, sword ready, pounding down the deep red hallway with Chug and Lenna on my heels. We pass several rooms, and I glance in, looking for more windows, but we definitely don't stop to check for loot. Our only goal is to find a way out of the fortress and back to Jarro and Tok, preferably without the brigands catching up along the way.

The red hallway opens up into a much larger, more open structure, with some welcome pops of black and gray stone. We hurry down some strange, twisted stairs and nearly fall into a pit.

"Ouch?" Chug mutters, and as he stands, a flash of light appears, some strange creature made of spinning fire and smoke. It rushes at him, crackling, and I dart forward and smack it with my sword. A puff of smoke chokes me, and Chug is up and already swinging. Together, we take it down, coughing at the smoke.

"What was that?" Chug splutters.

"A blaze," Lenna says, as if it's perfectly obvious. She dropped her bow and arrow when the brigand told her to, but she now has her crossbow in hand and looks ready for anything.

With the blaze gone, we continue down the hall, and I hate to say it, but I'm already lost. We need to get out of this fortress, get back with Tok and Jarro, but it's a giant labyrinth full of scary new creatures. At each juncture, I dart into empty rooms, hunting for another open window.

"Mal, duck!" Lenna calls as I reenter the hall.

I hit the ground, and an arrow skims over the frizzy hairs coming out of my braid and lodges in—

"What is that?" I ask, my cheek against cold stone as I look up at the creature looming over me.

"Some kind of withered skeleton," Chug says. He jumps over me and bashes it with his sword. It's taller than regular skeletons and somehow angrier, and when it manages to get a hit on him, he staggers back with a cry of surprise.

"That hurt!" he shouts before angrily beating it down to dust, leaving behind a chunk of coal.

I leap up and we run on, but Chug is flagging.

"What's wrong?" I ask.

"Dunno," he gasps. "But I don't feel so good."

We tiptoe across a bridge over sizzling lava, and I turn back and hack away several of the last blocks to stall the brigands before facing Chug and Lenna. Lenna looks fine, her crossbow ready, and Chug should look fine, but he's . . . not. I can't point to anything in particular that's physically wrong, but he looks like he's slowly fading away. I know we have to hurry, but now there's the added pressure to get Chug out of here and back home where someone hopefully has something that can help him.

When we approached this fortress, we went straight to the only window we could see, which suggests that there are no more windows over here. I could start mining the spongy red block, but we could fall out anywhere, right into the lava—and without the benefit of Tok's Potion of Fire Resistance.

"We have to double back," I say, feeling like a terrible leader.

"Sounds good." Chug's voice is weaker than it should be.

"Are we out of golden apples?" I ask Lenna.

She nods. "We need to hurry."

I replace the blocks on the bridge and lead my friends back the way we came. We take down two more blazes, and when another withered skeleton appears, I place two blocks on the ground and hide behind them with Chug while Lenna puts her crossbow to good use. As soon as it's on the ground, we're running again, expecting at any moment to run into the brigands who must be as anxious to find us as we are to get out.

The fortress is a labyrinth, sure, but I've always been good with that sort of thing, and we mostly stuck to big hallways, so we're soon near Tok's room again. We slow down. I hear footsteps inside, someone pacing back and forth. Before I can stop and assess the situation, Lenna reaches into her pocket and throws something down the hallway, past Tok's room. It's one of those weird iridescent spheres, and it makes a musical clatter when it lands on the stones down the hall. Right on cue, one of the brigands appears in the doorway and automatically looks left, toward the thrown sphere. Much to my surprise, Lenna already has her shovel in hand, and she smacks the brigand on the back, driving him to the ground.

"Whoa," Chug mutters. "I didn't know you had it in—"

"Come on," I say, pulling him into the room. We can compliment Lenna later.

I'm surprised to find Tok's room empty. The brigands must've had Potions of Healing or milk around, as the leader looked like a berry sucked dry, the last time I saw him, but now he must be on the move again. All the more reason to hurry.

"What do we do?" Chug asks.

I rush to the window and look down. Tok and Jarro are on their striders, waiting.

"Let's go," I say. Chug motions for me to go first, but I shake my head. "You're the one who's hurt. You go first."

For once, he doesn't argue. As he levers himself out of the window and onto the little ledge I built earlier, he looks like he might swoon and fall over at any time. I edge out after him to hold him steady. Last time, we easily walked along this bridge. Now we crawl, and it takes everything I have to keep Chug on the right path.

"Stop right there!" someone shouts from within the fortress. I glance back, and Lenna is on the windowsill, one leg on the bridge.

"Jump!" Tok shouts from down below.

"But it's lava," Lenna shouts back.

Tok holds out a bottle, shaking it. In his singed pajamas, with his wild hair, he looks like an absolute maniac.

"I have plenty of potions. Whether you land on lava or stone, I can fix you." He gestures down, and I realize there's a lot more beach than there used to be. "But land would be better."

And maybe a normal person would pause, take a breath, think about it. But Lenna is Lenna, so she shrugs and just slowly falls backward out of the window in a weird sort of back flip, crossbow clutched in her hands.

Lenna tumbles through the air, almost in slow motion, and lands with a sick thump on the calico beach Jarro built. I want to hurry Chug along so I can help her, but he's going desperately slow. I can only watch as Jarro and Chug dismount their striders and go to Lenna, who looks beyond broken, even worse than when Chug fell out of that apple tree last year.

Kneeling over her, Tok pulls a potion out of his pocket and dribbles it in Lenna's mouth. She splutters and then licks her lips.

"Is that . . . Floor Potion I detect?" she says.

I'd love to watch the potion take effect and fill Lenna with health, but one of the brigands has appeared in the window—the one Lenna hit with the shovel. He does not look happy.

"We've got to hurry, Chug," I say as the brigand steps out onto my ledge to follow us.

"But I'm so sleepy," he murmurs. "I could just close my eyes for a little minute—"

"No! We have to keep going."

"Only for you, Mal. Only for you."

We're on the stairs now, and when I glance down to Lenna,

she's already standing up and has her crossbow aimed for the brig-
and. The frown on her face suggests she doesn't want to shoot a
human being, but she also doesn't want Chug and me to get
caught. Oddly, Tok reaches into his pajama pants pocket and
hands her a red-and-white-striped tube.

"Fire at the blocks right under the brigand," he tells her.

Lenna looks at the tube, then looks at her crossbow. She grins
and loads the tube like it's a regular arrow. With extraordinary
calm and care, she aims for the blocks right under the brigand
and shoots.

*Boom!*

It's as loud as any of Tok's experiments back home, as loud as
a creeper, and the effect is immediate. There's an explosion of
brightly colored sparks, and then the brigand falls into the lava.

We're at the end of the stairs now, and Tok hurries to help
Chug onto his strider.

"Tok, I'm so glad—" Chug begins, tears in his eyes.

But Tok interrupts him. "Save our big reunion for later, bro.
We're in a hurry, and you're messed up."

"Mal, come on!" Lenna says as she mounts her strider.

I'm stunned to see her back to full health so quickly, but she's
right. We have to leave, now, instead of waiting around to see if
the brigand is badly hurt or if his compatriots are on their way. I
climb up onto my strider before realizing . . . we can't go anywhere. There's a block fence around the lava. I leap down, break
a block, and scramble back up. Jarro leads us out onto the lava
sea, and our poor, shivering striders turn back to their usual robust
color and seem happy to run away from the fortress.

As we zoom across the lava, I look back to where the brigand
fell. He's crawling out onto the shore, reaching into his pocket,

where I'm sure he'll find a potion or a golden apple. Two more brigands stand at the window, watching us go.

"To the bridge!" someone shouts.

I wish there was a way to make these striders go faster. The brigands know where we're going, and they're not going to stop until they have Tok back.

# 28

# TOK

 I'm so sleepy that I'm delirious, but I'm definitely riding a monster that's walking on lava, and my brother looks fine but is about to croak. I ease my strider closer to him and hold out a Potion of Regeneration.

"Drink this," I command him, and believe me—I never command Chug. "It should help."

He takes the bottle and nearly drops it but manages to gulp it down. I guess there are times when it's helpful that he's so food motivated. "Not quite as good as Floor Potion, but still pretty good," he murmurs. He perks up a little, but not all the way, and that worries me.

"What got you?"

"Some freaky withered skeleton guy," he says. "Just hit me once, but it feels like a building fell on me. The potion helps," he hurries to add. "But not completely."

I frown and long to pull out my books and see what's really at work here. I didn't know there were things a Potion of Regeneration couldn't heal. I make him drink a Potion of Healing, too, but he's still not back to his usual Chugginess.

"When we get home, you're going to drink an entire cow's worth of milk," I warn him, remembering that it worked for Mal the last time she was fading away like this.

"As long as it's served warm in bed so I can just go directly into a coma," he promises. He looks at me, eyes swimming with tears. "Bro, I'm—"

"No," I say firmly. "No. Absolutely not. I will not tearfully reunite with you and have a tender moment when we're fleeing bad guys over lava."

"We're not safe yet, are we?" Chug says darkly.

I shake my head. "No. These guys mean business."

We stride along together for a few minutes in silence, with Mal and Jarro a bit ahead of us and Lenna behind us with her crossbow. Chug seems a little perkier, but he's still swaying in his saddle, his eyes unfocused. I would say I need to keep him awake, but no one can sleep here. I need to keep him steady.

"Okay, so two questions," I begin.

"Her name is Miss Twolegs, and no, Thingy doesn't know I'm riding another animal," Chug says weakly.

I snort. "Okay, I promise not to tell your pig that you're cheating on him with a monster from the Nether. But seriously, how did you guys find me, and . . ." My voice rises a little as I look up ahead to Jarro's back. "Why did you bring along the guy who bullied me my entire life?"

Jarro must've heard me, as he flinches. We were alone on the beach with the striders while we waited for the others, but it was a very charged silence. I still have no idea what's going on.

"Those answers are connected," Chug begins. I can tell that every word costs him, but we both know that if he goes silent, he'll really be in trouble.

"The brigands kidnapped Jarro—"

"I know! I heard him whining."

"—and stole all his mom's sweet berries, but they abandoned him in the Overworld. We found him, plus a trail of berries."

"I dropped them for you to find," I say, glowing with pride that my gambit worked.

"Smart thinking, bro. Thingy was especially grateful. We followed that trail until we found iron ingots and horse prints, then we followed those. Once we figured out that whoever took you had to be headed for the woodland mansion, we took a mine cart through the underground cavern. Found the secret room, stepped through the portal, and—"

"What did it look like? Was it cool? It felt cool, but I was blindfolded—"

"Boom!" Chug interrupts me, as if telling the story is the only thing keeping him upright. "We landed in the Nether. And then we followed more sweet berries until we found the skybridge that led to the fortress."

"And my bed exploded," Lenna adds from behind us.

"Huh." I nod along. "I guess that's why they wouldn't give me a bed or let me fall asleep. Are you guys getting any sleep here?"

Chug snorts. "No way, bro. That's the only reason I was loopy enough to get smacked by some janky old skeleton."

"And I fell out of a window," Lenna reminds us.

"I totally would've done that anyway," Chug says with a chuckle. "Like, as a joke."

"Speaking of jokes . . ." I stare at Jarro, who has fallen back a bit. He maneuvers his strider until it's right beside mine. My skin crawls, and I wonder what it says that I felt more comfortable in a Nether fortress with brigands than I do this close to Jarro. "I'm sorry, by the way," Jarro says quietly without looking up. "For everything I ever did to you. This trip has taught me a lot, and . . . I'm just sorry. I'm not that guy anymore."

"He's really not," Chug breaks in. "And he tamed horses. And caught and tamed these striders!"

"Oh, I rode a horse. But I was blindfolded and gagged, so it wasn't really fun." I look down and pat my mount. "What's up with these guys?"

"They really like warped fungus from the warped forest," Lenna says. "We call them striders."

"Because they stride," Chug adds. "I wanted to call them two-legs, but Lenna argued that since we had two legs, too, that made things confusing."

Jarro finally looks at me, and his eyes are haunted. "The brigands kidnapped me and left me tied to a tree to die. What about you? What did they do to you?"

I gaze out at the never-ending lake of lava. "They took me out of bed, blindfolded and gagged me, made me point out all the useful things at Elder Gabe's shop, marched me to the horses, made me ride, brought me here, and then gave me a list of potions and weapons to make." I can't help sighing deeply. "The funny thing is, if they'd just asked me to do it and treated me nicely, it would've been really cool. I learned all sorts of things that I've been dying to know back home, but I couldn't enjoy it because I was away from you guys and couldn't sleep and didn't get enough food. And I was scared."

Against my will, I sniffle, and a tear sneaks out. I dash it away and glance back at Jarro, hating that he's here to see me in such a vulnerable moment.

"Don't worry about it, bro," my brother says. "We've seen Jarro cry and Jarro has seen us cry and after what we've all been through on this journey, it's okay. We're here, and we're together."

"And the whole point of having friends is knowing they'll share the burden of your difficult emotions," Jarro says, and my jaw drops.

He really has changed.

As we travel, I notice that Mal keeps glancing up at the bridge overhead, so I do, too, but I don't see any sign of the brigands. I can't believe how high up we were, that whole time. The brigands definitely didn't tell me that we were dozens of meters over a sea of lava, they just shoved me onward and told me to stay on the path.

We pass striders now and then, and a skeleton shoots arrows at us from the shore, and when a giant gray creature with tentacles appears, crying its lonesome song, Mal and Lenna work together to take it down. My brother looks at it with longing and murmurs, "So many fireballs I won't get to hit," and I start to wonder if I'm hallucinating.

I can't stop looking around, amazed at everything I missed the first time they brought me this way. I would've been so much more scared if I'd known the truth of this place. We pass waterfalls of lava and a giant, sunken black castle, and then I see a welcome and pretty patch of bluish green up ahead. Our striders chirp and walk faster as we near what appears to be a strange forest of fungi, but the moment they're on land, they start to shiver pitifully.

"We can't make them walk on land," my big-hearted brother says. "They hate it. They're so sad now."

He pats Miss Twolegs, and she makes a pathetic, whining chirp.

"Yeah, they hate this," Jarro confirms.

The bridge overhead ends, but there's been no sign of the brigands all this time. I hop down, and Jarro takes off my strider's saddle and offers him the warped fungus that's been luring him along. The strider takes the fungus and steps back onto the lava with a purring chirp. As the striders chomp their fungus, Chug rubs Miss Twolegs's cheek.

"You're a very good strider," he tells her before leaning close to whisper. "And you'll never tell Thingy about this, just like we talked about."

The striders all hurry away, striding across the lava and chewing their fungus. We store our saddles and fishing rods in our pockets, and Lenna collects more warped fungus to bring back home. She's pulling out her journal, and Mal steps up.

"Lenna, no. We have to hurry. They could be following us."

"But the Nether! We need to record everything—"

Mal shakes her head firmly. "Not now. Not this time. We can come back."

Lenna puts her journal away, looking utterly depressed. "You know the adults won't let us."

"They couldn't stop us last time or this time. How are they going to stop us next time?"

There are plenty of ways, actually, but Lenna trusts Mal. She takes out her crossbow and waits to take her place at the end of our troop, always protecting us from behind. We tromp through the warped forest, where Chug warns me not to look the Endermen in the eye, then enter the crimson forest, which is beautiful in an entirely different way. Lenna doesn't pull out her journal again, but she does take samples of everything that she can and stuffs them in her pockets. When a fierce sort of pig-thing snorts in rage and prepares to rush us, she takes them down with a few shots, and Mal finishes them and collects the meat. We walk faster after that.

"Hoglin," Chug tells me. "Nearly killed me. Here's a hint: They don't like to be scratched under their chins."

"Or anywhere," Jarro adds, and Chug nods.

We're so sleep deprived that it's like we're marching in a dream. At any moment, I expect the brigands to appear and charge us, but all we see are hoglins . . . at least right until the portal is in sight. Then I hear an entirely different kind of grunt and look up to find a half-man, half-pig rushing at us, axe raised.

"But piglins have never attacked us before," Chug says, looking conflicted.

"Well, they're attacking us now!" Mal shouts, parrying their strike with her sword.

Lenna gets in a shot, and Mal hacks away with her sword, but Chug stays out of the fray. I can't tell if it's because he's hurt, since my brother generally never misses a fight, but being Chug, he just has to shout, "I don't approve of this! I'm a big fan of pigs and piggish things!"

That piglin goes down, but another one runs in from the side. Mal throws me a spare sword, my old iron one, and Jarro gets his axe out, too. With Chug out of the fight, it's all hands on board. It seems like every piglin in the area hates us now, and when Chug tries to toss one a gold ingot—which makes no sense to me, because why would a pig guy want gold?—the piglin completely ignores it in favor of attacking us.

"Why are they doing this?" Chug cries from outside the fight.

Despite my potions, he looks grayish and smaller than he really is. "They didn't before."

"It must be Tok," Jarro says.

"What, do they hate nerds?" I shoot back.

"We're all nerds," Jarro says, swiping with his axe. "But you're the only one not wearing armor. Or gold. They really like gold."

As we all focus on the latest piglin, Chug roots through his pockets and throws me a pair of gold boots. I duck out of the fight to shove my feet inside, and we finish off the piglin, and then everything goes quiet.

"I hated that," Chug says.

"We all did," I tell him, wiping sweat from my brow.

We keep walking, and Chug looks worse, and I can barely place one foot in front of the other. I'm just about done with this place, so it's a huge relief when Mal points at a weird rectangle of black blocks and says, "There's the portal. Let's hurry."

We've almost reached it when I hear a familiar brigand's voice shout, "There they are!"

Much to my surprise, Jarro slings Chug's arm around his neck, and we run.

## 29

# LENNA

Brigands charge out of the forest, bristling with weapons. We've been running as fast as we could this whole time, terrified that they would catch up. I was always expecting it, and yet I still find it surprising. Mal doesn't have to tell us to run for the portal—we just do. Tok pulls up beside me and holds out another one of those striped things, and I take it and load it as I stumble over the rocky wastes.

I hear Mal saying, "Go! Just go!" to someone, but I can't look back and see who she's talking to. Tok and I are last, and as soon as I'm standing right in front of the portal, I turn and aim my crossbow just ahead of the charging brigands.

*Twang!*

*Boom!*

There's another beautiful, satisfying, louder-than-anything explosion, and Tok and I run for the portal together. Jarro is already gone, and Mal and Chug are waiting for us. Mal shoves me through the portal, and the world goes purply and swirly and wavery, and then I have to blink against the bright light of the Over-world.

I don't even have time to enjoy it, because Mal tumbles through right after me, followed by Tok and Chug.

"How do we stop them?" Mal asks, breathless—not to me, but to everyone.

"Destroy the portal," Jarro says softly. "No portal, no coming through the portal."

We all stare at him in utter surprise.

He's right, but I think we're all shocked that he figured it out before Tok could.

"When did Jarro get smart?" Tok mutters.

But Mal already has her original diamond pickaxe out, and she throws her other diamond pickaxe to Jarro. I pull out my pick-axe, too, and we all pick a block and start mining.

Except . . .

This black stone is insanely hard. It doesn't just crumble like it should. It feels even harder than diamond, somehow. My arms are getting sore, and my teeth hurt from slamming together with each strike. From this angle, I can kind of see through the portal, and I think a shape is coming through the purple. A hand reaches for me, a sword materializing—

And then the purple just disappears.

One of the black stones is gone, and now it's just a weird, bro-ken frame, sitting alone in an empty room.

"Hey!" someone shouts, and the guard pokes his head up through the trapdoor.

*Bonk!*

Chug clunks him on the helmet with his sword, and the guard tumbles back down to the ground below. "Hey to you, too," Chug says weakly, peering down through the open trapdoor.

Mal finishes mining her block, then mine, and shoves the odd black stone in her pocket. The portal is coming undone.

"So are they stuck there?" I ask.

"Seems like it." Tok runs a hand over one of the remaining stones. "I remember hearing snippets of conversation on the journey. They were talking about 'finishing the portal,' and when we got here, I heard the stone being fit. I guess they stole some blocks from town to complete it." He rubs his chin in that way he does that means he's thinking of something diabolical. "And if we take the stone, I bet we could build our own portal and come over here whenever we want to. I could get more potion ingredients, and Lenna could take samples and notes."

"That's pretty dangerous," Jarro says.

Tok whirls to glare at him. "Are you going to snitch on us?"

Jarro shakes his head. "No way. But if you need help, I could come with you. I don't like it here, but . . . if you need me . . ."

"I thought your mom never let you leave the Hub?"

Jarro grins. "Oh, I have plans. If you guys can move out, so can I."

Tok gives him a measuring look. "I didn't even know you could string more than five words together at one time."

"I told you, bro—he's changed," Chug says.

Jarro's grin gets bigger. "I really have. Either that, or you guys got less annoying."

Chug reaches up to give Jarro a noogie, and Tok is comically shocked, and we all laugh in the maniacal way that only happens when you haven't gotten sleep and you've been pushed beyond your limits and are starting to go loony. Not in the Loony Lenna way, but just . . .

I really need a nap.

Mal, Jarro, Tok, and I mine all the black blocks. Tok tells me he heard it called "obsidian," and I can't wait to write about it in my journal. We each take a few blocks until there's nothing left. While we work, Chug keeps watch over the trapdoor. Every time the brigand guard tries to come up, he gets clunked on the helmet with a sword.

"Stop bonking yourself," Chug says with each strike. "Bonk!"

Instead of using the trapdoor, we fit it with another block of stone and go out the window. I think we're going to head right back into the woodland mansion and back down to the cavern underneath, where the mine cart is, but Mal stops on the stairs and considers the animal pens the brigands have installed.

"We need rest, but first we need to get as far away from here as possible. If we take the horses, they can't follow us on horseback, even if they found new saddles," she says.

That seals the deal. We saddle up and ride, opening the pen so the other two horses can follow us or wander away, as they wish. A little farther away, we stumble upon a pen of llamas—our old llamas, which the brigands stole at the river crossing during our first adventure. Mal barely has time to greet Sugar before releasing them to follow us. We remember the route we took to get here last time, so we backtrack through the dark forest. At Chug's insistence, we stop to gather some wood for beds, but we definitely don't hang out long enough to attract any mobs.

The log we once toppled into the river is still gone, but they've built a nice, sturdy stone bridge in its place. We zig and zag up the mountain pass and follow the beacon to end up in the village at dusk. I have no idea how long we've been traveling and sleepless, but it's clear we can't go on. Our horses walk by the patrolling iron golem without incident, and a passing villager greets us with a curious, "Hm." Chug is too tired to move, but he asks Mal to trade for three bits of wool, which she's happy to do. The empty house we've stayed in twice now is still empty, thankfully. Mal, exhausted and lagging, hacks a paddock into the ground outside while Chug pulls out his crafting table.

"Bro, you brought my crafting table!" Tok walks over and runs a hand over it, confused. "But it's a little wonky."

"Oh. Um. Yeah, this one isn't yours. Yours is much nicer. We needed a few things on the journey, and I've been watching you make stuff, so I . . . kinda . . ."

"You made this?"

Poor, exhausted, weakened Chug looks so nervous about it, but Tok's face lights up. "That's so cool! Bro, I knew you had it in you!"

Chug glows with the praise but nearly faints. Jarro helps him to the ground. Although Tok looks like a puff of wind could blow him over, he fishes through his pockets for iron ingots and makes a bucket.

"Can you fill this with milk?" he asks Mal, and she takes the bucket and hurries off to find a cow.

I keep watch with my crossbow while Tok makes three more beds out of the wood we collected in the dark forest and the tufts of wool Mal traded from the shepherd. We set the beds up inside the empty building, which is a little more cramped than usual thanks to having Jarro around. Chug wants to help, but Tok and Jarro drag him to a bed and tuck him in tightly so he can't move. Tok makes him drink another Potion of Regeneration, and it does help . . . but not enough. Something is still killing him, slowly, from the inside. I long to write about the effect of the Wither in my book, but people seem to get mad when I pull out my book during tense moments. We poke around in our pockets for food, but honestly, it's getting pretty sad.

"I'm going to try to trade for some food," Jarro says. He heads outside, and I have my doubts about what he has in his pockets that might pique the villagers' interest, but I guess we'll soon learn if this is another skill he just can't pull off—or another instance where he'll totally surprise us.

"Do you think Mal's okay?" Chug asks, a breathy whisper. "She shouldn't be out alone. She needs me—"

"We all need you alive more than Mal needs you to babysit her while she milks a cow. None of us are really okay right now," I say. "You can't go that long without proper sleep and be okay."

"I don't even know how long we've been gone." Tok sits on the bed next to Chug's but doesn't lie down. He probably knows that the second his head hits the pillow, he'll be out whether he's ready or not. "Did anyone else from home come looking for me?"

Chug and I exchange uncomfortable glances. "They thought you and Jarro were just playing some kind of prank. That you stole the berries and potions and, I don't know, ran off to trade them," I finally say. "It makes no sense."

"They're idiots," Chug whispers.

Tok shakes his head sadly. "Why are grown-ups so unwilling to see the truth? Why can't they just believe us when we tell them stuff?"

"Because sometimes we lie about it," I say. "We've covered up a lot of our rule-breaking in the past."

"But none of us would steal things and disappear! Being eight and saying, while sweating a lot, *No, Inka, we definitely didn't borrow a couple of melons from your corner field and eat them with our bare hands* is one thing. A kid being stolen out of his bed is another."

"Nan believed us," I say. "Nan always believes us."

"Maybe you just have to get really old to remember how to be a kid," Tok says.

At that, we just laugh. There are plenty of old people in our town, and none of them are quite like Nan.

Much to my surprise, Jarro returns with pies, cakes, cookies, carrots, and a much juicier chicken than we've had in quite some time. Before we can feast, Mal arrives with a bucket of milk. She's got bits of grass in her hair and dirt stains everywhere.

"Wild cows," she says darkly. "Don't ask."

Jarro and Tok help Chug sit up, and Mal pretty much pours the milk down his gullet. He splutters at first but then starts sucking it down, and it's like watching a bottle go from full to empty. Whatever the Wither did to him, this was the cure. I'm just glad Tok's potions kept him alive long enough for the milk to take effect.

"I guess we need to add a cow to our travel caravan," Chug says, licking his lips. "That's the second time milk has saved me."

"Or we could learn how to milk a pig," I say, because I do wonder if it's possible.

Chug looks at me like I've said something scandalous. "We will do no such thing!"

We all laugh, but Chug heaves himself out of bed and, with no warning, launches himself at Tok, enveloping his younger brother in a hug.

"You can't stop me now," he says, right by Tok's ear. "I'm not half dead, and we're not in the middle of a sea of boiling lava, and I'm a lot stronger than you and not letting you out of this hug." Chug takes a deep breath and bursts into tears and shouts, "Bro!"

Tok buries his face in Chug's shoulder and wails, "I know! I know!"

"But bro!"

"Bro, I know! Believe me! I know!"

"I thought you were gone!"

"I thought I'd never see you again!"

"But you knew we'd come after you!"

"I know, that's why I left the trail!"

"I know, bro!"

"I know!"

They thump each other on the back for a while, and they must be speaking telepathically, because they're not saying anything out loud and yet there's so much emotion passing between them. As their sobs fall off, Mal joins the hug, and I know that I'm supposed to join, too. It's not very comfortable—Mal is dirty and smells like cow and Chug's armpits are a crime against noses and Tok mostly smells like gunpowder—but it's good, to be all together again, as we should be. When Jarro doesn't join the hug, Mal reaches back to grab his sleeve and drag him in. Finally, finally, it feels like we're home—even if we're not back in Cornucopia yet.

With the reunion finally handled, we feast on all the food and burp and laugh as we tell our stories. Then we sleep, and I swear it's the best night of sleep of my life and the most comfortable bed I've ever slept in. We sleep late in the morning and rub our eyes and eat our breakfast and mount our horses and head for home with llamas trailing behind. It was a little odd between Tok and Jarro at first, but Jarro somehow became one of us on the way here. If Chug likes Jarro, Tok will like Jarro. I think maybe even Jarro is learning to like Jarro.

The journey takes several days, but we're not in a hurry. On the way home, we stop to collect Poppy and Thingy and the horses we left behind in a paddock on our way to the Nether. My wolf wriggles and dances and yips with joy the moment she sees me, and I can't stop patting her head and kissing her nose and telling her how much I missed her. I felt incomplete, and now it's like I'm whole again. Chug goes through a similar dance with Thingy.

"Do you think he can smell strider on me?" he whispers nervously to me.

"Everything down there just smells like smoke," I tell him. "He would've been barbecued in the Nether."

When we're all back in the saddle and I've got Poppy trotting by my side, I ride up to Jarro. Now that we have twelve horses, I'm curious about something.

"What are you going to do when we get home, Jarro?"

He thinks for a moment before saying, "Get the chewing out of a lifetime from my mom, I guess."

"But you said you might set up your own place?"

He sighs heavily. "I'd like to. Maybe I could breed these horses. Or play around with trying to grow some of those weird fungi from the Nether. But I don't see how that's possible. My mom will never let me leave home."

"Kinda seems like she can't stop you. There's plenty of room outside the wall. There's the whole Overworld."

"And there's some space near us," Chug says. "If you don't mind occasional explosions."

"Oh, no more explosions, bro." Tok pats his pockets. "I've got the books I needed. I haven't exploded anything by accident in— well, I guess days, but it feels like a week."

Jarro looks up, hopeful and nervous. "You guys—I mean, are you going to keep your horses? Maybe I could keep them for you,

256 DELILAH S. DAWSON

or just horsesit them for a while to see if they're interested in having really cute babies?"

"You can definitely keep my horse for me," Chug says. "Thingy will lose his mind if I bring home Bee."

"Nan might like a horse," I suggest. "She always gets all wistful when she talks about them."

Jarro looks back at the rest of our herd. "Do you think she might like the white one? She seems particularly sweet."

I never thought Jarro could be generous, much less care about something being sweet, but that's just how far he's come along.

"I think she'd like that," I say.

We top the next ridge, and when we look down, there it is.

Our town.

"Oh, boy," Jarro says. "I hope my mom doesn't kill me."

## 30

# JARRO

 I was terrified when I was kidnapped. I was terrified to journey across the Overworld with people who justifiably hated me. I was beyond terrified to enter the Nether.

And now I'm terrified to go home.

Not only because my mom is going to be furious with me, but because I don't want to be friends with Edd and Remy anymore. The longer I traveled with the Mob Squad, the more I realized that my former friends aren't actually good friends. If I tried to hang out with Edd and Remy right now, they'd probably make fun of me for being kidnapped by adults and then hanging out with the town Bad Apples.

They probably weren't even worried about me, which hurts.

We ride through New Cornucopia, and people stop and stare at us. At first, I think it's because this is just how people treat the Mob Squad, and then I see the wonder on everyone's faces and the delight in a little kid's laugh and realize it's because they've never seen horses before. When a baby waves, I wave back. It feels pretty great.

We ride through the gate in the wall and down the road that leads to the Hub, and soon people are lining the streets, whispering and waving. Before we get into downtown proper, my mother comes roaring down the road, screeching, "What did you do to my son? Jarro, you get off that filthy thing right now!"

I stop my horse but don't get off. "It's a horse, and it's—" I chuckle. "Okay, he's pretty dirty, because it's been a long ride. But these kids saved me. I was kidnapped by the brigands who stole all your sweet berries."

"And where are my berries, then?"

"The brigands still have them. Or maybe they ate them. We were more worried about Tok than about berries."

"Those berries were valuable!"

"Mom, come on. You have a million seeds, even if you tell everyone you don't."

Her jaw drops and her face goes bright red. She's half crying, half furious. "Well, get down before you hurt yourself and come inside. Stop making a spectacle of yourself."

"You're the only one yelling."

Her eyes fly wide. That might be the first time I've ever talked back to her. She's just opening her mouth to shout at me some more when Elder Stu and Elder Gabe appear, hurrying toward us.

"Are you happy with your little prank?" Elder Stu says. "Stealing and hiding for a week! What will you kids get into next? And what are these—these big-nosed cows?"

"These are horses, and we were kidnapped," Tok says, loud enough for everyone to hear. "I was stolen out of my bed by brigands, who took Jarro when he caught them stealing the sweet berry bushes. The brigands carried us far away and forced me to go to the Nether and make potions for them. My friends and Jarro saved us."

Elder Stu shakes his head, just like he always does when we plead our case.

Everyone is totally silent.

And then Elder Gabe shouts, "Balderdash! Lies! Thief! I want to know what you did with my potions!"

Over the years, I've seen Tok express a variety of emotions, but I've never seen him turn this shade of purple. "You think I'm lying? You think I stole your potions for myself? I went to the Nether, you sniveling ignoramus!" He reaches into his pocket and pulls out a swirly, bright purple potion, which he gently hands to Elder Gabe. "That's a Potion of Harming. Ever heard of it? Because I have, and I can make it now. I can make all the potions you can and more, so I have no need to steal from you. And not only that, but I know your secret."

The Hub is so quiet that you could hear a pin drop.

"There isn't a— I don't have—" Elder Gabe splutters.

Tok pitches his voice louder. "Elder Gabe doesn't know how to make potions. The Elders left his family with a huge stockpile, and he's been charging high prices for them ever since. All those bags and chests in his closet were just for show. The only way to obtain potion ingredients is by going to the Nether. And we're the only people who know how to get there. Or survive there."

Elder Stu turns to Elder Gabe, whose bald head is burrowed down beneath his pointy shoulders like he's trying to disappear into his own neck.

"Is that true, Gabe? Do you really not know how to make potions?"

"I, uh, in theory. You see, potions are, um, very complex, yes, beyond the common person's understanding—"

"Do you even know what a blaze rod is, Elder Gabe? Because I didn't see any in your closet. You can't make a single potion without blaze rods."

Tok reaches into his pocket and pulls out several glowing sticks, waggling them in the air. "Good thing I know how to make potions, now that you don't have a single one."

Gabe shakes his fists furiously, his neck wattle wagging. "Now, you see here! My family was given the solemn task of—"

"Distributing much-needed potions for astronomical prices?" Tok asks.

"Withholding help in exchange for money?" Mal chimes in.

"Fleecing the people you're sworn to help and protect?" Chug adds.

"No! If someone didn't maintain strict control, we would've run out years ago!" Elder Gabe thunders. "It's not my fault we were left with a finite number of potions! You should all be thanking me for maintaining the stockpile so well!"

Tok smiles as he shoves the rods back in his pocket and holds up the only potion we all recognize—a Potion of Healing.

"From now on, as long as my friends and I are allowed to come and go to the Nether, I'll provide Potions of Healing and Regeneration to everyone in town who needs them at my usual reasonable prices," he shouts. "And you can thank the Mob Squad for that."

There's the smallest pause, and then the entire town . . .

Erupts in cheers and applause.

Elder Gabe is trying to shout his disagreement, but there's no way one old man can drown out a happy crowd of people who thought they'd never see a Potion of Healing again. Elder Stu could probably quiet everyone down, but he's too busy glaring at Gabe, who's been lying all along. I can't help looking around at all the people I know, elated, grinning, shouting, pumping their fists and stomping their feet and clapping.

"Mob Squad! Mob Squad! Mob Squad!" someone chants. More than a few people pick it up, but my mother doesn't join them. She just frowns, hands on her hips. Maybe she doesn't know I'm part of the Mob Squad, that I helped save the town again and ensure that we'd have the potions we need from here on out.

Maybe she doesn't care.

"You're welcome," Tok says with a bow of his head. "And good day, sir." He steers his horse right around the two stunned Elders standing in the street and then looks back over his shoulder. "You guys coming?"

Everyone follows him, and much to my own surprise, so do I.

"Jarro, you get off that thing and come home right this instant!" my mom screeches.

"No." I manage to pack a lot of feeling into that one small word as I follow my friends, bringing the rest of the horse herd and the llamas with me. My mom keeps shouting at me—first commanding, then begging, then saying some pretty mean stuff I wish I hadn't heard. I begin to wonder if maybe . . . she's the biggest bully in town. Maybe it'll be better, having some space.

I'm not sure where we're going until we enter the forest. I've never been out here before—my mom told me Mal's great-great-grandmother was a witch who would curse me with boils. Soon we see a nice little cottage with a pretty garden, and the door opens to reveal Nan. She looks annoyed for the briefest moment before her wrinkly face breaks out in a huge, gummy grin.

"Horses!" she squeals. "Ooh, hello, my beauties!" As she rubs the nose of Mal's horse, she adds, "And hello, children. It appears that you're multiplying. Which one is that?" She points at me.

"I'm Jarro, ma'am," I say, unsure if she has any idea who I am. "And we thought you might like a horse to keep?"

"I like this one already." She wanders back to the herd, and sure enough, she picks the white one. "I'm calling this one Hortense."

We all dismount and go inside to eat the best cookies in the world and tell Nan about our journey. Chug gets bored and goes outside to collect wood and make a fence for Hortense. Tok pulls several potions out of his pockets to show Nan, who grimaces.

"Nasty stuff, that," she says, recognizing them immediately. "Want me to keep them safe for you?"

"At least some of them. I wouldn't want anyone to get hurt," Tok says.

He unloads more potions than should ever be able to fit into his pockets, and Nan packs them into a sturdy chest.

"So you went to the Nether," she says, turning to Lenna. "And did you take notes?"

Lenna produces her journal and flips through it to show sketches and scribbles and mushy red splats that were once fungi. "As many as I could, but—"

"Rescuing Tok was our first priority," Mal fills in. "But we all want to go back, and it looks like the Elders will have no choice but to let us. Lenna wants to make better notes, and I want to mine the strange ores, and Tok will need more ingredients. He's going to keep the whole town supplied with potions. Nan, did you know Elder Gabe didn't even know how to make them? He was just doling out what the Founders left behind."

"I'm not surprised," Nan grumbles. "He always was a secretive little creep." She gets a bit of a wistful look in her eyes. "I always wanted to see the Nether, you know."

"We can show you," Mal says. "Probably not a long journey, just a quick jaunt, but we'll all go and keep you safe."

"I don't actually want to go back," I say, maybe too quickly.

"Me neither," Chug says as he walks back inside. "Any place with exploding beds is not what I would consider Chug friendly."

Right when I'm getting bored and tired, Nan stands. "Well, I'm glad you're all back safe and sound, but having you around is exhausting. Thank you for the horse and bringing my assistant back alive."

"And your great-great-granddaughter," Mal prompts, kissing her on the cheek.

Nan flaps a hand at her. "Obviously. I only have seven or eight of those. Goodbye, children."

"Bye, guys," Lenna says on Nan's doorstep. "Good job storming the Nether. See you tomorrow?"

"See you tomorrow!" the others call, and still, I'm not sure if I'm included, so I just wave.

She goes back inside, and the rest of us mount our horses, but no one makes a move to leave.

"I have to go home," Mal says. "My parents will be worried. And the cows will need milking."

"So you go on an adventure like that, and your parents are just worried about the cows?" I ask, incredulous.

"Your mom seemed pretty worried about her berries," Mal shoots back, and the old me would have lashed out, but the new me just chuckles.

"Parents just don't understand," I say.

Once we're out of the forest, Mal hops off her horse so it can rejoin the herd gathered behind me, takes her saddle, and heads down the dirt lane to, I guess, her farm.

"See you tomorrow!" she calls.

"See you tomorrow!" Chug and Tok say.

Chug looks over at me. "Bud, do you not plan on hanging out tomorrow?"

"I, uh, wasn't sure if I was invited."

His grin is a surprise. "You're part of the Mob Squad now. You're one of us. You're always invited. But not Remy and Edd."

"I don't think I'm gonna hang out with those guys anymore. They're jerks."

"They really, really are."

Mal's not quite out of earshot, so I call, "See you tomorrow!" and she waves over her shoulder.

"Dinner at our house?" Chug asks.

I smile. "Sounds good, bud."

It's a long ride back to New Cornucopia, and I'm worried that my mom is going to run outside and shout at me again as we walk through the Hub on our horses, but I guess we're old news now. The streets are quiet—except for one frazzled young mother who meets us outside her door and offers Tok a cake in exchange for a Potion of Healing for her toddler's broken arm. He smiles and happily accepts the trade. I know for a fact Elder Gabe would've charged twenty times as much, and it feels good, to know that even with that kind of power, Tok is a good guy.

Through open windows, I hear the sounds of food being served and bowls being scraped and families laughing or arguing at their kitchen tables. Our horses' hooves clop on the cobblestone, and then we're back on the dirt path, and then we're out beyond the wall. It felt crowded in town, after all we've been through, and I'm glad to be back outside.

I follow the brothers to their place, which I've never seen before. It's impressive, actually, a nice building with a big sign. Two cats come tearing out of the house and run directly at Tok the moment the door is open, climbing all over him while purring.

It strikes me that if I went home right now, I wouldn't feel this way. I wouldn't feel warm and fuzzy and glad to be there. Everything there is the way my mom likes it, just so, never out of place. She would yell at me. Ask me questions and doubt me and blame me for everything that's ever gone wrong. It would be terrible. But Tok and Chug have their pets and their space and the chance to do what they love. It's pretty inspiring.

Tok crafts a fence for the horses while Chug makes dinner. It's the best mushroom stew I've ever had, and it's so good to taste something that isn't dry meat. We chat and laugh over dinner, and afterward, I realize I'm stalling because I don't want to go home.

"I guess it's bedtime," Chug says, stretching.

"I'm going to sleep for three days," Tok replies, a cat on each shoulder.

"Okay, well . . . I guess I'll see you tomorrow. Thanks for dinner." I head for the door, trying to seem normal and, I know, totally failing. I really, really don't want to go home.

I hear whispering behind me and tense for the worst, because old habits die hard.

"You can stay here tonight, if you like," Chug says. "If you're too tired to head home."

I give an exaggerated yawn and stretch. "Thanks, bud. That would be cool."

I pull my bed out of my pocket and crawl in and sigh in contentment. It's so quiet out here, beyond the Hub. I can't hear a single other family—or my mom gossiping with Old Man Finn next door, who's the second meanest person I know. It's nice. Peaceful.

The thought that I could have this, too?

Well, I don't know how to say it, but . . . I'm glad those brigands kidnapped me.

# 31

# TOK

 Everything turned out just fine. Our parents on the pumpkin farm barely even noticed we'd been gone, the town is treating us notably better now that I provide their potions, and we helped Jarro build a little horse farm next door.

It's nice, having all the horses and llamas right there, and it's nice having Jarro for a neighbor. Chug is right—he's a completely different person, now that he's not stuck in the Hub with his mom. I guess staying in the same place with the same people all your life doesn't exactly expand your mind and give you the opportunity to learn and grow. I don't know if he'll ever want to go to the Nether again, but he's getting used to life beyond the wall. Most afternoons, if the weather is nice, he goes for a gallop across the prairie. I can tell Chug wants to go with him, but he still thinks it would hurt Thingy's feelings.

Now Jarro grows fungi and raises horses and llamas and rents them out when folks want to go on a journey—the horses and llamas, not the fungi. So many people from town are venturing to the village to trade on Jarro's horses that a trail is forming through the grass, a little brown dirt path snaking across the prairie, taking the citizens of Cornucopia out into the world for the first time.

Mal dug a nice-sized basement under my and Chug's bedroom, and we set up the Nether portal down there. We always leave one block out unless we're using it, because it turns out you can't activate a Nether portal if even one obsidian block is missing. Our portal doesn't come out where the one in the woodland mansion did—ours, luckily, spits us out in the middle of that nice warped forest. Whenever I need ingredients, Mal and Lenna and Chug are happy to go on a mini adventure and grab whatever I need. Well, Chug's not happy, but he'd rather go with them than know that Mal and Lenna are there alone, without a lug in armor constantly jumping in between them and danger.

Lenna's book is coming along beautifully, and Nan is Nan, so of course she acts like it's no big deal and she already knew everything about the Nether, but we know full well she didn't.

"Mm-hm, hoglins, yes, of course," she said, looking at the picture. "Good eating."

We don't correct her, though. They are good eating.

So that's how everything turned out. I stopped blowing things up and started supplying potions for the whole town. Mal has the market for weird ore cornered. Lenna's an expert with a crossbow and is writing her second book on the Nether. Chug and Jarro are buddies now, and Jarro eats lunch at our house almost every day. His mom got so mad that she decided to give him the silent treatment, and it totally backfired. Jarro's a lot happier, now that she's silent.

Oh, and the next time Candor and Clarity had kittens, Jarro

got the pick of the litter. Now he has his own cat to keep the creepers away, and he talks to her in a baby voice that the older version of Jarro would have ridiculed to pieces. Unfortunately, Chug named her before Jarro could, and now she's stuck being called Meowy, but Jarro has definitely learned his lesson regarding naming rights.

And me?

I finally got those books on potions I wanted so much.

Of course, that doesn't mean I'm not traumatized by the experience of being kidnapped right out of my bed. I'm a lot jumpier when I'm asleep now, which is not so great on stormy nights. We lock our doors, and I have elaborate traps set up around the house to deter anyone who might wish us harm—or try to steal our wares. There's this interesting stuff called redstone that I'm experimenting with that might help with even more elaborate traps, but first I'll need another book, which means we'll need to go on another adventure.

It's funny how nothing and everything can change. Maybe that's what growing up is—you become a different person bit by bit, figuring out who you really are. And from the outside, maybe you look the same, except for your hairstyle or clothing, but on the inside, you're a better, smarter, more creative, more confident version of yourself. And you still carry your fears around with you, but you learn to adapt and grow. And maybe the people you once hated become your friends. And maybe you realize who you want to be and work on becoming that instead.

We're all works in process, as complex as a potion on a brewing stand.

But hopefully not as explosive.

# 32

# CHUG

 Oh.

Hello there. What are you still doing here?

Tok told you everything is good, and despite what the Elders may say, Tok doesn't lie.

Maybe you're here to pet a pig and enjoy some of my delicious mushroom stew?

Or maybe you're here to buy your own sword and armor and head out on your own adventure. We have a beautiful new gold chest plate Tok just made, or perhaps you'd enjoy the sturdy feel of iron or the solid creak of leather. Try on whatever you like. I'm sure we can make a deal. We're known around town for our fair prices.

And when you're ready to explore the world outside, might I recommend renting a horse from Jarro next door? You'll see the Overworld from a new perspective as you follow that dirt path out to the village, or maybe you'll forge a new path to a place even the Mob Squad has never seen.

Yet.

# ABOUT THE AUTHOR

DELILAH S. DAWSON is the *New York Times* bestselling author of the *Star Wars* books *Phasma*, *Galaxy's Edge: Black Spire*, and *The Perfect Weapon*, as well as *The Violence, Mine, Camp Scare*, the Blud series, the Hit series, *Servants of the Storm*, and the Shadow series, written as Lila Bowen. With Kevin Hearne, she co-writes The Tales of Pell. Her comics include *Star Wars Adventures* and *Forces of Destiny, Firefly: The Sting, Marvel Action Spider-Man, Adventure Time, The X-Files Case Files*, and *Wellington*, written with Aaron Mahnke of the *Lore* podcast, plus her creator-owned comics *Ladycastle, Sparrowhawk*, and *Star Pig*. She lives in Georgia with her family and loves Ewoks, porgs, and gluten-free cake.

delilahsdawson.com
Twitter: @DelilahSDawson
Instagram: @DelilahSDawson

## ABOUT THE TYPE

This book was set in Electra, a typeface designed for Linotype by renowned type designer W. A. Dwiggins (1880–1956). Electra is a fluid typeface, avoiding the contrasts of thick and thin strokes that are prevalent in most modern typefaces.